£3.50

INNER CITY

INNER CITY

by

Iain McGinness

POLYGON
Edinburgh

First published in Great Britain in 1987 by Polygon,
48 Pleasance, Edinburgh EH8 9TJ.

Copyright © Iain McGinness 1987
All rights reserved

The publisher acknowledges subsidy from the
Scottish Arts Council towards the publication
of this volume.

Typeset at EUSPB, 48 Pleasance, Edinburgh EH8 9TJ.
Printed and bound by Billings, Worcester.

British Library Cataloguing in Publication Data
McGinness, Ian
  The inner city.
  I. Title
  823'.914   PR6063.A218/

ISBN 0-948275-27-8

INTRODUCTION

I once heard a man on the number 9 bus ask why kids were taught history in schools because it's all aboot deed peepul isn't it and whit's deed peepul goat tae dae with anythin' anyway?

So, this is not a book about history although it describes events which happened in the past. It is a book about astronomy, about life on a dead planet. It is a book about pathology. It is a book about looking into the eyes of a dead dog and seeing the world reflected in watery glass.

It is a book about some varieties of dream which masquerade as reality.

WHY?

Well, as far as I can tell, there was once a holy man called Kentigern, or Mungo as he was known to his close friends. And he worked for another holy man called Fergus. And Fergus, he was a bit, you know, "funny". And he told Mungo that when he died he, that is Fergus, wanted to be placed on a bullock cart. And planted in the ground when the bullocks were too knackered to go any further. So he died. And Mungo did it. And where the bullocks stopped was at the side of a burn called the Molindinar. And there, Fergus had the earth kicked in his face for the last time.

Obviously, after these exertions, Mungo/Kentigern would have been feeling rather tired, so he decided to have a rest. A long rest. He settled down, set up a religion factory, and called it "Glaschu", meaning "the church within the enclosed space" — how apt. Everything was OK until — guess what? Someone decided he didn't like Mungo's religion. So Mungo was turfed out and had to go to Wales where he stayed until someone overturned his persecutor's objections by killing him. Then Mungo came back. Then he died. About one thousand, two hundred years ago.

FACT!: The Molindinar Burn exists. It is in the East End of Glasgow. It is now an open sewer running into the River Clyde.

FACT!: St Mungo is the patron saint of Glasgow — at least that's what they told me when I was a nipper.

FACT!: I went to a school in Glasgow called St Mungo's Academy, run by men in black robes who always talked about god — even during Maths lessons.

FACT!: There was an annexe of St Mungo's Academy called St Kentigern's.

FACT!: St Kentigern's Annexe, which I attended for three years, stood on the banks of the Molindinar Burn.

FACT!: A lot of boys from the school, although I was not one of them, fell into the Molindinar and came out covered in shit.

FACT!: Strathclyde Regional Council have now built a new St Mungo's school, and I don't even know where it is.

SAM DUNBAR

Pat McKenna, a small, sallow-faced man in his mid thirties, leant with his back towards the bar as the pints were being poured. He was studying the television set which was high on a shelf in the corner of the pub.

"Bloody things," he mumbled, half to himself. "A pub is a pub!" he proclaimed suddenly to his companion, Sam Dunbar, a much larger figure, looking younger despite their similarity in years. "Someone should ban TVs from pubs. And the rest of all that crap — jukeboxes and one-armed bandits and pool tables and everything. Let's get back to the basics."

Here Pat paused, turned full on to the bar and, lifting his pint, eyed it appreciatively: "Bevvy!" he gasped, after draining half of the contents of his glass.

"No one could accuse you of not getting your priorities right anyway," sighed Sam, fingering the thick moustache which flourished on the top lip of his large, square face. "Anyway, who's going to do the banning under your scheme? That's just another example of your flabby thinking. You always say things that don't mean anything, usually because you've heard them from someone else. I suppose you want a return to real ale too, despite the fact that you always drink lager."

"At least pubs were pubs then, back in the old days. You could go in and have a drink and a good crack without hearing the 'Black and White Minstrel Show' in the background."

"How do you know? Even you weren't drinking in those days."

"I started early, Sam. Don't let these youthful looks fool you. I was born at a very early age."

Sam looked at Pat's ravaged face, more closely resembling a pickled walnut with every passing day, started into his watery, bloodshot eyes and sighed: "Did anyone ever tell you you're a clown, Pat?"

"Did anyone ever tell you you're a prick, Sammy?"

Both men swivelled back to the television, still holding their drinks.

"Look, look!" a jowly, well-built little man standing next to them shouted to no one in particular. "They'll be taking over here soon too. That's what this government will do to us as well," he continued, pointing vigorously at the TV screen. "There'll be nothing but wogs running about, taking over the schools, the hospitals, the jobs, every fucking thing."

The fat man was pointing to a film of a new university being inaugurated in Zimbabwe by Robert Mugabe. The film had a voice-over delivered by the newscaster:

"The new university, named after Nelson Mandela, the South African A.N.C. leader still imprisoned on Robben Island, was financed mainly by contributions from Britain, the E.E.C., and the United States. Prime Minister Mugabe said he hoped it would be a symbol of the continuance of the liberation struggle in Southern Africa, and also of the help extended to emergent black nations by the former colonial powers.

"Now, here are the main points of the news again, with subtitles for the hard of hearing. The summit meeting of ..."

"Hey," interrupted Pat, "did you hear the one about the Irish news programme? They put on special subtitles in Braille for the blind."

"A cracker, Pat," responded Sam with a sigh.

"Did I tell you the one about the Irish brekfast cereal? Well, instead of going 'snap, crackle, pop', it went ..."

"They're just as bad, son," interrupted the fat man, placing a podgy hand on Pat's arm.

"What the fuck are you talking about, pal?" asked Pat, looking down at the sausage supper grasping his jacket.

"The Irish! Micks! Paddies! Bogmen! They're probably even worse, because they're white. You don't even know who they are half of the time when they're out of their wellies. And there are more of them too: millions of them! And they all have about fourteen kids. They're like rabbits. We'll soon be sinking under the weight."

"Sure now, and is dat a fact?" asked Pat in an Irish brogue. "If youse'll excuse me den, oil away and throw mesell under de nearest bus, to take me weight off the poor, groanin' island."

The fat man quickly removed his hand from Pat's sleeve, then patted his arm soothingly: "Only joking, old son. I've worked beside Irishmen all of my life. Great bunch of blokes. What I was really getting at was . . . Them." The fat man gave a slight nod of his head in the direction of two Sikhs leaning on the bar close to the door. "They're even coming in here now," he continued in a conspiratorial whisper. "I've seen them working on building sites too. They'll soon be taking over *your* job!"

"I don't work on a site, pal," said Pat very calmly. Sam, spotting the signs of an approaching explosion, stepped in between the two:

"Listen, mate, why don't you just move away a wee bit and let me and my friend have a quiet pint, eh?"

"No bother! No problem! We're OK! Just having a wee chat, you know. Aren't we, son?" he asked, nudging Pat.

"Yes, dad," replied Pat, gazing into his pint, "a chat is what is occurring. But if you . . ."

The fat man drained his drink and disappeared into the toilet.

"Those bastards get on my tits!"

"Pat, Pat, a cool brain. Who is he? Some little wanker who's worried because he thinks darkies have got bigger willies than him. Humour him."

"But what's he got against Irishmen, then?"

"Pat, Pat," said Sam, glancing down at Pat's groin, "don't denigrate yourself, for God's sake."

"Fuck off."

At this point, the small man waddled back into the bar and ordered himself another drink: "What's for you, son?" he asked, addressing Pat. "Guinness, is it?"

"Listen, pal . . ."

"Pat, Pat . . ."

"No, it's not Guinness, it's lager."

"Lager it is . . . And what about your mate? Is he on Guinness too?"

"Very good of you. I'll have a pint of lager as well."

"Janet, Janet, put two pints of Guinness on that order please, will you?" asked the little chap, beaming at the barmaid.

"Jesus Christ!" swore Pat.

"Listen, son," the man continued as his hand returned to Pat's arm, "we've got to stick together. We might have our differences, but we've got more in common, right?" His nod was again directed towards the two Sikhs. "They're taking over. Everywhere. You just have to go along Paisley Road West near the Toll and all you see is brown faces. It's like fucking Bombay. Woodlands is even worse, because they've got the curry shops there too. The smell! And the curtains. You can always tell where the Pakis have reached by looking at the windows: newspapers, old rags, any fucking thing over them except a proper curtain. And they never clean them either. Never."

"Bombay is in India."

"What?"

"Bombay is in India," repeated Sam. "It's not in Pakistan."

"You know what I mean, anyway. I mean, they're all brown. India, Pakistan; Pakistan, India. they're all manky. They all look the same, anyway; what's the difference? I don't want *any* of them here. Son," the fat man continued, placing his other hand on Sam's arm, gazing into his face with tears welling in his eyes, "son. Do you know where my boy is?"

"What, him do you mean?" asked Sam, pointing at Pat. "He's standing in this pub drinking a pint of Guinness that's supposed to be a pint of lager."

"My son," porky went on, "is back there." He pointed over his shoulder towards the TV screen, which at that instant was showing a repeat performance of an episode of 'Dallas'. Both Pat and Sam looked at the screen:

"In Texas?" asked Pat.

"Back there where they've sold us out!"

"In Texas?" asked Sam.

"He went across there, thinking he could make something of himself. To find something better than he would have found here. He had a swimming pool; and his wife had a maid. He was talking about moving to a bigger house and hiring a gardener. He was talking about inviting me and the wife out for a visit. Maybe to stay. My boy. Who'd expect a lad from Maryhill to have a swimming pool?"

"I think everyone in Texas has a swimming pool," mused Sam.

"He wrote to us last week: they're coming home. He said they had put some big darkie in charge of his department, and that he couldn't understand a fucking thing he was talking about. He said that the maid was asking for more money. He said that he couldn't get any more promotion unless he blacked up and pretended he didn't know how to read or write.

"He went out there; he made that country what it is today. Now he's coming home. We were going to visit him. And do you know what our government's talking about now? They're talking about stopping the white Rhodesians coming to Britain. They're talking about not letting them in. Let in all the sambos you like, but keep my boy out.

"They're all leaving. They stayed there for years trying to build, trying to build a little Britain out there in the jungle, and now they're being squeezed out by these communist nig-nogs. They're loyal. They all are. Ian Smith fought in the Battle of Britain. Now they're saying they won't let them in, as if we don't know them. It's my boy. These people are our kith and kin."

"What are you talking about?" asked Pat. "What's this 'kith and kin' business? My old man was a darkie, Why didn't you let him in?"

"Ah," replied the fat man, "but he was a white darkie, wasn't he?"

"What do you mean, a 'white darkie'? He was as black as Al Jolson, and he worked in Rhodesia and South Africa. Cleaning swimming pools. Then he went from there to Belfast, where he had a job as a lavvy attendant, and he cleaned white Protestant arses, and built wee piles out of the sixpences they gave him as tips. And then he must have got a bit whiter, because he caught the ferry from Larne to Stranraer, and got in because he passed the test. And then he came to Glasgow and he lived in a mud hut for years. But he trained, and got fit, and he juggled a football and polished up his skills. He played in Saturday Morning League football, then Juvenile, then the Juniors, then Senior Second Division, then provincial First Division up north, until he came to the attention of one of the top clubs in the country because of his outstanding play. And they gave him a trial, liked what they saw, produced a contract, uncapped the pen, and then threw him out because he was a left footer. He turned black again after that."

"A left footer," mused the fat man. "These modern football teams are balanced, you know. Left foot here, right foot there. A balanced side. My boy was part of a balanced side. What is there now? We were supposed to go there. A swimming pool! What is there now? He said in his letter that gangs of darkies gather in the centre of Salisbury every night and deliberately piss on the statue of Cecil Rhodes. And the police, whites too, just stand around and let them.

"He's coming home. He's had enough. He's a Rhodesian citizen, but let them try to stop him coming in! He's coming home. I used to think about sitting round that swimming pool, too. Just like in 'Dallas'."

***

"Was your old man a darkie, Pat?" asked Sam much later, after the fat man had left the pub on unsteady legs.

"No, no; at least, I don't think so. He used to tell me sometimes that he felt like one, though."

"What do you mean?"

"I'll tell you some day. Another pint?"

"No, I've got to make a move. I've got some marking to do."

"It's not like you to let work interfere with the important things in life," said Pat mockingly, fingering his glass.

"Well, there comes a time . . . Everything's piling up. I'll have to get through some of it or I'll get my balls chewed." Sam slid from his bar stool and half turned towards the door, raising one hand in farewell: "See you."

"Aye, see you Sam. Listen," added Pat, detaining him with a hand on his coat, "where will you be tomorrow?"

"I don't know, why?"

"Well, any chance of tapping a few quid? Just till Friday?"

"You already owe me five," said Sam despairingly.

"Just till Friday. I'm really strapped for cash. I had a short week, what with having those days off on the sick. I'll pay you back on Friday."

Sam sighed: "OK, I'll see you in the Horseshoe any time after five. I'll be having a drink with some of the staff from the school. OK?"

"Cheers, Sam," replied Pat, raising his glass. "See you tomorrow."

"See you, Pat."

***

Outside, it was unnaturally still. Snow was falling steadily, adding to the layer which already carpeted the ground, filling in the footsteps of those who had preceded Sam along the pavement. There was not much traffic on the road, and what there was moved slowly, the car tyres making a splashing sound as they ground the snow into slush and sprayed it in soiled heaps in the gutters. The traffic was so light, and the temperature so low, that parts of the road were beginning to freeze, the falling snow refusing to melt. In a few hours time the road would be as white as the pavement, even the places where tracks marked the progress of vehicles. If it snowed on through the night, many roads would be impassable by morning.

This thought cheered Sam as he walked along the street with his hands in his pockets, coat unbuttoned despite the weather. He liked snow. It brought a promise of disruption, of order breaking down, almost imperceptibly. More things seemed possible during inclement weather, during the long winter nights.

Hurricane force winds blowing down power lines, dislodging roof tiles and chimney pots, whipping the sea into a frenzy, smashing over sea walls and pounding the ferries to the islands; boats sunk at their moorings; walking, head down, straining and back bowed; a car smashed by a fallen tree, flecks of blood on the windscreen.

Thunderstorms: the heavens opening; cars cutting a wake

along main roads, abandoned with doors open at the bottom of a hill; sandbags at the front door, dead sheep with bloated bellies floating to market down High Street; trees like islands in aerial photographs; waders, rowing boats, granny carried to safety, burst banks, the pitch of a roof above a new lake.

Snow howling in from the steppes: helicopter shots of isolated hill farms, fodder dropped to stranded livestock; corpses in metal tombs under the drifts; deserted city streets, white mountains stacked against walls, objects becoming anonymous bumps in the monotonous landscape; unspeakable horrors pulled from an icy shroud.

All of these things brought with them a sense of dislocation, a vague hint of disintegration, and if things disintegrate . . . no one pursues you any more. The mail gets lost, so bills do not arrive. Appointments do not have to be kept because transport is disrupted. There are excuses for almost everything! You can walk into pubs and order double whiskies, excusing your profligacy with a shiver, a rub of the hands, and a vague nod of the head towards the snow/sleet/wind/rain. You can ask people for favours and they feel terrible if they refuse because you can look very pitiful if you are soaked to the skin or have snow on your boots. If people ask *you* for favours, you can turn the pitiful expression to double advantage by slipping it on when you turn them down. I would if I could, but . . . And no repercussions! You get off scot free!

You can walk into work hours late and people let you off, even though they know the weather did not cause you any *real* difficulties. If they question your story about ten feet snowdrifts or vast lakes flooding vital roads, then someone might question *their* stories.

Cars were remarkably handy in that respect too, because they froze up during cold weather, had to be dug out of snowdrifts, and things happened to their sparkplugs. Public transport was not so good, because people could check up on your story by phoning British Rail or Glasgow Corporation, although they rarely did. The real misery in winter was when the snow thawed, unless it brought flooding in its wake; when the fog lifted; when the rains stopped, unless they stopped permanently, which would be pretty good too. Then we have to return to normality: trains run on time, appointments are kept, offices are reopened, burst pipes are mended; chaos retreats; people *expect* again.

Sometimes, Sam woke up in the morning and hoped that a nuclear war had broken out so that he could have a long lie in bed and forget about work that day. Other times, he would contemplate hurling himself down a flight of stairs, or launching himself in front of a car, hoping to sustain some not too painful injury which would, nevertheless, entail an extended leave of absence from his place of employment, and relieve whatever minor pressures he was being subjected to at the time from the world at large. He would look with envy at news films from the Middle East and South America which showed an endless procession of revolutions and coups d'état, most of which, he was sure, were organised by people who had done something wrong at work and did not want to face the boss on Monday morning.

As he walked along the deserted pavements, Sam experimented with his footing on the icy surface, half hoping to crash to the ground, perhaps sustaining mild concussion, or a simple ankle sprain which would cause an impressive swelling. At home lay mountains of examination papers written by his first, second and third year classes, all, as yet, unmarked. They were due to have been handed to his principal teacher some time during the previous week: "God," he thought despairingly. "God, God, God. Come out, come out, wherever you are. I want you to come and take me away. Come on, come on. I'm waiting."

A ten-minute walk brought Sam to the street corner opposite the entrance to his close. Across the road, up three flights of stairs, door open. His flat lay near: his house, his home. He leant against a street lamp, its orange glow making his face look ghastly, staring at the gap in the dark grey sandstone. Above, he could see his window: black, with an almost derelict air. Lights from other windows surrounded it, and behind a drawn blind he could see a female figure, pausing before moving on. From the ground level windows all around him he could hear television music blaring, interspersed with the sound of New York shootings and the screech of fast sedans. He shivered slightly and hunched his shoulders as a cat howled in a back court like an abandoned child. From somewhere came the sound of breaking glass, followed by silence: an incident leaving no echoes.

A crowd of teenagers came lurching along the pavement, shouting and jostling one another, bending to pick up snow from the ground to mould into missiles. Three wore fawn duffel coats, a fourth, taller and fatter than the rest, wore a huge, olive green parka. In the middle of the horseplay, the fat one slipped on the ice and lay on his back, cursing, then laughing as he gave up attempts to regain his footing. The other three gathered in a huddle, spluttering and giggling, then moved menacingly towards the stranded fourth, gathering armfuls of snow from hedgetops and car bonnets. The youth on the ground, recognising their intentions, tried vainly to raise himself up but fell back, striking his head off the pavement with a sickening thud as his legs splayed in the air. The others, seeing his attempts to rise, ran towards him with wild yells and as they reached him, dumped their loads on top of his head, rubbing snow on his face and stuffing it down his neck. They rolled him over bodily into a drift at the side of the road, one of them grabbing the hood of his parka and slamming it over his head after filling it with snow.

"Bastards!" screamed fatty, even this sounding slurred as he floundered in the snow with limbs flailing. "You fucking bastards! I'll fucking get you for this, don't you worry."

The others ran off, gasping for breath as they roared with laughter, slapping one another on the back, staggering on rubber legs, bumping into one another.

"Willie's a snowman! Willie's a snowman!" they sang, accompanying the chant with hand claps to a football terracing rhythm as they disappeared round a corner.

"Bastards," muttered Willie as he rolled on to his belly. "Fucking bastards." He crawled on his hands and knees to the iron railing which ran outside of a close mouth and raised himself on unsteady legs, parka hood still over his head, dripping snow. He angrily knocked the hood down, shaking snow from his hair, and rested there a moment, hands on the spikes, his legs making involuntary movements, buckling at the knees as his upper body swayed to and fro, shoulders dancing. At last, regaining what to him seemed to be equilibrium, he lurched on up the slight hill, weaving from side to side, occasionally stopping unsteadily to brush snow and ice from his hair and clothes. He had progressed a further twenty yards in this fashion when he slipped and fell again, sliding on his back a few feet down the slope. This time, he pulled himself up by grabbing on to a hedge which lined the building, fencing in a tiny garden. No sooner had he settled on his feet than he crashed forward again, flattening a large section of the privet under his body, snow erupting around him, with only his legs protruding on to the pavement.

He lay motionless for about thirty seconds, surely injured, bleeding; dead. Gradually, however, he stirred to life again and having pulled himself erect, moved gingerly to the street corner, taking advantage of all possible support en route. He too leaned against a street lamp, from where he was clearly visible to Sam, although now more than fifty yards away. Suddenly, Willie's whole frame convulsed and he retched a steaming fountain into the street. Two coughs preceded a second fountain, this one less violent. Further roaring brought only a small trickle of vomit from a now empty belly. Willie paused for breath, his right arm wrapped round the lamp post, his left hanging limply at his side. After a few seconds he straightened, wiped his mouth on his sleeve, and disappeared round the corner on slightly steadier legs.

Sam remained motionless under the lights, feeling his face numb with the cold. A flake of snow fell on an eyelash and blurred his vision. As he blinked it off, a couple walked up the hill and paused before his close. It was a neighbour, Eddie Callaghan, with a woman who was a stranger to Sam. Eddie was a fifty-five-year-old bachelor, a former shipyard rigger who had retired prematurely due to a heart condition or, as some people suggested, because his bottle had gone. A stocky, red-faced man, these physical features were accentuated by his bulky winter clothing and by that night's intake of alcohol.

His companion was a peroxide blonde hatchet, hair a mass of tight curls, wearing a black, flaired woollen coat with a nylon fur collar. Over the top of her shiny, plastic boots, two knobbly knees protruded from spider's legs. As he stared at her face, Sam thought he recognised her as one of a pair who haunted the local pubs; those they were not barred from.

The two walked tightly together, the blonde an inch or two taller than Eddie, a difference accentuated by the slope of the pavement: higher on the inside where ladies *always* walk. Their shoulders, hips and thighs pressed together as they made progress, heads down against the wind, arm in arm, warming one another with their bodies. Eddie carried a bulging plastic carrier bag in his right hand, the woman a huge white handbag under her left arm. They made no conversation as they progressed along the pavement, but as they reached the close mouth the pair stopped and exchanged a few words and nods and gestures before they both laughed and turned to climb the entrance stairs. Just as they reached the top of the short flight, just as they left behind them the downy carpet of snow on the pavement outside, just as Eddie turned to exchange a joke with his lady, the bottom fell out of the plastic bag.

There was a horrible crashing noise as bottles fell on the stone surface of the close mouth, amplified by the vault of the stair well. Eddie and his companion stared at the broken glass and the stream of liquid which spilled down the steps to melt the snow outside. Neither spoke for at least five seconds:

"You stupid wee bastard!" screamed the hatchet, breaking the ice. "I told you to use two carrier bags when you bought the carry-out in the pub, but, oh no, you knew best: you'll put them in one bag, won't you, you daft wee cunt."

"Mary . . ."

"That's it," said Mary, shaking off Eddie's placating arm. "And you can get your big paws off of me! I'm off. You can clean up your own mess. I'm away home."

"Mary . . ."

"You stupid cunt," exclaimed Mary in an agony of helplessness as she watched the last of the liquid drain away. "Some of my money was in there too."

"Mary . . ."

As Eddie made this latest conciliatory noise, Mary's handbag performed a brilliant arc in the yellow light and landed on top of Eddie's head.

"Mary," pleaded Eddie, attempting to ward off the blow, "it's OK. I've got some more booze in the house, honest."

This information seemed to calm Mary somewhat: "Are you sure now?" she asked him after a pause, prodding his shoulder with her handbag. "You'd better not be codding me or I'll gut you," she continued in a more certain tone.

"Honest, Mary, honest," replied Eddie. "I'll make it up to you, you'll see. Come on," he cajoled. "Come on up."

"All right," conceded Mary. "But I'm warning you!" she added, pointing a finger square in his face.

Eddie kicked the remains of the plastic carrier bag and the broken glass to one side and attempted to relink arms with his lady love. She rebuffed him violently. As they disappeared into the close, Sam saw a last flash of white plastic as the handbag sought fresh revenge.

Hands deep in his pockets, Sam bounced himself from the lamp post with a shrug of his shoulders and slowly crossed the street. As he was about to enter the close, he spotted a dog limping its way towards him, head down, rolling like a sailor on three legs with only a stump where the fourth should have been. It balanced its disfigured body with practised ease, tossing snow into the air as it flicked its solitary rear leg in pursuit of its still intact front pair. It was a mongrel: nondescript apart from its obvious disability, grey black hair matted, lean flanks showing the suggestion of ribs, tongue hanging and panting as if it were recovering from a cheerful summer's day romp in the park with its master. It was a scavenger, no doubt disturbed from its resting place among the rubbish bins by a housewife removing the day's smells from the kitchen before retiring for the night.

The dog did not see Sam until it was nearly upon him, whereupon it started and circled suspiciously through the snow to avoid him until it had passed safely. When it felt it had placed sufficient distance between himself and Sam, it resumed its progress up the incline, head bowed once more, staring despairingly at the ground. Despite himself, Sam felt touched and saddened. He crouched down, patted his right thigh with the palm of his hand, and quietly called the mongrel to him:

"Here, boy; here, boy," he coaxed. "That's a boy. Come on, I won't hurt you. Come on, boy."

The dog, hearing these words which perhaps struck a chord in its memory, stopped, turned and approached Sam, sniffing and wagging its tail. Tears seemed to stand out in its eyes as they reflected in the street lights.

"That's it, come on, boy," continued Sam encouragingly. "You're OK. That's it. Come on, I won't hurt you."

Sam held out his right hand, palm upward for the dog to sniff, but as he did so, it started back and growled, remem-bering other hands, not empty, not comforting, not consoling. It growled threateningly from deep in its throat and shied away, limping along the pavement, turning its head only once to ensure Sam was not following.

Sam remained for some seconds in a crouching position, hands now back in his pockets as he watched the mongrel vanish into the next close. He gripped his coat tightly round his body as he raised himself to his feet and climbed the stairs to his flat.

FROM THE BRAINWAVES OF A SLOTH

I looked around me, still dressed in my outside clothes. There were three sets of examination papers lying in neat bundles on the table, each wrapped in a sheet of double foolscap with the number of the class written in pencil on the outside. Next to these piles of essays were two red pens placed on top of the class lists on which I was to enter the marks I awarded for each paper. I had arranged them in this neat fashion ten days ago, just after the examinations, and there they had remained, untouched. They had begun to worry about me. The work involved in not correcting them was becoming more onerous than the work involved in correctin them. I had exhausted myself with excuses; I was fagged out inventing stories to explain my failure to produce the marks. They had to be done tonight.

I made a start by switching on the television and pouring myself a whisky, still flapping about in my coat and leaving damp footprints on the carpet. I threw off my duffel and flopped down on the settee, crunching a crust of bread concealed by a newspaper. A film was showing: French, with subtitles. That meant I had to concentrate. I slugged back my drink and stared blankly round the room, losing track of 'The Butcher' as a grey hole stared back at me.

I had only been living in the flat for around eight months, since the end of April when I had left Oban Drive and my potted palm and all that went with it. Now, I looked around me and saw yellow walls and dark yellow paintwork and yellow curtains and yellowing posters and books with curling, yellow pages. The carpet was sort of yellow too: sort of yellow black.

The winter had defeated the cockroaches where I had failed but it had spared the neighbours, and I could hear them now, above and below me and from both sides. Shouts, thumps, bumps, yells, whoops: a record player played Dolly Parton then there was silence. An accordion struck up, accompanying a hoarse female voice. Sad songs. It was time for weeping 70° proof tears and hugging the punter you had punched at half-past eight. It was the wind-up to the festive fortnight: the rockets were on the launch pad, fuelled and pointing towards the sun. Krypton was about to explode, flinging radioactive particles in every direction, spreading tartan Kryptonite to every Thistle and Shamrock Club from Toronto to Sydney. Here was I, at the heart of the super-nova, wrapped in a lead casket.

I lay back, staring at the ceiling, listening to "Your Cheatin' Heart" being rasped out for tin ears:

> "Youra cheatin' hearta,
> Willa tella ona yooaa."

I wanted to join in but my heart wasn't in it. I poured myself another drink. The film was continuing in the background, unintelligible French conversation filling in the empty spaces. I eyed the examination papers.

"My, my, myaa, Delilaaah!
Why, why, why, Delilaaah?"

The first paper in the second year bundle was covered in spidery writing which depressed me even to look at, so I put it to the bottom of the pile. The second one looked more promising: neat, nicely rounded; a good hand. The number "4" appeared in the margin. I looked at number 4 on the question paper: "You are trapped in a lift with someone you do not like. Write an essay describing your thoughts and actions." I looked at the budding Tolstoy's answer paper: "One day I was trapped in a lift with a big darkie who was boggin he was stinking something terrible he was really smelly so I took my . . ." I put that one to the bottom of the pile too.

"Well I was sittin', in a honky, in Chicagohhhh,
With a broken heart and a woman on ma maiiiindaa."

I realised I had to approach the problem scientifically. I picked up the second year papers and threw all ninety into the air. Those which landed with the author's name showing I placed to my left in a pile on the floor, those which had the name hidden I placed on my right. I then picked up the right-hand bundle and again threw them into the air. On landing, I separated them into two groups in the same manner as before. I repeated this for the left-hand bundle. I now had four piles of papers. Bundle number one was going to be awarded a mark in the range 0-25, bundle number two was going to be awarded a mark in the range 26-50, bundle number three was going to be awarded a mark in the range 51-75, and bundle number four, the high fliers, was going to be awarded a mark in the range 76-99. I couldn't give 100, of course; not for an essay.

I now had a good spread of marks for the year; well done. I quickly marked the papers with my red pen and transcribed my assessments into the class lists, having repeated the process with the other two year groups. I had finished. All over. All done. "I knew you'd come through, Sam." "Well, you know me — I might be late, but I get it done eventually." Laugh, laugh. What a character.

Time for bed. The film had finished. A humming noise was coming from the back of the television. Only dregs remained in my glass. I packed the papers in my briefcase, stretched, locked the front door and stripped my clothes off. I felt tired. Lying in bed, lights out, staring at the ceiling, thinking last thoughts, a loud crash came from above followed by a muffled curse.

> "Take these chainsa,
> From ma heartanda
> Seta meefreeeeea."

IN THE BEGINNING

The Glasgow coat of arms is really neat, and a truly fascinating story lies behind them. Unfortunately, I'll be forced to provide you with the abridged version. For reasons of economy. OK?

First of all the arms themselves, set in a traditional form with a little mitred and sceptred saint perched on top. We all know who that is, don't we? But the arms: there is a bird, a tree, a fish, a bell, a mound, a ring, and a motto. The whole thing has got something to do with religion.

The bell is one that St Mungo (remember him?) brought from a trip to Rome which, someone once told me, was then the CENTRE OF THE CHRISTIAN WORLD. When he came back from there he wanted to talk to everyone, so guess what? A mound rose up for him to stand on. Miraculous, wasn't it? While he was back in Scotland, he restored a bird to life for a friend of his, a Saint called Serf. Do you see how it all fits in? The tree represents the frozen wood which Mungo blew upon to get a light for Serf's lamp. I can do that too, but I need a hell of a lot more to drink than I've got in me now.

But it's with the 🐟 and the ⭕ that the real story lies.

Queen Languoreth was married to the king who ruled over the land round Glasgow. She gave a ⭕ of hers to a fellow she shouldn't have given it to. It was a courtly love: chastity, honour, respect; adoration from afar. It boils down to the fact that there was no, was no, eh . . . sex involved in their relationship. Strict adherence to the code: Lancelot and Guinevere. The man thus favoured by the Queen was lying asleep on a river bank when the

King happened to pass by. He spotted the ⭕ on the lover's finger, removed it without rousing him from sleep, threw it in the river, then asked Queen Languoreth to produce it. Clever, eh? The Queen approached Mungo: "What can I do, O Holy Man?" "Go fishing in the Clyde, O Virtuous Queen." So she did. And

she caught a 🐟. And found the ⭕ inside its mouth. Problem solved.

I said earlier that each part of the coat of arms had something to do with religion, but this might not be immediately apparent if

you look at the ⟨MOTTO⟩ at the foot, which reads a pretty secular "Let Glasgow Flourish". But. The original text. As preached by Mungo. "Let Glasgow flourish by the preaching of thy word and the praising of thy name". And we all know whose word and whose name he's referring to. Don't we? The spiritual reference was deleted when the arms were established in the mid 1800s. The energetic capitalist ethic which dominated city life thought people might get the wrong idea and sit around on their arses preaching and talking about God instead of bursting their guts in the glory of labour. Everything in its place.

Go on, flourish, you bastards, or I'll kick your teeth in.

Pat McKenna

The alarm went off long before dawn. Pat let it ring and the bell ran down until it finally stopped. He relaxed again. His eyes began to close. There was a nagging pain in his left socket which, he knew from a million Mondays, wouldn't go away unless he had another few hours' sleep. Sleep.

His eyes closed but only for a few seconds because a set of sharp toenails raked the back of his leg:

"Get up."

Pat feigned sleep.

"Get up!"

Another kick.

"Get up, you!"

Pat closed his eyes more tightly, holding on to the edge of the bedclothes until his knuckles turned white. Even louder:

"Get up! You're not going to lose another job, you! I can get up for my work — why can't you? You're OK spending the money but not out grafting for it. Get up, you lazy sod!"

When he heard this, Pat spun round with his right hand in a fist. His wife rolled back on the bed, her hands holding the bedclothes to her chin, nylon 'Comfi-Warm' armour.

"I've told you before," she threatened through her tight mouth. "If you lay a finger on me again, I'm off to my mother's with the kids."

Pat fell back on the bed with a long sigh, his hands rubbing his face, trying to squeeze the pain from his head, trying to erase years of memories which engulfed him with the nausea of despair. "Go! For Christ's sake, go!" he snarled to himself. But Pat did not say it. Instead, he leant over and looked at the clock, although he knew what it would say: 6.15.

He threw back the blankets and stood up, staggering slightly as his legs took the strain. His work clothes were below him, lying where he had thrown them the previous night. First, he dragged on his pullover, scratching where the wool rubbed against his skin, then felt for his trousers in the gloom. No Y-fronts. His fingers crawled down one leg and found them rolled in a ball where the trousers bagged at the knee. They smelled. He pulled them on, followed by his denims, picked up his boots and socks and, through the blackness, made his way to the bedroom door. His wife, still and silent, watched him go.

Outside in the hall, Pat switched on the light and tiptoed to the kitchen over cold linoleum, a sour belch filling his mouth as he went. Starting to shiver, he lit all of the rings on the gas cooker and sat down on a chair to put on his socks and boots. He could tell from the muffled silence outside that snow had been falling during the night. Looking out of the window, his heart flickered with the hope that the weather conditions would prevent the bus service from operating.

FROM THE BRAINWAVES OF A SHEEP

The bastards are always on when you don't want them, aren't they? My head was still thumping. I needed a cup of tea. When I was lacing up my boots I had to laugh when I remembered some of the crack from the night before. Jesus, I'd been bevied! Wee Tam Watt had been worse, though. The wee man can't hold it any more. His gut's away, same as his brother. Judging by the antics of him recently, his head's away too for that matter. The old bevvy, that's what it does it to you — you mark my words. Sam. Bingo! I'd to get the cash off him in the pub!

I put the kettle on to boil for tea and looked inside the cupboard and the fridge for some grub. Nothing. What does she do with the money I give her? At one stage I thought of going back to the bedroom. But what was the point? There were still a couple of slices of bread in the bin so I took them out, put on the pan with last night's bacon fat in the bottom, and fried up the bread for breakfast.

I felt in my trouser pockets: not a light! It came back to me that I'd bought the last drink the night before. I went back into the hall to get my jacket where it was hanging behind the door and went into the pockets for cigarettes: nothing but a few crumbs of tobacco at the bottom. There was a tear at the seam under the right arm. Fuck knows how that had happened.

The smell of the bread frying brought me back into the kitchen. I turned the slices in the pan, poured boiling water into a cup then added a teabag and three spoonsful of sugar. There was no milk.

I took my cigarette papers from the drawer under the kitchen table and looked for some likely looking douts in the ashtray. There were some right crackers. I knew from the size of the fag ends that the wife's sister must have been over the night before. I could just imagine the two of them sitting round the table moaning and whining — probably about me. I picked up two of the douts, broke off the hard end where the fag had been stubbed out, split the rest and rolled a home made. That's about all you get out of that cow — her leavings.

The bread was ready, so I put it on a plate where it sat steaming, surrounded by spots of grease. It was done just right: crunchy, not soggy, and I could still taste the bacon through it. I drank the tea with the fry and my mouth made the rim of the cup all yon greasy way. I started to feel a bit better, if you can feel good at all at half-past six on a December morning with a day full of crap stretching out before you.

Sixty pence for fags, a pound for bus fares, ten pence for a paper. I needed two quid to get me to work. It would have solved everything if I'd been able to tap that cash off Sam the night before. I knew I could get a tenner off the moneylender once I reached the plant. That would have given me enough to go for a pint that night, pay wee Tam the fiver I owed him, and leave me my bus fares for the next morning. And I would have the fiver from Sam too. Then I remembered I had nothing for my piece. And what would I do for money for the rest of the week? I could borrow twenty from the moneylender. That meant I would have to find twenty-two notes on the Friday, but I'd have some readies for a few days anyway. Who the fuck cares?

Two quid. It doesn't sound much, does it? I looked in all the usual places for the kids' dinner money. No chance. I knew she'd have it stashed somewhere because she likes to keep all her cash in wee compartments: the insurance money behind the clock on the mantelpiece, catalogue money in the Toby jug, Provy cheque money under the table lighter in the front room. I knew she had paid the insurance and the catalogue but I was sure the Provy man didn't come round until Wednesday. I sneaked into the front room and looked under the lighter. Ha ha. Big fucking joke. There was no money there, just a note from you know who saying: "I learned my lesson last week — walk to work."

The bitch! I knew that cow of a sister of hers had put her up to it the night before. I was fucking sure I wasn't walking anywhere. The bitch wanted me to ask her for the money. She knew I was always skint on a Monday. She wanted me to go crawling in there and beg for my own cash, so she could gloat at me again. I could just imagine the two of them the night before, laughing.

I went to the Toby jug just to check. Nothing. Not even a note. The clock. Nothing. I knew she was lying in there, giggling, cuddling her handbag with the big, fat purse inside. Bitch! I wasn't going to grovel to her again. I decided to take the day off. I felt like a wee holiday, anyway: lie back and watch the kids' programmes on the telly. I wasn't going to get down on my hands and knees. She could rant and rave when she got up if she liked; I wasn't moving.

I crashed out on the settee and began to feel quite comfortable. Then all of a sudden my brain exploded and I could feel the shit moving inside me: Stewart! He'd said he'd bag me if I took any more time off without a doctor's line. The big, fat bastard! He's always been out to get me. Fuck it! OK, I would get my jotters. This time it wouldn't be my fault; it would be down to her.

I stood up and began to walk across the floor, thinking what I was going to say to various people. Stewart. That turd wouldn't believe a word I came up with anyway. There was no point even thinking about it. What I wanted to say was: "Listen, you big, fat, Orange prick: stick your shitty job up your shitty arse." The wife. What was the point of thinking what to say to her either? She hasn't listened to what I say in years. The only thing she'd understand would be a bat in the mouth. I thought about the doc.

What were the chances of me getting a line out of him for a few days on the sick? Middle-class cunt. It's OK for him sitting in his nice, cosy office. He doesn't give two fucks about the poor mugs off grafting for their cash.

I walked to the window and looked outside past the curtain. If only the snow had been a couple of inches deeper: no bastard would have been going to work. I looked up to see if there were any clouds in the sky but it was too dark to tell. Bitch! It's my money, anyway. What does she do with it all? There's never even anything for my pieces. The pain was coming back in my head. I needed a drink.

I looked at the time: seven o'clock. That meant I was going to be late no matter what happened. I searched behind the clock again, just to make sure: nothing. I wondered if I could sneak some money out of her handbag but I knew for certain she was still holding it. I knew for a fact that she was still awake in there, listening, waiting on me coming in. Christ, that bastard Stewart! Two quid, that's all I wanted. Two quid. Even a pound, just for my busfares.

I wondered if the kids had any cash. I thought maybe that cow of a sister-in-law had given them something last night. I walked back to the window to think this one over. No chance. Even if I could have found the dough, the brats would have screamed the place down if they had copped me taking it. They take after their mother that way. I was getting desperate. I really felt like going in and putting one on her chin.

I didn't even know what I was doing when I picked up the tin of fish food from the table nearest the window and took the lid off. The stink from it seemed worse than usual and it made me feel sick in my guts. I pinched a speck of the gunk and held it over the goldfish bowl. The fish was darting about like crazy: it must have seen my hand over its head and known it was in for some grub. As I dropped the flakes in, I saw a green, fuzzy shape through the water. It was a green, fuzzy, "hello, I'm the answer to your problem" shape. I lifted the bowl, slapped my hand on the kids' dinner money, and tucked it into my trouser pocket.

As I opened the front door, I planned what I would say to

Stewart: "Sorry I'm late. The wife was taken ill. OK, Fatarse?" Come off it. Give us a break.

I've only hit her once, anyway, and that was eight years ago. And it wasn't fucking hard enough.

* * *

Pat closed the front door behind him and descended the stairs, each step worn down the middle through a hundred years of use. Outside, it had stopped snowing, but a bitter wind blew through his coat, striking a chill in his bones, especially under his right armpit where it had found the hole in his jacket. He walked along the middle of the pavement, along a path in the snow marked out by the feet of others as they walked to work, walked in the darkness lit by street lamps. He walked two hundred yards in between rows of identical tenement blocks, their close mouths lit up by a bare bulb at the entrance. He turned two corners and reached the main road and the bus stop where he waited for transport into the city centre.

The long queue of people meant that a bus was due at any moment, but he decided to take the risk of crossing the road to the newsagent's for cigarettes and a paper. He moved off the kerb and his foot sank into the snow which had formed a drift in the gutter. He tried to shake the snow from his boot and lower trouser leg as he crossed the road, looking like some bizarre, limping stick insect as he progressed to the other side.

The shop was warm with the smell of a paraffin stove and Pat felt like asking the woman behind the counter if he could curl up in a corner for a snooze. Instead, he asked for twenty 'Embassy' tipped and a box of matches, and picked up a *Daily Record* from a pile on the counter. He handed a pound of the kids' dinner money to the woman, and glanced through the paper as he waited for his change. First, the naked girl in her regular position on page three, today called Cindy Lou and aged seventeen, the owner of very large mammaries. Then the sports pages at the back with their out-of-date reports of Saturday's football matches: "'Gers Turn On The Style"; "Dons Caught Napping"; "Last Gasp Celts".

The woman gave him his change, but Pat suddenly remembered he needed the exact fare on the bus, so he had to cash another of the pound notes. Cigarettes and matches in coat pocket, paper folded under the arm, change in trouser pocket: off into the cold.

The bus was at the stop when he left the shop, so Pat trotted across the road, putting his other foot into a drift as he reached the kerb.

"Shit, I'm not going to get on," he thought to himself as he stood at the back of the queue, edging his way towards the door with the others. The bus was crowded, upstairs and down, and the people in front of him who were getting on were being forced to stand on the lower deck. Four in front of him. Three. Two. The driver twisted in his seat to see how many were standing. One person in front of him. Now Pat.

"Sorry, pal; no more room."

"Aw, come on. I'm late already."

"There's another bus behind me."

"Listen, I'm going to get bagged if I'm not at work soon."

"And I'm going to get bagged if I let you on and an Inspector sees me."

"Come on, act the white man. There's no sign of an Inspector. Someone'll get off at the next stop."

"Aw for Christ's sake, let him on," shouted an old man sitting near the door. He looked like an engineer, wearing a bunnet and a checked jacket over faded blue overalls, a haversack slung round his neck. "There's no Inspectors out at this time in the morning. I'm getting off at the next stop, anyway."

"OK, OK," sighed the driver, turning again to face Pat. "What do you want?"

"Thirty-five."

Click. He was on. As he moved past the driver, the old workman, sitting on the front seat of the bus, gave him a broad wink. Pat returned it.

He felt too tired to stand, so he sat down on the steps leading upstairs. Fumbling in his pockets for cigarettes, he remembered there was no smoking on the bottom deck. He wondered if sitting on the steps meant he was on the bottom or the top. Fuck it. He lit up. Two stops later a passenger from upstairs pushed his way past him, which meant an empty seat. Pat climbed to the top deck where the atmosphere was blue with smoke and peered into the fog, searching for the vacant space. Right at the back. Making his way there was like crawling into a sock. The air was thick, and warm with the heat of two double rows of bodies. All the windows were closed. No one spoke and the only sounds were the rustle of newspapers and the noise of people racking their bodies in paroxysms of coughing, bringing up smokers' phlegm which the more discreet swallowed, the less particular deposited in glutinous gobs on the floor, despite a sign at the front of the bus which read: "No Spitting". Some wag had rubbed out the "p" and replaced it with a spidery "h", so that at a quick glance the sign said "No Shitting".

Pat sat down with a sigh of relief, his cigarette jammed between his lips, his right leg splayed out into the passage. His neighbour, a young boy of around fifteen or sixteen, slumped with his head against the window, rattling with every bump on the road, dead to the world, hunched in his donkey jacket.

Pat opened his paper again and re-examined the nude on page three. Years ago, almost without fail, he would get an erection on the early morning bus journey to work. Not because of nudes in the newspaper: they were not allowed in those days, anyway. Perhaps it was the rocking movement of the bus's suspension, maybe it was idle, subconscious thoughts, perhaps it was because his erotic dreams had been disturbed by the shriek of the alarm clock. Pat did not really know or care. All he knew was that he wasn't getting them anymore. Most times, when the thought popped into his head, he regretted the loss; after all, it was quite a pleasant condition in which to pass an unpleasant bus journey. Sometimes he worried about it.

The article next to the nude told of a drama on the A74, where a stranded motorist had caught her skirt in the boot of her car when pulled up at the verge, revealing her knickers to passing motorists. "An AA spokesman said . . ." The next page told of the anguish of a sex-change peer as he struggled to annul his marriage. "A Vatican spokesman said . . ." Further on was the page devoted to readers' contributions: "Scotland's Liveliest Letters". One was headed "Proud Service": "I served in the Home Fleet on the Russian convoys in World War II, a very hazardous life indeed for the princely sum of just over £1 per week. In the spring of 1943 I was serving on HMS *Glasgow* when King Geroge VI reviewed the Fleet. It was an experience of which I am proud." E. McNish, Glasgow. Another was headed "Top Tip":

> "When you're feeling down,
> When you have lost your zip
> Don't wear a frown.
> Just do as I do,
> Pick up the *Daily Record*
> And read it through,
> 'Cos that's my way
> For not feeling blue."
> Jim Curdie, Thornwood Avenue, Glasgow.

Pat flicked to the sports pages at the back of the paper. When he reached them, he leaned over the unconscious figure next to him and rubbed the condensation from the window. Peering out into the still darkened streets, he looked for landmarks. The Kelvin Hall. Nearly there. Pat refolded the paper, saving the sports page for later: once; twice to make a long rectangle. Then in half again to make it into a wallet shape. Slipped into his inside pocket, it sprung open to make a bulge in his jacket over his heart. He settled as deeply as he could into the scantily padded seat, waiting for the remaining bus stops to pass. Hands deep in coat pockets, collar up, buttons buttoned, second cigarette dripping ash from his mouth, feet tapping a nervous dance on the floor. And thought. Of nothing very much, except at one point he dreamed of a farm gate, rusted, creaking, with a small boy swinging, feet lodged on the bottom rung and arms outstretched, head back to stare through clear eyes at a blue sky. But it passed.

* * *

Pat trudged through the streets of the city centre, his feet automatically leading him towards the bus station at Anderston Cross where he would start the second leg of his journey to work. It was not yet 7.30. The streets were alive with the silent progress of workers wearing heavy boots, brown and blue overalls, soiled denims, pullovers, anoraks, donkey jackets — some with 'Wimpy' or 'Bovis' tattooed on the shoulders — parkas, trenchcoats, woollen tammies — usually in the colours of football teams such as Rangers, Celtic, Partick Thistle, Manchester United and Leeds United — bunnets in all shapes, sizes and colours. In pockets thick with tobacco dust were crammed pieces wrapped in greaseproof paper which had once covered a loaf of 'Mother's Pride'. Or perhaps the package was stuffed into a small duffel bag or a green, ex-army haversack slung around the neck. All members of the throng had collars or hoods turned up against the wind, with hands reaching for warmth in coat pockets. It was possible to identify some trades: engineers showing a glimpse of baggy, blue overalls beneath their coats; the handle of a trowel and the rusted metal of a spirit level protruding from under the flap of a brickie's toolbag; a plumber making an early start, carrying lengths of copper pipe on his shoulder.

Very few ties or suits or smart shoes, or hats of the pork pie or bowler variety were to be seen. Office staff would not be arriving in this, the commercial centre of the city, for at least another hour. It was only twenty-five minutes to eight when Pat reached the peeling concrete facade of Anderston Bus Station. He was over half an hour late.

Winos were still dossing on the benches outside the station, risking death in the ice and snow. As Pat walked down the hill towards Argyle Street, he saw a bus waiting at bay number six: a single-decked, red and white hearse. A queue was snaking its way towards its entrance and Pat recognised a few of the passengers' faces as those of fellow workers. This recognition made him feel a little better, as if his problem was eased by being laid on many shoulders.

"How's Jimmy?" asked Pat, placing his hand on the shoulder of the little man at the end of the queue.

"Hello there, Pat. How's it going?" asked Jimmy in reply, spinning round in surprise.

"Oh, great, Jimmy. Stewart will use my balls as a bolas when he sees me walking in late again."

"I'm not in too great with my superintendent either," sighed Jimmy, shaking his weasel face from side to side, the bus station lights reflecting in his polished black hair. "I'd have taken the day off, but I've already been given a verbal warning for that."

"Same here," sighed Pat in understanding, putting on his hangdog expression. "I need the spondulcks anyway, what with Christmas and the New Year coming up."

"Ay, it's some life, eh, Pat?" philosophised Jimmy, inching his way ever forward.

"You're right there, Jim," agreed Pat.

"Still," said the pocket Spinoza, his back to Pat as he counted out his money for the driver, "I suppose these days we should be grateful we've got any sort of job at all."

"Too true," agreed Pat. Secretly he was not so sure.

"Well, see you, old son."

"See you, Jim."

Pat paid his fare and walked to the smoking area at the back of the bus, passing Jimmy, who was already seated halfway up the aisle, engrossed in his paper. There was a tacit understanding between most of the people at the factory that, unless they were friends as such, as workmates they exchanged greetings but did not socialise. If two met in a pub, they would nod to one another but stand apart at the bar. In the same way, on meeting on a bus, they would acknowledge one another's presence as acquaintances but would not impose by becoming neighbours on a seat. It was safer that way. It meant you could screw up most of the people you worked with without getting a conscience about it. After all, you would never see them again, anyway. And if you did, you could just ignore them, couldn't you? You see?

Pat was the last passenger to board. The bus throbbed to life and pulled slowly out of the station in a wide, arcing path, to become part of the stream which ran through the city centre. Over the dead river: dark; no vessels showing their lights; Christmas stars on the far bridge switched off. The bus was having a clear, fast run. The stops flashed by, empty of passengers. Perhaps it will make up some time. Lights. Just missed the red. Catch one and you catch them all. The whole way to Linwood.

The bus Pat used was usually crowded with men heading to work in Paisley and beyond but this morning, because of the late hour, Pat had a seat to himself. The floor was littered with crumpled, day-old newspapers, cigarette packets, trampled dog-ends and spent matches. Somewhere at the front, a bottle was rolling to and fro with the motion of the bus as it cornered and accelerated. Pat lit another cigarette and peered out of the window at the lightening streets. The bus was really picking up speed now, hammering along Paisley Road West, the road clear and fast, most of the traffic heading in the other direction. Pat reached into his pocket for his *Daily Record*, unfolded it and turned to the back, opening the first page: "Stay Right On The Ball With Super Record Sport". He tried to decipher the photographs, which were of a highly ambiguous nature, usually with a caption which bore little relationship with the action on view, then glanced at the report of Saturday's Celtic versus Kilmarnock match. Reading through it, he began to doubt if he had actually attended the same game. The article seemed to be totally at variance with his recollection of the play. It contained the usual phrases, comforting in their familiarity: "a game of two halves"; "lively Killie stunned Celts with an early goal"; "a late counter by the Celtic number nine before the interval"; "the men in hoops in command in the second half"; "a breakaway on the left brought a goalkeeping blunder which stunned the home fans into silence"; "last gasp equaliser by McAdam salvaged a point"; "the big number five soared above a stranded Killie defence to nod home"; "reshuffle for Wednesday's crucial top of the table tussle"; "new faces"; "freshen up the side"; "midfield supremo"; "lively striker"; "nippy winger"; "long-striding Fifer".

Pat's eyes flickered over the other football reports, looking for something of interest. He had already read the sports news in Saturday's *Evening Times* and in the *Sunday Post* and *Sunday Mail*, but he still had a last pang of hunger for news, as if unwilling to allow the weekend to vanish into the past, submerged by five working days. Finished with the football stories, but far from satisfied, he turned to the Racing Section to see if he could pick some winners.

Two meetings were listed: one at Plumpton, the other at Fontwell. Not being a regular punter, Pat had never even heard of Fontwell before, and, although Plumpton struck a familiar note, he did not have even the vaguest idea of where the place was. Somewhere in his mind he connected it with trains, but that was only because of the similarity between the town's name and that of a children's television puppet show which featured an anthropomorphic choo-choo.

The prizemoney offered for winning the races at the two meetings was meagre, to say the least: "Street Selling Handicap Hurdle, £426, about 2m., 10 runners"; "Chailey Novices' Hurdle, £584, about 2m., 12 runners"; Adur Amateur Riders' Handicap Chase, £617, about 2¾m., 18 runners". Perhaps, understandably, the prizemoney did not attract the cream of the country's jockeys or horses. Picking winners was like standing at a street corner and guessing the make and colour of the next car to pass. Betting on these races required the same amount of skill and held forth the same chances of success as the above activity.

Pat looked at what 'Garry Owen' and 'Newsboy' tipped as the likely winners of the races at the two meetings and compared their selections, looking for correlations. Both of the ace tipsters picked Balmuick Boy in the 4.15 at Plumpton. Pat felt in his pocket for the stub of a pencil, took it out, licked the point, and carefully put a cross next to Balmuick Boy's number at the edge of the column. This selection system he repeated for Good Intent in the 2.15, then, turning to Fontwell, for Swordsman in the 2.00 and Ragusa Imp in the 1.30. Six cross 5p doubles, four cross 5p trebles, 5p accumulator: a 5p Yankee. No, better make it a 10p accumulator: a small increase in the roll-up stake could make a tremendous difference in the winnings. Total stake: 60p. Jesus, if all four came up he would be quids in. He could pay back all of his debts . . . well, some of them . . . and still have a beano. Wait a minute: 8-1, 7-2, 6-4, 13-2. Ten pence at 8-1 equals 90p, going on at 7-2 equals £4.05p, going on at 6-4 equals ... No. Bad luck. Just let the money roll in.

Pat repocketed the pencil with some satisfaction, folded up the newspaper and stuffed it back inside his jacket. He would place the bet with old Archie when he reached work. Nearly there now, anyway: the sky lighter now despite heavy cloud; Paisley long passed. In front of him, the other latecomers were buttoning their coats, reslinging their haversacks, and slowly shuffling to the head of the bus where they stood in silence. Pat followed them, feeling fairly jaunty as a result of his calculations, and descended into the cold air as the bus drew into the kerb and breathed open its doors.

Turning round into the road where the plant was spread out, they were met with a stinging wind which took their breath away and reddened their cheeks. Collars were turned up, scarves tightened, as the workers bent their heads into the wind. A transporter thundered down the dual carriageway, six cars balanced on its double back, dragging the roaring air in its wake. Under the railway bridge which screamed the name of the workers' fate to passing motorists, urging them to buy. At intervals, individuals peeled from the stream, passing through the perimeter fence to head for their section, some disappearing into the underpass which tunnelled under the traffic to the sprawling complex on the opposite side of the road. Above them, a bridge protected from the elements led over the road: this not for men but for machines.

Pat usually entered the plant at the earliest opportunity, walking through the roar of the factory to his section, nearest to the motorway to Glasgow. Today he walked on alone, outside the perimeter fence, passing the gateposts manned by uniformed guards, his heart sinking again as he gazed through the bars to the squat factory beyond. Today, he wanted to remain at liberty for as long as possible.

People Inside Buildings I

Glasgow has old places and new places. When I say "old", I don't mean from thousands or even hundreds of years in the past, although the city has places of antiquity by the score — look at any tourist brochure. I mean those parts of the city where you can clock an old codger and his missus and know, just know they've been tramping those same streets for sixty or seventy years. You know they've lived up the same close since they used to wipe the snotters off their noses with the sleeves of their jerseys. You know that inside those two dotty old brainboxes there are enough memories, there is enough local history to fill the City Chambers with books.

When the two of them shamble out together to do the shopping it's an epic journey because every ten yards along the pavement they bump into some old crony who fills them in on the latest news about who's snuffed it and who's not talking to who because they missed their turn at cleaning the stairs. It's impossible for any ordinary person to progress normally along the street because the pavement is littered with pow-wows from one end to the next.

The "old" areas of the city have names like Govan, Partick, Calton, Dennistoun, Springburn and Maryhill.

I see them all now, the old districts spread out before me as I float across the city in a Zeppelin shaped like a Guinness bottle. Most of them have gone. Just disappeared in a cloud of dust. Abandoning my Zeppelin, I travel south under the Clyde to emerge from the Underground at Govan Cross. It looks like the end of the world. The new subway station stands in isolation amidst roads leading nowhere, crisscrossing abandoned building sites. A few crazed survivors of the holocaust roam aimlessly through the debris, looking for their false teeth.

But still in little pockets, a distorted version of the old life continues: geriatrics huddle for warmth outside close mouths which gape in awestruck silence at the devastation wreaked with ball and chain on their now deceased neighbours. Knots of survivors shake their heads fatalistically at the edge of screaming expressways, and reminisce about the good old days: the rats, the dampness, the cold, the public baths, the steamie, the outside cludgie. The time Aggie's wean caught meningitis and died. What happened to wee Bertha, her that had rickets? The old men cling to worn bunnets, perched like concrete slabs on shrunken heads. The women wield empty shopping bags and remember pots of porridge poured like cement down cheap-cheap chick throats. Son, you don't know, you just don't know, I tell you.

And then there are the "new" areas of Glasgow. When I say "new", I don't mean as in yesterday or even the day before, although there are areas in Glasgow like that as the District Council will tell you. I mean "new" like the news you read about in the papers: one day it's bright and white and real and crinkly fresh, next day it's something you eat your fish supper out of.

These places can be found on the outskirts of the city and they have names like Easterhouse and Nitshill and Castlemilk and Drumchapel.

As I swing above in my Zeppelin, the housing estates are below me like graveyards. Row upon row of identical tombstones press in on one another, separated by narrow paths. But the dead walk: the lost souls gape heedlessly at the endless monotony, and are in limbo once they have lost sight of their own marble block. These antiseptic loony-bins are personalised by gang slogans, meaningless scrawls, drawings of pricks and fannies, and splashes of blood from outbursts of violent frustrations.

Whole streets are boarded up and abandoned as civilisation retreats from the outer perimeters, leaving tumbleweed areas to the dog packs and the glue sniffers. Plaster facades crumble from walls to reveal stitched concrete below. Rone-pipes lean at crazy angles and weeds creep up to window level, leaving the building looking like a forgotten tusk. Fires break out, leaving the pill-boxes blackened with soot, and crows perch on the eaves, searching for carrion. Parked half on the pavement, half on the road is a rusted skeleton, stripped of seats, wheels, engine and wipers. The front windscreen, miraculously still intact, has along the top a sticker bearing two names: BILL — BETTY. A cat peers suspiciously from the open boot.

A row of shops stands isolated in a windswept piazza, steel shutters drawn permanently over their windows. Those still occupied bristle with barbed wire and burglar alarms, and a dim, yellow light can be seen shining through the grilled door. Others have closed for good, the carcass gutted and left to rot. A ball thuds montonously against the end wall as ragged-arsed kids dream of glory. Outside of the Co-op, prams are parked. A glance into a chipped pink one reveals it to contain a bag of smokeless fuel and five pounds of spuds.

At night, the streets are deserted. Where is there to go? The evening is still apart from the banging of a loose shutter in the wind and the light scramble of a discarded newspaper as it cartwheels amongst the debris in the gutter, until it is caught in an endless whirlpool of rubbish spinning wildly in a freak turbulence at the junction of two blocks. Then the silence is broken by a shout and the sound of broken glass and running feet, and a skid on concrete as someone falls to the ground to be treated with boots, bottles and bricks. Another bloodstain seeps into the anonymous earth and, far away, the siren call sounds from outside the ghetto.

Alec Dowdeswell

Alec knew something was wrong as soon as he entered the kitchen. He had come home to Bedford Street as normal, 5.30, Thursday evening, donkey jacket buttoned to the neck against the wind which was swirling powdery snow against his reddened face, plastic shoulder pads streaming with melted ice. He had climbed the tenement stairs to the third floor landing which was in gloom because someone had removed the bulb from the light fitting. This had caused him to fumble with his key as he opened the door, making a noise which probably alerted those inside to his approach. Inside the flat, he laid his grip and a plastic carrier bag on the floor, then removed his jacket and hung it on the clothes stand in the corner of the narrow hall, placing his checked bunnet on top of it. He removed his folded-up newspaper from the capacious inside pocket and searched for his pipe, tobacco, cigarettes and matches at the side, at the same time lifting each leg in turn and giving it a gentle shake to remove some fragments of snow and ice from the trouser bottoms, like a genteel dog drying after the rain. All was quiet, apart from the trilling of the budgerigar from the front room.

Alec picked up the carrier bag, opened the kitchen door, and saw Betty sitting at the table in her curlers and dressing-gown. He knew from her smudged mascara and swollen face that she had been crying, and could immediately tell from the expression in her eyes that this was no ordinary bout of depression. A slight movement of her head caused Alec to turn round and there, behind the door, he saw a man leaning insolently against the wall. The man's eyes, bullet holes below a lumpy forehead, studied him closely, a smug smile on his face. He was a huge figure, his small head topped with a helmet of black hair through which he ran square fingers.

"There you are, love," said Alec, turning back to the table and placing the plastic bag in front of Betty. "I've brought you a wee present. What's the matter?" he asked. "Are you not well? Don't you want to see what I've brought you?" Alec pulled a chair out and sat down opposite her. "What's the matter?" he repeated. "Are you not feeling up to par?" Alec heard a snort of derision coming from behind him:

"Up to par? Up to par?" mocked the large man. "Is that the patter you pick up on the golf course, your honour?"

Alec knew from his voice that the man had been drinking, and a shaft of fear ran through him.

"So you've decided to come home, have you?" continued the man in a voice heavy with sarcasm.

"What was that?"

"You've decided to come home after a hard graft on the road, home to the wee woman. And you've brought presents with you too, eh? Let's see what we have here."

The man shoved himself off from the wall with the palms of his hands and moved unsteadily towards the kitchen table. Alec put out his hand to prevent him reaching the plastic bag, but was restrained by a mute appeal from Betty.

"Let's see, now," murmured the man, opening the bag. Then louder: "'Lena Martell's Greatest Hits, Volume II'. Did you get her Volume I last week? You're doing well for a man who's saving hard for a fortnight's holiday in Saltcoats at the Fair, eh? And chocolates too? Jesus, you're a toff all right. Do you not think she's fat enough already?" he asked with a harsh laugh which turned into a hacking cough. "Give us one of your fags, hen, will you?" the man asked, tossing down the chocolates and removing a cigarette from Betty's packet which sat on the table.

"Has your loving brother been getting at you again, Betty?" asked Alec as the man lit up.

"Me, getting at her?" snarled Betty's brother through thick, blue smoke. "Don't you fucking start, pal. I've been telling her some home truths, that's all. And I'm just in the mood to knock your fucking head off if you start to act it with me. The only reason I haven't done it so far is because of her," he continued, nodding towards his sister who by this time had begun to cry again.

"Betty, Betty, come on, it's all right," Alec soothed, patting her arm. "Don't let him get to you. You know he's always trying it on. Tell me what's wrong."

"What's wrong! You should fucking know what's wrong!" screamed Betty's brother, lunging forward and slamming his fist down on the box of chocolates as he leant towards Alec.

"Come on, Betty, go in next door for a wee lie down while I sort this out," urged Alec, trying to ignore the atmosphere, heavy with violence.

"She's staying here, she's not going anywhere. She's going to listen to what I've got to say to you."

"Just a minute, Tam. It's your sister I'm speaking to, not you. Is she not allowed to answer for herself anymore? Come on, Betty." Alec stood up and grasped Betty's arm, meaning to lead her out of the room, but Betty remained seated, only looking at him through anguished, tear-stained eyes before she turned away with another sob which rocked her substantial body and caused her front curlers to bob up and down.

"Listen, pal," said Tam, moving towards him, flicking ash on the table as he did so. "'Do you think we're all stupid in here just because she is?" he asked, nodding towards Betty. "Do you think my head buttons up the back? She's saying no more to you, do you hear, no more. I'm talking for her now so you'd better listen or you'll have your head in your hands. Do you think we're all daft?"

Alec continued to look at Betty, willing her to turn her head so that he could look into her face, but she stared at the floor in silent resignation, a huge lump of bowed, dispirited flesh, fingering the frill on her dressing-gown with plump fingers on which there were two rings.

"I'm asking you: do you think we're all daft?" repeated Tam, his voice rising.

"You've already asked that question," replied Alec. "Do you really want me to answer it?"

"Oh, Mr Smartie, eh?" Tam lunged towards Alec, grabbing hold of his pullover with his left hand. Alec could smell cheap wine on his breath and automatically turned his head away. "Oh, sorry, your lordship, does my breath bother you? I forgot to bring my throat spray with me today."

"Look, Tam, you're drunk. I'm not going to argue with you. We just go on about the same things and it only upsets Betty." Alec stood up and attempted to lift Betty from her seat: "Come on, love. You go in and have a lie down and we'll sort everything out later."

"Oh aye, drunk am I? I'm telling you, I'm not drunk yet, but I'll get that way after I've sorted you out. I've never liked you since you started sniffing round here, but I didn't say much because this stupid bitch thinks the sun shines out your arse. You never seemed like one of us, and it wasn't just me that noticed it. Everyone down at the pub said so too. Even Betty did when she wasn't mooning over you, but all she could talk about was, 'Oh, he's so gentle', 'Oh, he's so kind', 'Oh, he's so thoughtful looking when he's smoking his pipe'.

"I couldn't put my finger on it, but I knew you weren't just right. I thought you were some kind of snooper at first: a screw, or someone checking up on the social security, or one of those university punters, but you stayed too long for that. And then you took up with her. You don't talk like us, not really. Sometimes, when you're not paying attention, I can see the plums in your mouth. I knew something was wrong, but she just couldn't see it. She kept on saying: 'Oh, he's just a nice man; too nice for the likes of you'. That's a laugh! I knew something was wrong, so I decided to find out for myself."

Tam moved from the table and walked towards the sink which stood below the window. When he reached it, he turned and rested his hands on the edge. He took a long draw on his cigarette and blew the smoke triumphantly high into the air: "Well," he continued, "now I know. Last Sunday night when you left here saying you were off to work, I followed you."

Alec's face went white. For the first time since he had entered the kitchen he looked at Tam directly: "What did you say?"

"You heard. I said I followed you last Sunday night. The game's a bogey, wee man; I know it and she knows it. All it needs is for you to get it into your skull. I followed you. I even know your name now: your real one, that is. Now all I want to know is just what you're playing at, messing with my sister."

"How dare you!" screamed Alec, losing control for the first time. "How dare you interfere in my life! How dare you follow me! How dare you invade my privacy! Oh no, you've never liked me — do you think I don't know that? You've never taken any great pains to conceal the fact. I've had nothing from you except a constant stream of innuendo and veiled abuse and whining and attempts at breaking up the relationship I have with your sister. And why? Not because of any protective feeling you might have towards Betty, because you consider no one but yourself. Not really, in the final analysis, because you feel any enmity towards me as an individual. Oh no. Do you know why you've tried to break us up? Do you?"

Tam did not expect this violent counter attack and the look of triumph was fading slightly from his face, but he attempted to transform it into a sneer of contempt: "No, I'm just thick: I don't know anything. You tell me, big man."

"It's because you're scared, that's why. You were scared then and you're still scared now."

"What, me scared?" asked Tam incredulously. "What have I got to be scared about? A wee jumped-up barrel of shite like you? I could knock you down by farting on you."

"Oh yes, you could, Tam. I have no doubts about that. You're the tough man; everyone round here knows you. You're the man who's been inside; the man with the battle scars, the man with the reputation. No, it's not really me you're scared of, at least, not directly."

"Oh, that's a relief," said Tam sarcastically, "you were really getting me worried there. There was me thinking I'd better flee the country to get away from you."

"No, it isn't me you're afraid of. You're afraid of losing Betty: to me, to the man next door, to a job, to anything."

"Her? What are you talking about, you wee prick? Have you lost the place or something?"

"No," replied Alec, cooler now. "I've not lost the place. And you know it. You're frightened of losing her because, inside, you're still just a vicious, overgrown kid, and you need your sister to mother you. You know women hate you, so Betty is the only wife you're ever going to have. You need her to cook your meals and wash your clothes; you need someone to shout at; you need to make someone feel miserable; you need someone to borrow money from; you need Betty to clean up after your drunken riots; you need her to feel frightened when you bring that scum you associate with into the house; you need to have someone trapped."

"Is that right, is that right?" said Tam quietly and hurriedly, a nervous flurry of movement as he tried to restrain himself from leaping at Alec's throat.

"Yes, that's right!" roared Alec. "And what's more, you need her because, despite your bluster, you get frightened when you realise you haven't got a real friend in the world. You're frightened because you know that, without Betty, no one will give a damn when you die. No one will mourn, no one will even notice. You'll lie in your house, rotting, until the police break down the door to investigate the smell. No one will attend our funeral. Within a few days you'll be forgotten. It will be as if you had never existed. No one will ever say your name again. You'll disappear without trace."

"Is that it then, have you finished?" screamed Tam, veins throbbing visibly on his forehead, face contorted. "Because when you've finished I'm going to pick you up and pap you through that window."

"No, I've not finished," replied Alec in a calmer voice. "This time you can hear me out. I don't care if you throw me out of the window. This time it has got to be said." Alec could not believe he was hearing himself speak.

"I'm warning you, wee man. The only reason you're not on the deck already is because of her." Tam nodded towards Betty, who was staring dumbly at the table, hands tightly clasped, the nobody whom everyone wanted. "She's asked me to let you go; she's been threatening to do herself in if I touch you. I'm only going to tell you once: any more of this shite and I'll forget my promise: I'll stiffen you. And if you top yourself," he continued, turning towards Betty, "I'll stick you in the same plastic bag as him and dump both of you in the Clyde. Comprendo? Take my advice, wee man: fuck off while you can still walk, and take this shite with you." On saying this, Tam picked up the record from the table and bent it in half before throwing it on the floor.

"No," stated Alec flatly, "I'm not going yet. I've still got something to say, and I'm not leaving alone. I'm not going to stand by any longer watching you ruin Betty's life. You've told her for years that she's fat and unattractive and of no use to anyone, and she believed you. You knew how to scare off any friends she made, at least until I came along. You tied her closer and closer to you until her life revolved round your squalid existence, with no hope for the future. Until I appeared. I provided the hope, and it frightened you. It's over now. We're going, Betty and I. You can stay behind and die alone."

"That's it," spoke Tam quietly. He walked the two paces to where Alec still sat in his chair, bent down, and lifted him into the air by the throat. Alec made no resistance and when his feet touched the ground, Tam moved him closer by flexing his arm. When he judged the distance to be correct, Tam viciously butted him in the face. Instinctively, Alec twisted his neck to somehow avoid the full force of the blow which, instead of smashing into the bridge of his nose, glanced off his cheek and lower ear. As Alec twisted, a scream sounded in the silence.

"Leave him, leave him for God's sake, Tam!" shrieked Betty, finally stirred from her torpor. "Leave him be. Oh, please, please, Tam, I'm begging you." As she said this, she rose from her chair and placed her hands imploringly on her brother's shoulders. "Just leave us alone for ten minutes. I'll sort things out. You know I will. If you hit him again, you'll end up back in jail. Please, Tam; let him be."

Poised to strike another blow, Tam turned to his sister, her hands now clasped over her face, body shaking, convulsed with sobs. He dropped Alec like a sack of oats, turned his back to the crumpled form and placed both hands on Betty's shuddering shoulders:

"I'll leave him alone, Betty; for your sake. But you know what I've told you. I'll leave you for ten minutes. And you!" roared Tam, turning again to face Alec who was now back in his chair, rubbing his throat and his cheekbone, choking for air. "If I come back and find you here, I'll swing for you. That's a promise. And if I see you again in this area, you're not going to be able to walk out of it: that's another promise.

"I'll be back, Betty," said Tam, moving towards the hallway. "Remember." He left, closing the door silently behind him.

* * *

Alec watched Betty as she moved to the door in Tam's wake. He was still sitting at the table, rubbing his cheek, the flesh numb to his touch, tongue exploring bruised gums, testing teeth. From shoulder to shoulder, Betty seemed an immense width of yellow nylon, crosscrossed with white ruffles. Her arms hung limply at her sides, hands motionless. Silently, Alec counted the small curlers at the back of her head.

Their eyes did not meet nor did they exchange words as Betty turned and walked to the cooker, picking up the kettle which she filled from the cold tap at the sink under the window. The rasp of a match lit the gas and Betty fumbled for teabags on the top shelf of the cupboard, dropping two into the empty teapot.

"Betty . . ."

Betty moved back to the sink and rattled a few dirty dishes, scraping left-over food from the plates into a bin at her side.

"Betty, for God's sake . . ."

Betty slammed a plate down on the aluminium draining board and spun round towards Alec, bottom lip trembling, sending shock waves over the rest of her face: "What?" she cried helplessly. "What do you want from me now? You sound as if you're the one who deserves an explanation, as if *I've* done something to be ashamed of. Do you make *her* feel guilty too?"

"Look, Betty, you've got to listen."

"Listen?" asked Betty despairingly, eyes raised to heaven, hands raised in supplication. "I think I've listened enough, don't you?" She turned back to the sink and filled a blue plastic basin with warm water from the tap, squirting washing-up liquid on top of the dishes while agitating the water with her free hand. Her shoulders rocked slightly with silent sobs.

"Betty," pleaded Alec, "you've got to understand. You don't know what I've been through."

"What you've been through?" gasped Betty, spinning round in incredulous anger, pointing a finger dripping with soap suds at

Alec's chest. "What about me?" she questioned, turning her finger towards her own breast. "Doesn't anyone ever think about me? I used to think that you did, but now I know I was just being taken in again. God," she cried, raising her hands to cover her face: "Betty Muggins. The soft touch. Everybody's friend. Everybody's mug. Good old Betty. Poor old soul. But you," she continued, hands now back at her sides, soap adhering to her face as she leaned forward despairingly. "I thought you could change things, I really did."

She shook her head and turned back to the sink, washing the dishes and stacking them on the rack to dry: "I suppose you did change things in a way," she continued, calmer now as she wiped the soap from her cheek with the back of her wrist. "Who would have thought they would hear big, lumpy Betty talking like this? I suppose you brought me out, showed me things, taught me things; and I'm grateful. But I hate you now too. I opened myself up and showed you what's inside, and I thought you showed me what's inside yourself too. But now I know I was wrong. I don't want to see you again, and I don't want to talk any more either. I'm tired."

Betty, her back still towards Alec, turned to the now boiling kettle. She took a cloth from the sink and used it to grip the handle as she poured steaming water into the teapot: "You can take a cup of tea if you want," she continued in a monotone, "but I won't drink it with you. I'll pack your things and you can collect them tomorrow morning. I'll be out. Use your key and then leave it in the Toby jug before you go."

"Betty, look . . ."

"I don't want to talk any more!" she screamed, now in a fury. "I've told you! I'm tired and I'm sick and I can't take it any longer. Now leave," she went on in a calmer tone. "Leave for God's sake before Tam comes back and kills you. He'll do it, you know, if he finds you here; believe me. Not for my sake; I know that. You taught me that much. But he'll do it just the same, and this time I won't stop him. So go; I can't lose the two of you in one day."

"OK, I'll go, Betty," said Alec evenly. "But I won't be going for good. I'll be back because we've got to discuss things, whether we want to or not. That much I'm certain of. I owe it to myself to explain what's happened; then you can judge. I've just got to work it all out, maybe for the first time, and I need your help for that. And I owe it to you, even if we never see one another again afterwards. We can't split up with just bare, second-hand facts between us. There's surely much more to it than that."

Betty did not reply but stared silently out of the window, hands gripping the edge of the sink. Her slippered feet, protruding like furry paws from the hem of her dressing-gown, rippled as she flexed her toes against the floor. Alec noticed a small cigarette burn at the back of her left-hand pocket.

"All right, Betty," he said resignedly, "you don't have to speak now; there's plenty of time for that later. I'll go now, but I'll be back: not for my clothes, but to get this thing settled for both our sakes. And if you're not in, I'll be back again, then again, then again, until I eventually see you, Tam or no Tam. I'll see you tomorrow, Betty. I'll leave the chocolates: I know they're your favourites."

* * *

Alec picked up his grip from the hallway and turned the Yale lock to open the door. As it closed behind him, he was left in silence in the sterile close. Where was he to go? He could not return to Pollokshields dressed as he was. If he returned to the office to change, the police would probably arrest him for breaking and entering. What excuse could he give them for returning so late dressed in such disreputable clothes? As he reached the close mouth, he suddenly realised he had just been ordered from his own house. A flood of anger and resentment welled inside him, also a feeling of contempt which had lain barely concealed beneath his consciousness. He thought of Tam with his fat belly and black teeth and threadbare trousers. He thought of Betty, and disdain and a new bitterness fought with the old tenderness. He remembered the gifts he had showered her with, she who had probably never received presents in her life! He remembered with irritation attempting to explain the simplest facts to her, information which he considered to be self-evident, part of the natural make-up of any civilised being, but which was totally alien to the underdeveloped sensibilities of Betty and her brother. Alec's lip took on an involuntary curl. He thought of the burn on her dressing-gown, of her curlers, of her huge brassieres. He thought of the mounds and dips of flesh which had once so transfixed him, with the beginning of a sense of disgust and loathing. She was turning him out of his own house! Where the hell did she think she was?

As he walked along the pavement, Alec touched the bruising inside his mouth with the tip of his tongue. One of his teeth felt slack. If he had not instinctively turned his head, his nose would most probably have been broken. Animals! He thought he was beginning to see more clearly now. He laughed softly to himself. Maybe he had been a bit of a fool. What Tam needed was to be locked up and the key thrown away! He felt as if he was wakening from a dream, a dream which had been threatening to assume all the qualities of a nightmare. This was his chance! Now he could make a clean break. Imagine picking her brother instead of me! After all I've done for her! I've practically remade her! Thrown out of your own house by a drunken yob and his overweight sister!

In the street, Alec passed in front of a billboard advertising 'Old Holborn' cigarette tobacco. He looked to his right, then to his left, then to his right again. Seeing all was clear, he heaved his holdall into the air over the hoarding, and was gone before it hit the ground.

People Inside Buildings II

Glasgow is quite a big place, but it's getting smaller. It's getting smaller just like a grape shrinks when it's left in the sun to dry, and, like the raisin the grape becomes, Glasgow is turning black and wrinkled and disfigured as all of its lifejuices evaporate into the atmosphere. Also like the raisins, Glasgow is wrapped in an appealing cardboard and cellophane package which diverts the eye from what lies within.

Many of the people who remain in Glasgow even look like raisins. Or human masks. It's difficult to imagine the old men you see on every street corner as young men in their prime. Many are pathetically small, wizened creatures, sucked dry years ago: faces deeply creased, shoulders hunched, eyes empty. They used to have knots of muscle across their shoulders, bulging disproportionately on their narrow frames, extending and contracting as they swung a hammer at red-hot rivets or hauled steaming ingots from a furnace heat.

Now, their mates are dead, their sons have disappeared behind strange postage stamps, their wives have nothing more to say to them. They can still gasp with pleasure as a wee goldie disappears down the gullet, but it is a pleasure rooted in the past, not the present. That familiar bite and burn reminds of long ago when a drink was a gill and dyspepsia tears did not rise to blind already misty eyes.

Some of the old men stand alone in pubs, shaking their heads over phantoms, sighing, staring blankly at the gantry, joint-rusted fingers gripping plastic carrier bags full of tins of pork luncheon meat and Kit-E-Kat. As if they were a fixed, unchanging point, the universe spins crazily about them, changing daily: sometimes resting for a moment, then taking quantum leaps, so that some mornings you wake up and don't recognise the view from the window.

The old men who live alone keep dogs and cats and budgies and goldfish, but they die too. Just like family and friends and football players and everyone you used to read about in the newspapers. Some of the old men wait quietly for their names to be spoken by the Big Man, living endless days, waiting for night to fall, until finally one morning they do not waken up. From time to time a tear wells up in the old men's eyes for no apparent reason. Maybe it was the fried onions you had for dinner; maybe it was a noise which sounded like a muffled rattle of a tramcar; maybe it was a half-imagined smell which brought back the harbour and the fishing boats and the patched nets of the village where you spent your holidays a thousand years ago.

Some of the old men give up entirely, taking root in their own filth, letting go of the threads which bind them to life. They have no ties, no family, no friends, no responsibilities. Better to dull the senses with a bottle of Lanliq. Eventually, they abandon their homes, or are evicted, and huddle in the night round an oil drum fire in the middle of emptiness. Wrapping cardboard boxes round themselves, they curl up in the nearest skipper and feel the seeping cold call them to the grave. Miraculously, most wake up the following morning to the scurrying of rats, and another day stretches ahead in the long winter.

Other men busy themselves with the routine of a previous life, waking at 6.30 sharp, ready for a job which no longer exists. They tell the time without recourse to watches or clocks, through ingrained habit: rise, wash, breakfast, hooter, teabreak, dinner, teabreak, hooter, pint, tea, bed. The landmarks are followed, but what fills the yawning gaps in between? The bookie, the *Daily Record*, long walks, TV, sleep, anxiety, loneliness, despair. As the years pass, a job which made them sweat and grit their teeth and freeze and dread seems like a far-off rosy heaven. The dream becomes distorted: no splashes of molten metal, no deafening noise, no sickening thump as a workmate falls from scaffolding, no short time, no thin wages, no bastard boss.

And the wives of the old men adhere to the seasoned routine: polish, scrub, scour, rub, sweep, wash, until their hands are all wrinkles and knots, and they can see their faded faces in the bottom of saucepans. The furniture gleams, the ornaments are dusted, all in preparation for the day when first one then both of them are laid out neatly in the front room, when the brass nameplate is taken down, when the whole lot ends up in a second-hand shop, ripe for curio seekers.

"I was sorry to hear about your dad, Billy."

"Thanks. It was a bit far to go for the funeral. Know what I mean?"

"Yes."

SELECTED INFORMATION FOR TOURISTS

BAR-L

Large PENAL ESTABLISHMENT in Glasgow. Official name: 'Barlinnie'. inmates include members of GANGS convicted of crimes of VIOLENCE, those incarcerated for crimes related to DRUNKENNESS, those who are SOCIALLY INADEQUATE, those who are INSANE, some of those who are INNOCENT but have been convicted by others who are GUILTY.

BATTLE OF THE BOYNE

Fought in 1690 near the town of Drogheda in IRELAND. Forces of KING WILLIAM OF ORANGE (PROTESTANT) defeated those of KING JAMES (CATHOLIC). POPE (Alexander VIII) sent congratulatory message to KING BILLY. N.B.: Date 1690 seen very often, written on walls and on the back of Corporation bus seats.

DRUNKENNESS

Common condition in West of Scotland. Basis of most JOKES and conversation. Extensive range of synonyms for state of DRUNKENNESS: "steaming", "steamboats", "pissed", "pished", "BEVIED", "jaked", "rubber legged", "blotto", "blootered".

GANGS	Usually based in a specific district, e.g. Brigton (Bridgeton) Derry, Govan Team. Also note Cumbie, Toi, Tongs. Chief of GANG known as "LEADER AFF": usually PSYCHOPATHIC PERSONALITY. Weapons used include boots, fists, HEAD, knives, swords, bayonets, clubs, razors, CLEAVERS, hatchets, chisels, meat-hooks. Inflict damage.
KING WILLIAM OF ORANGE	Known colloquially as "KING BILLY". Symbol of PROTESTANT SUPREMACY. Can be seen, usually seated on a rearing horse, tattooed on the chests and forearms of some ORANGEMEN. Victor over KING JAMES at BATTLE OF THE BOYNE. Name heard frequently at FOOTBALL MATCHES. Common usage: (i) Fuck KING BILLY; (ii) there's only one KING BILLY, that's McNeill. N.B.: Initials F.K.B. (see (i) above) seen very often written on walls and on the backs of Corporation bus seats.
PARANOIA	"A form of mental disorder characterised by fixed delusions, especially of grandeur, pride, persecution." (Chambers Twentieth Century Dictionary.)
POPE	Head of ROMAN CATHOLIC CHURCH. Spiritual leader of one third of the Scottish population. Wears large hat. Name heard frequently at FOOTBALL MATCHES. Common usage: (i) Fuck the POPE; (ii) The POPE is a poof. N.B.: Initials F.T.P. (see (i) above) seen very

often written on walls and on the backs of Corporation bus seats.

PUBS	Venue for much DRUNKENNESS and VIOLENCE. Can also be friendly and amusing. Lots of them to choose from. Many have changed to modern lounge bars, many remain traditional DRINKING DENS. Occasionally, CHILDREN may be seen ABANDONED outside, clutching bags of salt 'n' vinegar crisps and small bottles of 'Fanta' orange drink, awaiting re-emergence of one or more PARENTS.

RELIGION	TABOO subject in golf clubs, whist drives, etc. Important topic of conversation when DRUNK in PUBS. Glasgow's religions include Christianity (CATHOLICISM and various PROTESTANT faiths), Islam, Hinduism, Judaism, Taoism, Zoroastrianism, etc. From the age of five, CATHOLIC children go to CATHOLIC SCHOOLS. From the age of five, PROTESTANT children go to PROTESTANT SCHOOLS. In the CATHOLIC SCHOOLS the children learn the Catechism and frequently visit church. In PROTESTANT SCHOOLS the children are regularly guided by a Church of Scotland minister. The families of children who adhere to other religious beliefs have the FREEDOM OF CHOICE to decide which of the two forms of SPIRITUAL GUIDANCE they desire to be bestowed on their offspring.

VIOLENCE Often the result of DRUNKENNESS; sometimes the result of RELIGIOUS DIFFERENCES; sometimes inflicted by INDIVIDUALS on other INDIVIDUALS; when newsworthy, the result of GANG fights; at varying times, explodes spontaneously. Extensive vocabulary available to describe being assaulted: "CHIBBED", "timmed", "malkied", "hammered", "battered", "ripped", "done", "had". See also "stick the nut on"; "HAVE A SQUARE GO".

SAM DUNBAR

A12 measured twenty feet by thirty feet. On one side, a line of windows reached from a level three feet above the ground to ceiling height. The winter sun streamed through, making the strip lighting redundant, but it remained switched on. At the back of the room was a solid wall broken by a horizontal strip of cork board two feet wide, its centre positioned at adult head height. Pinned on to the board with thumb tacks were several yellowing posters and a couple of halfhearted graphs. On the third side, opposite the windows, was a line of coat hooks on which duffels and anoraks hung, steaming in the heat from the radiators positioned round the room. At the corner formed by the junction of this wall and the fourth was a door opening on to the corridor which connected the rooms along 'A' level. Next to the door, facing the posters on the cork board, was a large wooden cupboard with a year-old calendar stuck to one of its doors. About half of the fourth wall was taken up with a double blackboard, fixed in position, with altogether six sides which could be changed by revolving the board like the belt of a vertical conveyor round a series of drums. All six frames of the board were empty of writing. Next to the blackboard, under the examining light from the windows, was a table and a chair. Behind the table sat Sam Dunbar, hunched over a day-old copy of the *Glasgow Herald*.

Sam was dressed in light grey trousers which, if he stood up, would be seen to be bagging at the arse and at the knees, and a grey jacket which almost matched. His brown tie, draped over a yellow shirt, was tucked into the waistband of his slacks. Grey was the predominant colour in the room, it having been the main constituent of the colour scheme chosen for the walls. It looked like the wardroom of a Royal Navy cruiser.

In front of Sam, arranged haphazardly at double and single desks, sat thirty-two children, male and female, pens and pencils scratching jotters and heads, faces contorted in concentration, legs twisting, bums squirming. 2m2 had been at PE during the previous period, so the whole room was redolent with the smell of sweaty bodies. Despite the sunshine, it was too cold to open the windows, so the aroma lingered like a fetid cloud, undisturbed by a breeze.

The room was in silence. The hush had gripped the class to such an extent that even the normal noises of conscientious labour such as squeaking seats and muffled coughs were restrained. Still at an age when it was taboo to tamper with the collective will, no one wished to raise his or her head in case it was chopped off. Sam was grateful for the silence while it lasted. Soon, with awakening adolescence, signs of defiance would float to the surface and the more daring would attempt to call his bluff. Then, it would be a battle of wills to see who would come out on top. If he ever failed the test, he could pack up and go home, for the fragile barrier between discipline and anarchy would have been breached.

Meanwhile, he took advantage of the power his position bestowed upon him and relaxed, immersed in the pool of stillness around him, secure and confident his will was dominant. He could hear his watch ticking.

He glanced up from the crossword to scan the mass of hunched little bodies in front of him, and to his dismay saw one at the back of the room straighten and raise a hand. Wearily he struggled to his feet and squeaked his way over the parquet flooring towards the upturned face. As he neared the girl who had disturbed his coma, one of the brighter pupils in his class, he questioned her with a look before leaning both hands on the desk as he bent down to place his ear to her mouth.

"Sir," she whispered, "I've finished. Do I go on to the next exercise?"

Sam straightened and fixed her with a look of disdain, lips pursed, left eyebrow raised questioningly. The non-verbal message hit home: as he turned to walk back to his desk, he heard the girl turn the page of her textbook to exercise 415.

Creeping back to the top of the class, Sam smelled noxious fumes rising from a boy in the middle of the centre row: McIlhone had farted again. His neighbour suppressed a giggle. Standing silently behind them, Sam saw McIlhone give his neighbour, a boy called Snevely, a dig in the ribs with his elbow. Snevely gripped his pencil like a dagger and lunged for McIlhone's hand which was palm down on the desk, missing by millimetres. Sam picked up a ruler from the desk behind and with the speed of light gave both a crack on the head with the edge. The rest of the class darted a glance to see what was happening then returned to their work. Both Snevely and McIlhone withdrew their heads into their shoulders and feverishly began to scribble in their jotters. As Sam passed them, slapping the ruler into the palm of his hand, McIlhone sneaked a look after him. Sam stared back and the boy broke the tip of his pencil on the desk in confusion.

Regaining his seat, Sam again concentrated on the crossword. In thirty minutes he had managed to find the solutions to two clues. His mind drifted. Glancing out of the window, from his second floor vantage point he could see acres of houses drifting off into the distance. Below the window was a road, across from which was a row of semi-detacheds. In the front garden of the house directly opposite Sam's window, a man bent down to coax a dog towards him by waving a stick in its face. As the mongrel grew near, the man aimed a kick at it but the dog darted away, avoiding the assault, and trotted out of the front gate at a brisk pace. The man, dressed only in a vest and trousers, despite the cold, bent down to gather a handful of snow which he threw at the departing animal, missing it by three feet. He cursed and turned back towards his open front door, and as he did so, Sam noticed he was wearing carpet slippers.

Outside in the corridor a bell rang, signalling the end of the period. Thirty-two thirteen-year-olds started but restrained their conditioned response to dart gleefully out of the room in a bid for freedom. All of them pretended still to be working, at the same time casting anxious looks towards the front of the room.

"Pack up," Sam yawned, stretching himself, his reverie interrupted. "Complete exercise 414 for homework," he instructed them as they packed their books away. "Then start exercise 415 on the next page. The first ten questions only. Leave the room when you're ready."

2m2 finished their packing then filed out of the room, remaining subdued until they reached the raucous stream in the corridor, whereupon they joined in the shouting, jostling, whistling throng. As the last of the pupils filed past him, Sam crooked a finger and called a mite by the name of Bobby Gilmour over to his desk. Bobby approached apprehensively, wondering if he had somehow infringed one of the plethora of unwritten rules which varied capriciously from moment to moment, classroom to classroom, at the whim of the deities in crumpled suits.

"Bobby," said Sam questioningly, "what period was that?"

"English, sir," replied Bobby, puzzled and looking for traps.

"I know that, Bobby," rasped Sam in an exasperated tone. "I meant what number was that period?"

"Period three, sir," said the lad warily, still looking for the catch.

"Right, thanks," said Sam in a businesslike manner. "On you go."

Bobby left the room after his classmates. A conscientious boy, his whole day had been ruined as his mind entered tortuous paths, seeking an explanation for this bizarre interrogation. The simple truth was that Sam had forgotten how many classes he had taught that morning. Earlier, a glance at his watch had revealed the time to be half-past seven, in which case he should still have been in bed, or be drinking his sixth pint of lager in the 'Horseshoe' bar. Realising he was in neither cocoon, he had been forced to fall back on his rather unreliable recall of the day's events to orientate himself.

Period three over. The interval. Playtime. Fifteen minutes. Cup of tea. Two cups. Soft seat. Newspaper. Kit-Kat. Then two more periods. Then lunch. Then three more periods. Then the bell. Over for another day. Interval: in that case, why hang about?

Sam moved briskly to the door and locked it behind him. Outside in the now almost deserted corridor two small boys were wrestling on the floor. Sam stepped over them, passed through the swing doors, and climbed the stairs to the staffroom.

***

Shepherd's pie and caramel cake and custard lay heavily in Sam's stomach. It was now period six, first period in the afternoon, and twenty-five sullen faces stared at him from behind tiny desks. Before some, books lay opened; most leant their elbows on the covers, their heads resting on their hands bobbing up and down to the rhythm of chewing jaws. The silence was broken only by the popping of exploding bubblegum.

Most of the boys in the class sported wispy, silken moustaches, and rogue hairs could be seen sprouting from their chins at crazy angles. Their clothes were in a variety of styles. The two teds among them favoured pale blue drape jackets and string ties, with crepe-soled shoes protruding from the ends of drainpipe trousers which were hitched up to reveal an alluring glimpse of luminous, lime green socks. With their greased-back DAs they looked like Woody Woodpecker trying to impersonate Doc Holliday.

There was only one punk. He had used his old man's black 'Cherry Blossom' boot polish on his spiky hair, and wore a chic, off-the-shoulder leopard-skin effect T-shirt above black plastic bondage trousers. Round his neck was a leather dog collar, studded with metal spikes. There were several mods there too, pork pie hats perched on their heads despite being indoors, wearing black knitted ties and parkas with what looked like archery targets on the back. Right at the back of the room was a group of skinheads with cropped hair, black jerkins with tartan linings, and 'Doc Marten' lace-up paratrooper boots itching to crush a few noddles.

The girls were a pretty motley bunch, their only common denominator being the liberal use of red varnish on nails bitten down past the flesh on their fingers. A few affected the 'sixties mod look with short skirts and white stockings, but most couldn't be bothered dressing up in anything other than what they had worn yesterday. They were bored. Everyone was bored. All twenty-five fifteen-year-olds in the classroom were so bored with the entire universe they were crawling up their own arses.

The fact that the kids were bored was known to Sam, but it didn't really concern him. When it came right down to it, he was pretty pissed off too. What bothered him was when they *told* him they were bored, as if they expected him to put on a cabaret performance or something. He couldn't stand that.

Eight or nine years ago, when he had begun his teaching career, Sam had often probed into the feelings and aspirations of these third and fourth year classes: the "non-certificates"; the factory fodder; the ones everyone had long given up on. Most teachers saw them as troublesome arseholes who should be turned into briquets, saw them as a containment problem and nothing else. These teachers struck bargains with their adversaries: "don't bother me and I won't bother you". Simple but effective: play truant; do fuck all work when you're here; but whatever you do, do it unobtrusively. And the system worked: resources were devoted to the kids who could succeed even to a limited extent in the academic system, and every year about fifty or sixty deadheads were excreted out of the rear end. Some of them survived in the outside world through native wit and cunning, and indeed a few became successful in their own way. Most signed on at the bottom of the list of the world's casualties and joined the ranks of the chronically unemployed, the chronically alcoholic, the chronically insane, or the chronically in gaol.

Part of the tragedy was that these kids thought they were smart: they thought they were foxes. They would laugh up their sleeves when they truanted, when they held farting competitions instead of learning how to add up, when they avoided homework and used their jotters as bum paper. They thought everyone else was dumb, especially the teachers: they were *really* a bunch of wankers. Their teachers in turn tried to reinforce this world view, because if someone thinks he's beating the system, he's going to keep reasonably quiet: smug but containable. What they didn't want was a class full of self-aware failures: that would be a disaster. They reinforced this view all the way up to the time when the kids left school at sixteen years of age, when they signed off with shouts of "so long suckers" as they were abandoned in the outside world without being able to read the street signs.

Sam wasn't like that: he tried; for a while. He would spend his evenings searching for suitable, exciting, relevant, supermaterial, and bring it in proudly next day to present to his non-certificate classes. He would give dramatic readings of poems, act them out, organise drawing and poster work based on the general theme, highlight their relevance to contemporary urban life, motivate creative efforts on their part. At the end of it all, sweat dripping from his nose, heart bursting with pride, feeling like a holy man because he was spending so much of his valuable time on these rejects, at the end of it all he would ask the class what they had thought of the experience:

"Shite."

"What do you mean, 'shite'?"

"Shite."

"But you've got to explain that."

"Jobbies" (giggle, giggle).

And after a pause:

"OK, why didn't you like it?"

"It was boring."

"But why was it boring?"

"Because it was shite."

After a year he gave up. The final straw came when he gave his third year class a cartoon strip with blank bubbles coming from the characters' mouths and asked the pupils to invent dialogue to suit the storyline. He had spent four days copying the cartoons on to 'Banda' sheets for duplication. After a period's work he collected the sheets to discover the class had produced gems of repartee like "suck my cock, baby", and "the Pope's a poof", and "Big Tam's da's a darkie". They hadn't even got the spelling and punctuation right.

Now, Sam stared back at the rows of blank, sullen faces; faces of people waiting for something to turn up. Although nothing ever would. Except, one day, maybe a hearse.

"I'll be back in a few minutes," he said, making for the door. "Don't wreck the place while I'm gone."

His remark was greeted with an awesome silence. Leaving the classroom behind, he walked along the corridor to a quiet spot and stared out of a window at snow falling on the playground. Suddenly, he felt a tap on his shoulder. He jumped and turned round, half expecting to be face to face with the headmaster. With relief he saw it was a pretty girl about seventeen years old.

"Hello, sir," she said brightly. "Remember me?"

With a sinking heart Sam realised that he did. The girl had been in one of his classes last year: keen, but not very bright. Sometimes he thought the keen ones were the worst: "Oh, hello," he said halfheartedly. "How are you?"

"Oh, not bad," the girl replied. "Eh . . . D'ye think . . ."

"Yes? I'm afraid I'm rather busy right now."

"Well . . .," the girl hesitated. "It's just that . . ."

Slowly and with horror Sam realised he was going to be on the receiving end of some problems of a personal nature. What would it be? Pregnant? Possibly. Boyfriend? Perhaps. No job? Probably. He could see tears blobbing up in her eyes and knew he had to head the situation off quickly: "It's really nice seeing you again, Janet," he said briskly, "but . . ."

"Mary."

"What's that?"

"My name's Mary, sir," said the girl sadly.

"Yes, it's very nice seeing you again, Mary," continued Sam, "but I'm afraid you've caught me at a bad time. I'm extremely busy just now. Exams and everything, you know?" He began to lead her along the corridor towards the stairs.

"It's just that . . . I wonder if I could have a word with you?" asked the girl, looking up at him with the suspicion of a tremor in her voice. Sam reached the stair-well and stood with one foot poised to ascend the first step:

"Any other time," he lied, "I'd be pleased to have a chat, but unfortunately I've got to head for the staffroom just now for a conference with Mr Allison. You know: the principal English teacher."

"Oh, I see," whispered the girl, now staring at her feet.

"Look," said Sam brightly, "pop in some time next week and we'll have a nice long chat, OK?"

"OK," said the girl softly, still staring floorwards.

"Well," said Sam, already halfway up the flight of stairs, "I'll be seeing you." On saying this, he bounded the rest of the way up to the staffroom, not looking back in case he met the girl's accusing stare. Throwing open the staffroom door he saw Bennet, the Maths principal, sprawled in a corner drinking a cup of coffee:

"Hello, Sam!" Bennet shouted in his usual jovial manner. "Free period?"

"No," replied Sam, casting his eyes around the room. "I'm just in for..." He frantically scanned the table in front of Bennet. "I'm just in for..." He leapt towards a heap of papers. "I'm just in for this pamphlet," he cried, waving a sheaf of papers in the air before pocketing it. "See you later!" he called over his shoulder as he left the room.

"See you, Sam," replied Bennet, a huge grin spreading over his broad face.

Outside again in the corridor, Sam looked to his right towards the staircase, at the bottom of which he felt sure the girl stood. He looked over his shoulder at the staffroom door, now closed, behind which he knew Bennet was smirking, having caught Sam skiving off. Looking straight ahead, he saw the entrance to the toilet. Sam stepped forward, opened the door, and stepped inside. Both cubicles were empty. He chose the one in the corner of the room, entered it, and turned the lock. Dropping his trousers he sat down on the pan with a deep sigh and relaxed as he felt his bowels loosen.

FROM THE BRAINWAVES OF A SLOTH

Why do they whine at me? I've got fuck all to do with it. I didn't neglect them when they were babies. I didn't give them weak fathers. I didn't beat them up and reject them when they crawled on to knees in search of comfort. I didn't give them sexual hang-ups: I didn't set them a bad example: I didn't teach them to say "fuck" and to kick other kids in the balls. I didn't give them a world with nowhere to go except to crawl into a bottle or a cell or a mental ward. Why take it out on me? I can't be held responsible; I didn't make the world like it is. If you've got any complaints, find out who was behind all this shit and kick fuck out of him. Only save some for me.

But you won't do that, will you? It's too difficult to take any positive action which might make your life more tolerable, more meaningful. You prefer hanging around on street corners, laughing at the poor doughballs passing by. You prefer making farting noises by squeezing the palm of your hand under your armpit and flapping your elbow. You prefer practising spitting through your teeth, looking round to elicit praise from your cronies. You would rather concentrate on developing a hard man strut and a scowl to match. You pathetic little pricks, counting all the buttons on the pockets of your shirts and trousers, saying "gallus" and "pure gemme". Toytown tough guys learning to be the real thing.

And you've plenty of models, haven't you? Wee Rab round the corner, he's a success: List D School, then Detention Centre, now graduated to the Bar-L; "Young Team ya bastard!" Started off with fists, looking out for a bit of boxing on the waste ground: just kid's stuff but the praise comes and you've never had any before, at home or at school. Then fourteen and the Tiny Toi attack in front of the Community Centre: an iron bar on the head blinds you with pain and blood but you get him down and a half brick is in your hand and it pounds his face to a pulp. The reputation draws the girls too, and it gets even better as the blood runs freer.

But then you're inside, and the screws are all ex-army bastards who scream and shout and shave your head. Quick march! Attention! Double time! Scrub that floor! Come here, you little shit! And a knee sinks into your groin and the pain doesn't end until you conform. You get used to the blankets and the uniform, rubbing red, and enjoy the boxing in the gym and the real thing behind the laundry block when the screws turn a blind eye to subculture discipline. Another reputation. You make a name for yourself: you find out what earns respect, if not friendship.

And then you're out, and everyone wants to know you: "What's it like, Rab?"; "Do the screws batter you?"; "I heard you sorted out Big Charley Murray".

Older now, no school, and a bayonet down the back of your trousers. Give it to the girlfriend most times because the cops search you on the street nearly every night. They know you too: "How's Rab?"; "Are you not back inside yet? We'll have to do something about that". Everyone looks on as you banter with them when they search your clothes. Admiring. A local figure. Known. Assuming heroic proportions as you swagger off into the stark night, arms bearer in your wake.

But you're carrying when you see 'Cisco' Henderson walking down Renfield Street on Friday night and you shout after him and he runs as he sees you, but he's drunk, and falls outside of the Boot's the Chemist. And as he raises himself up you reach him and leap in the air as the bayonet arcs in the night light to slam into his back with a thud which leaves him flat and gasping. "Young Team, ya bastard!"

Yes, you can look up to Rab, who's inside now, detained "During Her Majesty's Pleasure", only it'll be *His* Majesty's Pleasure by the time anyone finds the key. His wee brother feeds off his reputation and you jump about with him, and already you're feared, and you can boot other kids up the arse and take their dinner money.

But your brain's already shrunk to the size of a walnut and your soul has been submerged, and if anyone looks into your eyes, they see only sullen resentment. You don't even know what you resent, but the hatred and violence it spawns brings a form of success. Besides, you've nothing else to put in its place. You've got sores on your top lip and around your nose from sniffing glue and one of your mates drowned in the burn last week when he was stoned. You've already forgotten him. You knock sweets out of the Paki's and you stole a woman's purse once in a supermarket. Billy's got hold of his old man's tools, and the two of you are going to break into R. S. McColl's next week to steal fags.

OK, follow your chosen career, but don't do it near me. I can't be bothered anymore. If you think that school's crap and that I'm a boring old fart then fuck off out of it. Go away and fill a plastic bag full of 'Bostik' and stick it over your head. Stab one of your mates with a screwdriver. Screw your old dear's gas meter, buy a couple of bottles of Lanliq with the money, and fall under a car. Just make sure it's not mine.

Stop whining, all right? Stop demanding to be entertained; I've retired. Go home and put your head in a television tube and your finger in the mains socket. Eat the goldfish; strangle the dog. Burn the house down. Steal a car and wreck it. Put a concrete sleeper on the railway line. Drop plastic bags full of piss from your bedroom window on to the heads of passers-by in the street below. Pull down a few trees. Drown a toddler in the reservoir. Put in the neighbours' windows with half bricks. Pour petrol through their letterboxes and set it alight. Tie Mrs Halcott's cat to the back of a bus and run after it, throwing bricks at its head as it bumps along the road. Amuse yourself, but do it away from me. I've had enough. I'm all locked up and closed until further notice.

I close my eyes now when I drive through your shitty streets, running with trouserless two-year-olds and mangy Alsatian crossbreeds, like a Mexican adobe village. I don't see your Stalag houses with the boarded-up windows and the lead ripped off the roofs. I don't see the barbed wire round the electricity sub-station or the skeletons of cars at the roadside, or the abandoned fridges and sofas on the waste ground. I don't see the writing on the walls: F.T.P., Young Winey, BOYDY RULES, F.K.B., U.D.A., Derry Land, GOVAN TEAM, Partick Cross, I.R.A., GLUEBOYS.

I ignore the young/old shapeless women in short baggy trousers flapping at the ankles, hair tied in a greasy pony tail, purse, cigarettes and lighter gripped in one hand. Teeth like an Eskimo matriarch, laugh like a rasp on the psyche, hacking cough in winter, flesh that never sees the sun. Ageing overnight from sixteen to forty, buying one tin at a time from the corner shop, feeding the brood on bread and jam. Hanging out of windows, arms resting on the sill. A pound is dropped, wrapped round a 10p piece, to a tiny messenger below: "Twenty Embassy Tipped and don't you stop to talk to those neds on the corner or they'll have the money off you."

Within a few years, daughter looks like mother, married to another sixteen-year-old man. Five months gone at the wedding in Martha Street. Sky blue suit and a rose; floppy hats; platform shoes; Uncle Benny was sick in the pan and lost his false teeth and couldn't eat his dinner. Living with your granny because there's no room at home. A woman now, your ma talks to you as an equal: "They're all the same, believe you me, Bella. Your father's been a good-for-nothing shite all his life and your man's turning out like that too. I've seen him, down outside the Off Sales with those layabouts he goes about with, poncing drink, laughing and joking as if he'd never a care in the world. Believe you me: this isn't a real life for a woman."

And now Bella's off to the Bingo with her ma, swapping fags and dirty jokes with ma's friends: accepted: shaking heads, nodding in agreement, rocking with laughter. Stop for a gossip outside of Willemena's close, clucking and preening, girths expanding, never to return to girlish dimensions. Childhood ends with a guillotine cut. Adulthood is a second, and years stretch ahead: gathering your own flock; passing it on.

And your kids disappear and you don't know where the fuck they are until the cops bring them home by the scruffs of their necks. Gangsters at nine. "It's my nerves, Willemena: I'm a wreck with all this worry about James out of work and then coming home with a drink in him: I don't even know where he gets the money from. And last night he tried to strangle me in bed. I had to scream and the kids came running into the room. Wee Tommy went wild when he saw it and jumped on his dad's back and bit him, so James threw him against the wall and split his head open. And the Social Work warned James the last time when they saw those marks on Billy's legs. And then Robert's to go in front of the Children's Panel next Thursday, and I know he'll be put away this time. He threw that wee girl's bike in the canal then broke her mother's front room windows. I don't know, I really don't know."

So she enters a Valium dream and, although Robert does get taken away, it doesn't seem quite so bad: "The only thing is, I keep on forgetting things, Willemena. Last night I forgot to make his dinner. James cracked up when he came in and put his fist through the door of the kitchen cupboard."

The kids think it's so bad they want to escape from home as quickly as possible, preferably to Dallas. So they get married at sixteen too, and within a few years it's turned full circle. There seems to be no physical escape, so the buroo money goes on drink, the kids' pocket money goes on glue, until some morning another one is found belly up. Well done; you've made it.

* * *

As Sam came out of the door of the toilet, he looked both ways before turning left towards his classroom. He glanced at his watch: still five minutes of the period to go. Two more periods before it was time to go home. He felt a twinge in his abdomen and considered the possibility it might be appendicitis, weighing the surgeon's knife against an extended lay-off. The twinge passed. Nearly holiday time.

The corridor was cold. As he walked past the windows which ran the length of the school at shoulder height, his hand brushed along the the top of the radiators which gurgled and grunted in their painful struggle to heat the surrounding air. Drawing nearer his classroom, Sam heard an increasing volume of noise: shouts, bangs, squeals; the scraping of chair legs along parquet flooring; a thud as some object rebounded from a wall. He stood for a moment with his hand on the door handle, peering into the room through the small pane of glass which served as an observation hole.

Throwing the door open he stepped inside and all noise ceased abruptly as twenty-five heads turned towards Sam, the intruder. In the front row, Tommy Harkins, a large boy dressed in a parka, had his hands round the throat of his neighbour, and, judging by the movements of the victim's head, had only at that moment stopped a vigorous throttling motion. At the back of the room, Rose Galt, the girl with the biggest tits in the school, was standing on a chair with a shopping bag over her head.

"Rose," said Sam wearily, stifling a yawn as he scratched the back of his head, "I like the headgear: it really suits you. Do you think you could continue the millinery show sitting on your bum? And Tommy," Sam continued, "if you want to strangle someone, do it in your own time, eh? If you murder Dalrymple in the classroom, I've got to fill in all sorts of forms."

Both attacker and attacked looked at Sam with blank expressions, then both sniggered as the would-be murderer whispered in his victim's ear.

"Sir, sir!" clamoured a deep, sonorous voice from the back of the room. "Can we get away early?"

"Early?" asked Sam of a stubbled fifteen-year-old muffled in a

Rangers scarf. "Why on earth do you want to leave the classroom early, son?"

"I just want out of this place, that's all."

"But you're only going to another boring, meaningless class. What's the point of getting there early?"

The boy retreated into a glowering sullenness: "I just want out," he stated defensively, "that's all I was saying."

"But won't you be just as cheesed off in your next class?"

"Oh, forget it."

"No, tell me, I really want to know. Where do you actually want to go to? What lies behind this tedium? What light is shining at the end of the tunnel, beckoning you on? What great event are you saving up your life for? When does all the good stuff start?"

Sam did not receive an answer, for at that moment the period bell rang and in a confusion of noise, the classroom emptied leaving Sam standing alone, a satirist without an audience.

A few minutes later, a new class filed into the room. First year. Little baa-baas following the butcher's knife. Some still in the tattered remnants of a once hopeful school uniform. As they passed, some of them glanced at Sam to ascertain whether he was in a benevolent or a cantankerous mood. Sam liked to keep them guessing. It kept them on their toes. He sighed again and glanced at his watch, hoping it had miraculously leapt forward in time.

"Jotters out. Open your textbooks at page eighteen. If you have not already done so, complete exercise six. When you have finished exercise six, turn to page twenty and begin exercise seven.

Silence quickly fell on the classroom. Sam settled in his seat and re-examined the *Glasgow Herald* crossword. In a matter of moments the black squares began to blur in front of his eyes. He rested his head on his hand, elbow lodged in the angle between desk and wall. Slowly, his eyelids began to close. Two periods to go.

LINGUISTICS

Eskimos have lots of words for snow. It's because their whole lives are spent surrounded by the fucking stuff. There's wet snow and dry snow, powdery snow and clay-packed snow, killing snow and light, eyelash-feather snow. Years ago, before they started pickling their livers, Eskimos even lived in houses made from snow, little bowl-shaped structures called "igloos". There was fuck all else available to build with: no wood, no concrete, no bricks, no plastic, no cement, no mud, no paper. Kids were born with the sunlight filtering through an ice canopy. If there were too many girls born in any particular year, small, wrinkled, red, cord-cut human beings were tossed outside to die with the white stuff clogging their air holes.

When Europeans go north in Canada, all they see is a landscape draped in white sheets, as if the furniture has been covered, awaiting a breath of spring air. During the long days, the only break in the monotony is a twenty-watt bulb glowing dimly in the sky, reminding them they're on the same planet as Paris and Amsterdam and Vienna. The deadening impact sends some of them crazy, makes some of them blind, but meanwhile the impassive, hood-eyed Eskimo is comparing the day's fall with the time twelve years ago when his uncle harpooned three fat slug-seals in one crystal morning.

Snow is life: it's underfoot, in the air, melting in the mouth to douse a winter thirst. Snow is iron-clad, fur-flaked, tendril-touch, wild wind, teeth-bite, death mantle, life-melt, igloo-warm, seal-sleek. an Eskimo who only talks of "snow" is going to be stuck for conversation.

Similarly in Glasgow. We don't have much snow here and what does fall is quickly turned to dead, brown slush. Snow is not a big factor in our lives so we call it . . . "snow". No more, no less. Some things do, however, impinge themselves strongly on everyday life, things like drink and football and violence. Many conversations revolve round these topics, usually in anecdotal form, so an extensive vocabulary is required in order to raise social intercourse above the level of the banal.

Unfortunately, sporting conversation has been corrupted by the easy jargon of newspaper and television pundits. People slip easily into the now meaningless and devalued phraseology of sleep-walking typewriter jockeys with their emptyheaded talk of "a game of two halves", and "midfield generals", and shots "cannoning from the woodwork". Occasionally, gems do emerge, as in describing the height a labouring centre forward reaches when attempting to head the ball as being of insufficient altitude to slip a copy of the *Daily Record* between his studs and the ground. Talk of drink and violence, however, still retains its vibrance and gut feeling, spilling out words you can touch and savour, phrases which well up from your boots and liberate tongues in metaphorical ecstasies.

What is "electric soup"? Put plainly it is cheap wine, fortified with spirit, but embodied in its evocative, gut-churning argot it is a combined anaesthetic and speed trip which has the effect of plugging a ten-thousand-volt cable into your ear. "White lightning" splits your cranium and atom smashes your brain, hurling the disparate particles to every corner of the universe. "Red Biddy" creeps up on you like a rising hot-blood bath until you drown beneath its calm waters, the last few bubbles to break the surface signalling a Morse code SOS. What are you doing next morning when you're "calling 'Hughie' down the big white telephone"? You are contacting thousands of kindred spirits who are also shivering and sweating, kneeling in prayer before the porcelain receiver which is summoning its stomach-racked correspondent home to the soil. How are you feeling when your eyes are like "dugs' balls", or like "pissholes in the snow"? Certainly worse than you were last night when I heard you "gi'ing it laldie" when you were "scooped".

And can you remember wellying that guy last night? You cracked him one on the jaw then stuck the nut on him. Later on, when we were walking through the town, we saw a block getting chibbed. He was shouting for a square go but some cunt came up behind him and malkied him. I was going to jump the block, but then I sobered up and knew I would just get my heid in my hands. Simple as that. I shot the crow. Got on my bike. Fucked off. Fuck that!

PAT McKENNA

"Aaoooow! Owowowwww! Owwww!"

The howling came from down by the spot welding section and was taken up by others all along the line.

"Owwwww! Owowowwwww!"

Pat raised his head to the vaulted ceiling which was crisscrossed with steel supports, and gave forth:

"Wowwwww! Wowwowwww!"

He glanced over at Big Jimmy the fork-lift driver and grinned. Big Jimmy stopped his truck, cupped his hands over his mouth, and howled in reply, flapping his elbows to give the baying resonance. The sounds of the wolf pack came from every corner of the section: from people concealed behind mountains of pallets, from passing rubbish waggons, from maintenance men hanging suspended from the over head track. An entire shift was howling at the hidden sky, drowning the sounds of ordered chaos from the plant. The wave of frustration and directionless anger swept swiftly over the hundreds of men around Pat, and just as quickly subsided. The work continued, prompted by the relentless tempo of the metal track as it ground its way through each section of the factory, dragging car shells to each section along its length. Big Jimmy restarted his truck, the maintenance men became flies once more, the men behind the pallets resumed their silent labour.

Billy Paterson came up to Pat and tapped him on the shoulder. Relief. Most sections, manned by four men, worked a system of half an hour on, half an hour off. By bursting their arses, two men could do the work of four for this short period, allowing the other two a half-hour break. In an eight-hour day only four hours were worked by each pair, but it was four hours at a frantic pace. It helped a bit, but not much. Sometimes it seemed to make the day longer: no work to numb the brain. It was tradition; it was done.

In any case, the pair who were resting couldn't leave the immediate vicinity of the station in case any bigwigs came round. The foremen knew what was going on but ignored it because that made life easier for all concerned. If a senior manager appeared on the scene, however, the foremen would warn the line workers and for the duration of his tour of inspection the stations would be fully manned. The unofficial system caused delays and accidents and botched work but it existed, it was rooted in the past and therefore did not have to be justified by anyone. Senior management knew the system operated, but were content with things as they were as long as lip service was paid to their standing within the plant by halfhearted attempts at camouflage while they were present. Everyone knew, and everyone knew everyone knew, and everyone knew everyone else didn't really give a fuck as long as Laughing Imp won the 2.10 at Hackney, or the weather cleared up for a spot of golf with the boss.

Pat nodded to Billy, removed his light blue industrial gloves, and stepped off the raised metal grille at the side of the track. He sat down at the table next to the factory wall, on a wooden bench scratched with years of initials and doodles and obscenities. Above his head was a photograph of a girl with big tits lying naked on a bed covered with red silk sheets, and a bubble came from her mouth into which someone had pencilled: "Hello, I'm your new foreman".

Big Jimmy roared along the passageway, inches from Pat's back, carrying a tub of the struts which were used to keep the car doors slightly ajar as they were raised twelve feet above the ground past Pat on their route towards the paint shop.

Jimmy sounded the horn of his truck as he passed and burst into one of his unintelligible songs, roaring out the words against the clamour of the line. Pat waved at his back and waited, sitting hunched at the table. As he returned carrying an empty tub, Jimmy swerved into the side and parked next to the table, swinging his bulk down from the seat to land on ballroom dancer's feet:

"Top o' the mornin', Pat!" he shouted in greeting, a huge grin covering his face. "And how's life treating the Irish today then?" he asked, slamming a huge paw down on Pat's shoulder.

"Couldn't be better, Jimmy," replied Pat, brightening. "You know me."

"Whenever I hear that, Pat me old son," said Jimmy, staring down at him with eyebrows raised and eyes rolled upwards in mock admonition, "I know you're going to give me a tale of woe. I've been hearing you've been a naughty boy again. Is that right?"

"See this fucking place," complained Pat. "You can't do anything in here without it being someone else's business. You can't even fart in the bog without it being round the place in minutes."

"Knowing your farts, Patrick, that's something none of us want to experience."

"You know what I mean. Half of them have got nothing better to do. They're like old sweetie wives. All they need is a big basin of washing and a bundle of clothes pegs stuck in their gobs."

"Come on, now; give us the story," insisted Jimmy. "I saw you weren't in on time this morning anyway."

"Too true. By the time I got in, my card had been lifted from the clock-in and I had to go to the office to collect it. Stewart got me again." Jimmy pulled a face and drew in air through his teeth. Pat went on: "The big bastard gave me a written warning for latecoming."

"Haven't you already had one?" asked Jimmy.

"No, that was for taking days off."

"Well, you're OK then," said Jimmy sarcastically, "that's just another one for your collection."

"Anyway," said Pat knowingly, "it's common knowledge that Stewart's got it in for me."

"How come?"

"You know," stated Pat flatly, clasping his left hand with his right and shaking both up and down at the same time, darting a fox-like look in his direction.

"Oh, for fuck's sake, Pat," spluttered Jimmy in exasperation. "I've told you a thousand times before: Stewart's not in the Masons. According to Joe Gilroy in the paintshop — and Joe's brother is Grand Master of the Renfrew Lodge this year — Stewart's got nothing to do with it. In fact Harry McArthur in

'Crazy K' drinks in the same pub as him, and he says that Stewart's always taking the piss out of the chargehand because *he's* in the Masons."

"Well then," said Pat, unabashed, standing and stretching, suppressing a yawn, arms raised to the roof. "He's in the Orange Lodge or some fucking thing because he's had a down on me since he heard my name was Pat McKenna and he clocked my Celtic Supporters' Club badge. Anyway, he wears the ring — that big, black thing on his pinky."

"Shite. I'm telling you, Pat. Martin McGill even saw him in the stand at Parkhead with his two boys in tow. He saw him a few weeks ago. You never know: he might even be one of your lot."

"No chance!" stated Pat categorically, becoming suddenly animated. "I can spot real huns a mile away, believe you me."

"Well, what about me then, Pat?" asked Jimmy.

"You're different. You're OK: know what I mean? You're not a bastard like Stewart. He wouldn't piss on you if you were on fire unless you were true blue."

"For God's sake, Pat," exclaimed Jimmy, leaping to his feet and peering down from a great height into his friend's watery eyes: "has it never occurred to you that Stewart's got a down on you because you're a lazy bastard? Eh? Has it?"

"There's a lot of lazy bastards in this place," replied Pat, calmly and evenly, the height of reasonableness. He stretched out two palms questioningly and sank his head into his shoulders, tilting it beseechingly like a caricature Jewish tailor involved in civilised haggling: "All I'm asking is: why is it always the Catholic lazy bastards who get it in the neck?"

Jimmy clasped his hands over his face, let out a despairing sigh and silently retreated to his fork-lift truck. Regaining his seat, he flicked the engine to life and manoeuvred the gears, preparing to drive off. He looked across, seemingly about to add something, but seeing Pat repeat his questioning gesture, this time with eyebrows raised quizzically, he shook his head and roared off, his song silenced.

Pat looked at his watch. Ten minutes until he had to relieve Billy Paterson. He stuffed fists into the pockets of his overalls and sauntered off in the direction of the toilets, whistling softly. He was allowed to leave his station only at official dinner and tea and piss breaks, but fuck it! He could say he had the runs.

The toilets were at the bottom of the section, round the corner past the main doors where the fork-lift trucks roared in and out, laden and unladen, past the huge ventilation fan which thundered non-stop, its tone changing in quality and becoming louder as Pat approached. A constant stream of overalled figures meandered aimlessly in and out of the washhouse doors, some stopping to exchange a few words with passing acquaintances, others kicking nuts and bolts along the oil-stained concrete floor as they slouched, heads down, staring into nothingness as they counted the minutes and the hours of their lives. Inside, Harry Whitby was staring into a brass plate set into one of the WC doors, tongue extended and contorting as he tried to catch its reflection in the dull metal.

"Boot polish on it again, Harry?" asked Pat, peering over his shoulder.

"What do you want, McKenna?" asked Whitby sourly as he straightened and turned towards the circular sink unit in the centre of the tiled, echoing room.

"What, me? Want something?" asked Pat incredulously, following him. Whitby dipped his fingers into one of the tubs of Swarfega which were suspended over the sinks and smeared his hands with the glutinous jelly. Pat followed suit at the next sink, and both washed the resulting oily mess off with hot water.

"Listen," said Whitby sneeringly, straightening from the bowl, shaking loose water from his hands on to the already swimming floor. "Just tell me what you want. I've got better things to do than waste my time with the likes of you."

"I know, I know," agreed Pat vigorously, still rubbing his hands together. "You're an important man round here." He hesitated a few seconds, staring down at the dirty water in the bowl, busying himself, avoiding Whitby's stare: "I want twenty quid until Friday."

Whitby sniffed derisively and turned towards the roller towels on the wall. When he saw their condition he stopped, rubbed his hands on his overalls, and completed the drying process by sweeping his thin hair back over his head, shaking a dandruff storm on to his blue collar. Having finished his ablutions to his satisfaction, he fished a greasy notebook from his side pocket and unclipped a pen from a row adorning his breast. He thumbed the pages with a moistened digit until he came to one headed "P. McKenna". He glanced over the columns of figures and dates, only once raising his eyes to steal a look at Pat who was vainly trying to find a dry space on the towel with which to dry his hands. He made a fresh entry in the book.

"Right," Whitby exclaimed loudly, snapping the notebook closed as far as its decayed condition allowed it to be snapped. With one hand he replaced the pen and notebook while with the other he delved deep into his overalls, through the lining into his trouser pocket, pulling out a tight wad of fivers: "Usual terms," he rapped out briskly as he counted the notes. "You should know them by now," he said slowly in an attempt at sarcasm.

"I know, I know," replied Pat, nodding his head, glancing at Whitby over his shoulder as he tried to squeeze some water from his hands with the sodden towel. He turned and stretched out his palm towards the proferred money which was hidden in Whitby's fist.

"Tell me," quizzed Whitby, delaying the transaction in order to wring the maximum amount of triumph from it. "Are you sure you'll be able to pay up on Friday all right? I hope you're not going to sneak out without paying me like last time."

"You'll get paid," spat Pat, prising the notes from Whitby's fist and swiftly pocketing them. "Tell me, Harry," he asked, "has anyone ever taken that big wad from you?"

"Twice," said Whitby into thin air as he headed for the door. He stopped on the threshold and turned to face Pat straight on. "But if you're thinking of doing it, you wee Fenian cunt, tell me now and I'll organise a whipround for a bunch of grapes to send to you when Arthur puts you in hospital. You know who I'm talking about?"

"I know," replied Pat, facing Whitby, trying to stare him down. "I know who he is. The next time you see him, you can tell him from me that he's a leeching arsehole who should be put down. Do you hear me?"

"Oh, I hear you all right," said Whitby with a sneer. "And don't worry: I'll deliver the message. Arthur likes a good laugh."

As the door closed on the moneylender's back, Pat clenched the notes tightly inside his pocket. As the toilet flushed inside one of the WCs, he turned and launched a kick at the washbasins with steel toe-capped boots.

* * *

"Well, well, well; if it isn't Pat McKenna."

Pat looked down at the old, grey-haired man who spoke this greeting and grinned. Old Archie Campbell inhabited a part of the plant which seemed an oasis of calm amidst the grinding and sparking and banging of the track. Archie, one of the skilled elite of the factory, had a maintenance job, but he seemed to have run out of things to maintain. In this tranquil eddy, separated from the mainstream by high walls of boxes packed with components, Archie passed the last days of his working life contemplating his shortening future, his lengthening past, and concentrated on running his bookmaking business.

"How's Archie?" Pat asked brightly. "How are the corns? How are the piles?"

"Oh, I'm falling apart, son," complained the old man, still seated, peering at Pat over the top of a pair of spectacles which had only one supporting leg. His gnarled, large-jointed fingers rolled the pen with which he was selecting horses in the racing section of the newspaper folded over his crossed leg. "But then I hear things aren't too clever with you either."

Pat's grin disappeared: "News certainly travels in this place."

"Only the bad news, son," philosophied the old man, "only the bad. Here," he went on, sliding his backside along the highly polished bench, "take a pew. Settle yourself down."

"I'd like to, Archie, honest, but I've got to take over from Billy Paterson in a few minutes."

"That wee shit," said Archie in wonder. "Is he still here? I thought he'd left years ago."

"Yes, wee Billy's still here. Still picking his nose and chewing it."

"Ah well," sighed the old man, rubbing his red nose with thumb and forefinger, "I don't get about as much as I used to. People have got to come to me now."

"Which is why I'm here, Archie," said Pat feeling in his pocket. He drew out a crumpled piece of paper and handed it to the old-timer: "Put this on for me, will you?"

The old bookmaker looked at the names of the four horses on the betting slip and glanced up at Pat quizzically.

"I know, Archie, I know," said Pat, nodding his head, "they haven't got a fucking chance. Just humour me, will you?"

"Oh well, it's your money, son. I won't touch it. With the luck of the Irish, all four will probably win. I'll lay the bet off." The old man looked at Pat's hands as he peeled a five pound note from his small, newly acquired bundle: "Now, the only explanation for you having a bundle of fivers on a Monday morning, Pat," reasoned the old man, "is either you've won the pools, in which case you wouldn't be here at all, or else you've been tapping from that weasel Whitby again."

"I've won the pools, Archie."

"You know the trouble you got yourself into last time with those sharks," said the old man, fumbling in his pockets for change. "For Christ's sake, watch yourself, son."

"You know me, old-timer: I always land on my feet."

"There comes a time for everyone you know, son."

"Anyway," said Pat, nodding at the betting slip in Archie's hand, "by the time those four beauties romp home, my worries'll be over. right?" Pat bent down and gently slapped the old man on both cheeks with the palms of his hands, dislodging his glasses.

"Hey, hey, watch the specs, watch the specs," cried Archie, trying to conceal his pleasure.

"Don't worry," shouted Pat over his shoulder as he hurried off. "I'll buy you a new pair tomorrow." He raised his hand in a final farewell as he left the old man's cocoon.

* * *

"You're five minutes late," complained Billy Paterson, glancing at his watch while picking his nose with the index finger of his right hand.

Pat jumped on to the raised grille by the side of the track, removing a pair of protective gloves from his back pocket, pulling them on to his hands: "Billy," he observed: "one of these days you're going to inflict major brain damage on yourself doing that."

Billy quickly withdrew the finger from his nostril, rubbing it on the leg of his overall, pulling his glove back on to his hand: "All I'm saying is you're five minutes late. I don't think it's fair. I do my half hour, then you should do your half hour: that's fair. Not me doing thirty-five minutes and you doing twenty-five minutes: that's not fair. It's just not fair, that's all I'm saying."

Pat elbowed Billy to the side and took up his position at the track: "I get the impression you don't think it's fair, Billy. Would I be right?"

"You're bloody right I don't. It's not bloody fair."

"Well, I'll tell you what: I'll work for the next forty minutes, then you work for the next twenty; that'll bring us back on an even keel, right?"

Billy thought for a moment, scratching a head which sported an affront of red hair, gloves gaping on his hands: "That's not the point. I could have arranged to meet someone five minutes ago. I could have missed an appointment."

"An appointment?" asked Pat incredulously, "what appointment? You never do anything except sit at that table, digging for gold with your finger."

"That's not the point. What if I needed the toilet?"

"Billy, for Christ's sake, go away somewhere and shut up. I've not had a very good day today, and you're making it worse."

"Well, all I'm saying is . . ."

"Billy, do me a favour: just fuck off, will you? Come back in forty minutes; come back in an hour if you like. Just go away right now; please?"

Billy wandered away to the table by the wall and sat down on the bench, grumbling and muttering, his pedant's sense of probity still smarting. Almost immediately he became engrossed in the bazookas belonging to the *Sun* page three girl, imagining her glossy mouth moving softly in his ear, whispering appeals for him to assuage her insatiable appetites: "Come on, Billy, one more time, big boy." From time to time he would probe either nostril for exciting discoveries.

While he had been carrying on this conversation, Pat had been holding down the jobs of two men by coping with the work of both himself and Billy at the station. Stark silver skeletons inched their way towards him from the welding and lead infilling sections at the top of the block, the chassisless, emtpy body shells positioned on trolleys which were dragged from station to station by an endless, underground track. Above Pat, the orange sprayed overhead track began its climb into the paintshop, and it was the allotted task of his station to transfer these embryo cars from ground to air. Pat was a small, grey speck in the grand design.

Before the shells reached Pat, another team had inserted metal bars into the body at front and rear. Attached to these bars were eyes into which hooks were inserted which would haul the car into the air as they climbed with the metal track. Pat put the hooks into the eyes.

A shell approached. Above, the overhead track pulled a metal bar around in a slow arc. Attached to the bar, fore and aft, were two steel crescents tipped with hooks. The bar, synchronised with the track below, glided over a shell, the hooks scraping the roof. As the front of the bar began to rise with the overhead track, Pat pulled the first hook through the empty windscreen and forced it through the eye of the support. It began to take the strain as the two tracks moved onward in unison. Pat moved swiftly to the hook at the rear of the bar and pulled it through the back window to mate with the eye of the second support. The front of the car began to rise. The support was jolted round so that the eye pointed to the roof: the shell was being lifted from the trolley. The back support took some of the strain as it too was jolted into place by the pull of the hook. The whole structure lifted and swung from side to side in the air as the bar supported its whole weight. Up, up it climbed until it levelled out fifteen feet in the air, soon to disappear forever into the maw of the paintshop. The empty trolley was moved by truckets back to the beginning of the track. Eventually, Pat would see it again as the system turned full circle, but he would not recognise it. It would drag another car with another with other supports with other eyes, which would be pierced by other hooks.

Occasionally, a support would burst free from a car as the hook pulled it aloft. On good days the front support would collapse at the top of the rise, leaving the car swaying nose down, suspended by its rear. This calamity ensured a stoppage on the line and a lengthy delay as the car was removed with the help of a fork-lift truck. Pat would leap gleefully towards the emergency stop control which dangled on a cable above him, punching the red button which halted the overhead track and activated a flashhing light and a hooter. It was something to look forward to.

Within a short time people became so accustomed to the rhythm of the work they could perform it automatically. This left the mind free to explore other avenues, which was fine for those who had other avenues to explore, but wasn't so good for those whose imaginations were the metaphysical equivalent of small matchboxes. Some of the workers in the car plant went mad. Quite literally. They went gaga; they became cocopops; they went crazy, plumb loco, loony, loopy, bananas. Mad. So mad they were admitted to mental hospitals where doctors put electrodes on their ears and juiced them until their toes tingled. They had all that empty space in there and nothing to put in it. They were tied to the track, so they couldn't seek out any external stimulus, and their input receptors were crying out for something to fill in the blanks with. They would feel a choking sensation creeping over them, then it would seem as if they were drowning, lungs bursting, building up pressure, seeking release, then: owwwwwwww! owowowwwwwww! And you run at a car and, by fuck, you kick it good and proper; and once you tried to bite a piece from a roof but you broke your front tooth instead.

Jesus, another day, and there are eight hours stretching out endlessly, and after that, four more days, and after that you're on nightshift and you can't eat, can't sleep, you can't screw, you can't crap. You can't do anything because your system is all to cock and by the time it readjusts, you're back on dayshift again. Holy Mother of God, what's the answer? You're a tradesman, but who needs a cabinetmaker these days? And even if you do find a job, you'd never earn as much as you do now for doing this chimpanzee work. But where does it all go to anyway? You're still skint all of the time. You can't afford a holiday in Spain or even one of the cars you're making. You've got a colour TV and a display cabinet full of shit in the corner of the living-room, and a doctor who thinks you're an alcoholic because you drink non-stop to forget the next day. And as you work, you sing all the old, half-forgotten songs which remind you of when everything seemed full of promise, and dream of the gate swinging in the wind, and try not to count the minutes because that makes the time seem that much longer.

* * *

As the horn sounded at midday, Pat fled from the small emergency exit near the inspection station towards the car park. He had persuaded a reluctant Billy Paterson to take over the last five minutes of his spell to enable him to strip off his overalls and position himself on the threshold of the plant. He spotted the small, red Datsun immediately, revving its engine as it nosed its way towards the main gate. Breathlessly, Pat pulled open the passenger door and threw himself in beside the driver who immediately accelerated the car and sped past the security guards on to the main road. Behind Pat and the driver sat two other passengers, both panting, one still wearing overalls and gloves.

"Just made it, Pat!" congratulated the driver, a heavily jointed man in his late thirties with long, dark sideburns which ended far below his ears. "We were going to leave without you."

"Jesus Christ, Danny," wheezed Pat, "I've got to watch my step, you know. No skiving off early for me anymore."

One of the passengers in the back seat clapped his hand on Pat's shoulder and turned towards his overalled neighbour: "Pat's our bad boy, Liam," he explained. "Aren't you, Pat?" he questioned, rumpling Pat's hair with more vigour than seemed necessary. "He's going to get bagged any day now. By the way, this is my brother Liam, Pat: just started today. He's come to join us in the asylum."

"How are you doing, Liam?" asked Pat, nodding in greeting. "You take my advice, son," he continued in a paternal fashion to the boyish looking recruit: "You take my advice and fuck off out of it while you still can. That's the next best thing to not starting at all. Are you married?"

"Not yet," stammered Liam, "but I'm going to be in a few months' time. Gerry's going to be my best man."

At this brother Gerry looked up towards the roof of the car: "I've told him, Pat, I've told him," he insisted. "I've told him to go off and see the world instead of rotting in this shithole. I don't get you, Liam, I really don't. At your age I was travelling around from site to site, seeing a bit of the country, shagging a few females, sinking a few jars. You've got plenty of time later on to settle down. Look at us," he advised, pointing at his own chest as he nodded towards Pat and Danny.

"Don't you listen to him son," advised Danny. "Your brother's just an old reprobate, believe you me. You get married and settle down, and don't get involved with the likes of us. Eh, Pat?"

"Too true, Dan," agreed Pat. "Look at me: wife and two kids, and soon I'll be out of a job. And do you know why, son?" he asked, turning to Liam, who sat transfixed in the back seat, puppet hands still encased in pristine gloves, neatly creased overalls barely streaked with grease. "Do you know why?" he asked again. "This." On saying the word, he expanded its meaning by making as if to grip a glass with his right fist, and moving it in an up and down drinking motion with his arm crooked, a universal mime which left Liam in no doubt as to why Pat's life was, as he saw it at that melancholic moment, in tatters.

"Don't worry, Pat," encouraged Gerry, again reinforcing his feeling with a slap on the shoulder. "A couple of pints and a few halfs and you'll be as right as rain again."

Pat visibly brightened at the prospect as the car swerved into the kerb to park outside of their destination: a pub about three-quarters of a mile from the plant. He threw open the door and bounded on to the pavement as Gerry fumbled with the back seat, attempting to push it forwards to release him from the back of the two-door saloon. Danny danced his way round the bonnet of the car having slammed his door shut, and stooped to haul Gerry from his predicament: "Shut the door after you, kid," he shouted to Liam as he pulled his brother free. "Don't bother about locking it."

Gerry popped from the car and the three experienced hands burst into the maelstrom of the public bar. Feverish customers stood three-deep at the counter, raising fists which clenched five pound and single notes, hoarsely imploring the harassed bar staff for service as the minutes of their lunch break ticked away. Many were from the plant; others wore the muddied boots and wellingtons of building site workers. Standing quietly around the edge, nursing warm dregs, were the pinched faces of the bar flies, vainly hoping to cadge drinks from old or new acquaintances.

Suddenly, Gerry leapt into the air like Denis Law in full flight, seeming to hover in the air as his head snap-panned left to right to determine who was serving behind the bar. Landing back on his feet, he nudged Pat with his elbow: "Watch this," he advised. A second salmon leap took him into unobstructed space, and at the highest point of the jump he shouted over the heads of the wriggling, elbowing crowd: "Three pints of lager, Rita!"

A few heads at the back of the mob turned round and several muffled curses were heard, but time was too short to grudge other people their influence. Gerry held out his hands to the grumblers in mock supplication: "Can I help it if the girl finds me sexually attractive, boys? Now can I?"

"Has she still got a fancy for you?" asked Danny in amazement. "After you giving her a dizzy last week?"

Gerry shrugged his shoulders: "It's just animal magnetism, boys, that's all. Anyway, they like being mistreated a wee bit. It gets them drooling."

"Is that why you fuck the wife about then?" asked Pat. Danny nudged his arm and looked away.

"Pat, Pat," said Gerry calmly, with a hint of menace glistening beneath the surface like a shard of steel reflecting sunlight. "That's uncalled for. Don't you think so, Dan?"

"Come on now, boys," said Danny soothingly, his podgy hands smoothing the air. "Don't let's start all this again. We're here for a wee drink." At this point, a beringed female hand appeared above the heads in the crowd and an index finger pointed towards the right-hand side of the pub. "Hellooooh!" announced Danny triumphantly, "we're off!"

The three men fought their way through the throng to an oasis of calm beside the food counter where there was no bar staff and no beer pumps. There, Rita was waiting with three pints of lager. Gerry flashed a grin on his dark, still youthful face, showing white teeth which enhanced his slyly attractive features. He stroked his moustache like someone he had once seen on television:

"Rita, my wee beauty," he said throatily, extending his right hand to clasp hers.

"Don't you come near me, Gerry Mulhearn," snapped Rita, slapping his hand aside. "What happened to you last week? I waited over an hour for you and you never showed."

"Come here, pet," said Gerry, gesturing her towards him.

"No, I'm not coming near you. That's it as far as I'm concerned."

"Come here," Gerry coaxed, now leaning on the bar towards her. "I just want to have a wee word in your ear."

Rita feigned a look of displeasure then tilted her blonde head in his direction: "All right, then. But I don't know why I'm listening."

Gerry bent towards her ear and his tongue darted out, briefly licking the lobe, eliciting a muffled giggle from Rita. He whispered a few words and at the same time his right hand crept over the bar in a wide outflanking movement, slowly moving closer to Rita's ample backside, coated in a second skin of lime green satin. Suddenly his hand darted forwards, goosing Rita, who leapt into the air roaring with laughter. She slapped his wrist for the second time and moved off towards the other customers, darting a knowing look in his direction as she went: "I'll believe you," she said as her parting shot, "thousands wouldn't."

"Rita!" shouted Gerry at her retreating back. "Three half pints this time; and three halfs!" By this time both Pat and Danny were fingering glasses which had barely a trace of lager at the bottom, so Gerry placed his pint to his lips and rained threequarters of the contents: "See that?" he asked, gesturing with his thumb over his shoulder. "It's the old magic touch. Don't you wish you were in the super stud bracket, Pat?"

"She's a hell of a brainy lassie, isn't she?" mused Danny, scratching his ear.

"Fantastic, Danny," replied Pat. "There's miles of unexplored territory inside her head, just waiting to be discovered."

"Who's bothering about the grey matter?" asked Gerry incredulously. "Look at the body it's got on it. She's some fucking ride, I'll tell you that for nothing."

"Is that right?" asked Pat innocently. "I noticed you didn't bother to pay for the pints. Is that you starting to rent your prick out now?"

Gerry's dark features whitened slightly as he drained the rest of his lager: "We've just got a wee arrangement, that's all," he said softly. "You've been known to borrow money before, haven't you, Pat?"

"Not from women, Gerry."

"Oh, sorry, I thought you did. I must have been getting it mixed up with your kids' Christmas present money."

Pat slammed the empty glass on the bar.

"Boys, boys," pleaded Danny. "I thought this was all finished between you two! For Christ's sake, I'm down here for a quiet drink, and if you're going to ruin it for me I'm going to fuck off and the both of you can hike it back to the plant. Look," he said, gesturing towards the counter, "there's Rita with the bevvy." Rita set down a tray on the bar and placed six glasses before them. Three were half pint mugs containing lager, three tot glasses containing whisky.

"You're a wee darling, Rita," said Gerry. Rita flashed a brief smile:

"That'll be two pounds, ten pence."

"I'll get it," said Pat, fumbling in his pocket.

"No, hold on," argued Danny.

"Here, I'll get it," insisted Pat, handing over three pounds. "Get one yourself, Rita."

"Thanks, pet."

"Get us three halfs when you're ready, darling, will you?" asked Danny.

"OK."

All three men drained their whisky glass and poured the dregs into the lager.

"Where the fuck's that brother of mine?" demanded Gerry.

"The boy's just as well not coming in here in his first week anyway," counselled Danny.

"But he's supposed to be coming out for a drink with me. I told him I'd show him about. Daft wee cunt. He's off his fucking head, anyway. He's been going with the same lemon since he was fourteen: the wee prick. He's going to get married and he's only shagged one woman. Sometimes I think he hasn't even screwed the one he's going with."

"He's just a young boy," interposed Pat.

"Oh yes, a lot you know about it, Casanova. I've heard all about you."

"Leave off, Gerry, will you?" pleaded Danny. "Here's the drinks, anyway. Cheers. What's the damage?"

"One thirty-five."

"There you are."

"That's it exact. Thank you."

"Don't mention it."

"Another three halfs, Rita, eh?" asked Gerry.

"I don't think we've got time," said Danny doubtfully. "What do you think, Pat?"

"Oh, fuck it. Let him get them."

All three men drained their whisky glass and poured the dregs into the lager.

Gerry stretched and belched loudly over the heads of his two companions. He rocked off the bar: "I'm away for a slash," he explained. "Don't worry, Pat," he continued as he brushed past on his way to the toilet. "I won't ask you to pay for it: it's on me."

"Great, Gerry. That's a big relief. I'm not used to being out with such monied company." Then, as Gerry disappeared into the toilet, releasing a draught of stale urine: "Fucking prick!"

"Take it easy, Pat," warned Danny, placing a soothing hand on his elbow.

"He just gets on my tits, Danny, that's all. What the fuck do you bring him along for, anyway? We used to have good wee bevvies along here: me and George and you, before George got pumped. I know he's your wife's brother, but enough's enough. And now I see we've got two of them."

"Come on, now. Wee Liam's OK."

"Maybe so, but I suppose Gerry was like that once too. Where's the wee cunt got to anyway?"

Danny looked furtively over his shoulder: "I told him not to come into the pub."

"What? Jesus, if Gerry knew that . . . What the fuck did you do that for?"

"You know what can happen, Pat. The boy's only just starting. Let him find his feet first, then he can decide which side of the fence he's on for himself."

"Do you know, Danny, you're a big soft bastard at heart, aren't you? Always keeping the peace. What would we do without you, eh?"

"Laugh if you want, Pat, but I'll tell you one thing: sometimes I can go home at night and know I've done something good. You know, something really good, not just putting some fucking bolt in the right place."

"Take it easy, big man; I know, I know."

"Do you fuck, Pat. I'll tell you something: all you know is what you find at the bottom of these glasses, and it's showing."

"Come on now, Danny, cool it down."

"And I'll tell you another thing," continued Danny, laying a finger on Pat's chest as he again glanced behind him at the creaking toilet door. "Lay off the snide with Gerry. You know he can be an evil bastard. You've talked to Margaret."

"And I've seen her too," interjected Pat. "I've seen her on Sunday mornings with the dark glasses on to hide the black eyes."

"Well, just leave it out. I want none of it today."

Pat shrugged his shoulders and tilted the lager glass to his mouth, gulping the contents with a gasp of contentment: "At least we know where the money comes from to let Rita buy all of those drinks."

"What do you mean?"

Pat lifted his glass to eye level and shook the remaining inch of lager from side to side: "I haven't got any change back from my round yet."

Danny tilted his head back and laughed, the flesh on his throat and jowls shaking in waves: "Poor Pat. Fuck all's working out for you these days, is it?"

The toilet door slammed and Danny furtively snapped a look over his shoulder: "Remember."

"No drinks yet?" shouted Gerry questioningly, slapping Danny solidly on his upholstered back: "Rita!"

"Coming!"

Rita wobbled up to the bar carrying three whiskies. Gerry blew her a kiss as he searched for his glass: "You're a marvel, girl, a fucking marvel. Did anyone ever tell you?"

"Yes."

All three men drained their whisky glass and poured the dregs into the lager. With an automaton movement, Danny threw the beer down his throat:

"Come on, let's make a move. We've about thirty seconds to make it back to the chain gang."

Outside the pub they found Liam leaning against the car, systematically destroying a packet of salt 'n' vinegar crisps.

"Where the fuck have you been?" demanded Gerry, staring into his brother's eyes before he thrust him aside and pulled open the car door.

"Looking after Danny's car."

"What?" asked Gerry incredulously, staring at him again as he paused before he climbed into the back seat.

"Looking after Danny's car," repeated Liam. "He didn't lock it."

"Jesus Christ!" exclaimed Gerry as he threw himself in. He gestured with an index finger: "Get in, cunt face. Come on. and throw these fucking things out!" As he screamed his last instruction, he grabbed Liam's crisp bag and threw it on to the pavement as the boy squirmed in beside him. "I can't stand the smell of those things."

Liam settled in beside his brother, his legs cramped submissively in response to Gerry's assertive, splaying knees. He stared silently through the side window as his bony hands again found their way into blue-white gloves.

Halfway to the factory Gerry began to hum a tune, and after a few seconds he was accompanied by Liam who drummed his fingers clumsily on the back of the seat, glancing apprehensively towards his brother. In the front of the car Pat hummed half of a bar then broke into song:

> "Her eyes, they shone like diamonds,
>   They called her the queen of the land,
>   And her hair hung over her shoulders,
>   Tied up with a black velvet band."

Danny joined in the next verse, gently harmonising, and the song continued until the car pulled in through the factory gates. No one spoke as the car doors were slammed. Each individual hurriedly made for his own particular entrance into the complex, each swallowed up, vanishing like a pebble on the beach. It was Monday afternoon: only eight shopping days until Christmas.

VOCABULARY

Come here, son . . . I want to give you a little test . . . It's not painful. That's it; sit down. Make yourself comfortable. OK? Ready? Right?

Now, what I want you to do is tell me as many words as you can think of which describes a Rangers supporter. And you can wipe that smile off your face, you little snot: I don't want any obscenities. . . . Clear? Now, the only thing is, you can't stop to draw breath: you've got to breathe in deeply and cram as many words as possible into your sentence before your face turns blue. Blue . . . get it?

Ok, are you ready? All set? Brain ticking over? Deep breath. And . . . Go!

"Gersteddybearsproddieshunsbluebottlesorangemenbluenosesbilliesthatsallicanthinkof . . ."

Right, not bad for a first attempt. You can relax now. That's it for today. Now, I want you to go across the room and take a seat inside that little black booth there. Do you see it? The one with the white cross above the door. I want you to go in there and put on the headphones you'll see lying on the table in front of you. Put them over your ears then slip the blindfold on. You'll find that on the table too. Just wait in there until I send for you again. Clear? Right, off you go now.

Right, sonny, in you come. Take a pew. . . . Do you know what that means? Just take a seat. Don't be nervous. Settle down. Put your palms face down on the arms of the chair, on top of those pads. That's it. Now, what I want you to do is sit a little test. Will you do that for me? Good lad! It's quite simple. All I want you to do is to think of as many words as you can which describe a Celtic fan. Now, I know you've probably heard a lot of bad words at the games, but I want you to forget about them for the time being. You know the ones I mean? We'll come back to them later. Anyway, I want you to tell me the words, but I don't want you to draw a breath while you're saying them. Understand? Of course you can breathe in before you begin; we don't want you damaging those lungs, do we?

Now, do you think you can do that? You're not confused at all? OK, get ready; deep breath. And . . . Go!

"Fenianstimspaddiesmurphiestimaloyspapesteaguesmicksbogmen."

Right, right, you can breathe now. That's fine; relax. . . . Now, do you see that little booth across the room? The purple one with the crown on top? I want you to go in there and put on the headphones and the blindfold you'll find on the table, and stay there until I fetch you again. Why? What do you mean, "Why"? I ask the questions around here, not you, you jumped-up little shit. Go into the booth and do as you've been instructed or I'll warm your hands for you. Go on. . . . Get! . . . Kids!

Scottish Recipe Page

"SUICIDE SUPPER"

Ingredients:	Take one middle-aged, hungry Glaswegian, preferably two or three stones overweight, with a pot belly and flabby breasts. Extend his right arm, open his hand, and place a pound note in his fleshy palm.
Direction:	Point the Glaswegian in the direction of the nearest fish and chip shop, wind him up, and let him go.
The meal; Prelude and Postscript	The Glaswegian will walk slowly on flat feet, avoiding sunlight where possible, in case it damages his delicate skin. On reaching the fish and chip shop, he will queue behind similarly shaped customers, all smoking cigarettes, preferably untipped and with a mammoth tar yield. It being our own Glaswegian's turn to be served, he will order a pie supper with a pickled onion and two buttered rolls. Plenty of salt and vinegar.

Returning to his home, our ingredient unwraps his meal as the front door clicks behind him. Entering the kitchen, he puts more butter on the rolls, more salt on the pie and chips. He wedges approximately half of the chips inside the two prepared rolls, lays them aside, and deposits the remainder of the meal on a cracked plate. For maximum effect, the whole operation is carried out using the hand and stubby fingers which have been playing with loose change inside his trouser pocket. While all this is going on, the pickled onion is being munched as an aperitif.

The Glaswegian carries the meal to his living-room where he deposits the plate(s) on top of the television, which he switches on to warm the food. He returns to the kitchen where he pours out a huge mug of tea, into which he dumps four spoonfuls of sugar. Back in his living-room he sits on a chair with his plate on his lap, his mug on the floor beside him, in a good viewing position for the box. He removes all teeth not strictly required for the thorough enjoyment of the meal and places them on a nearby table. The meal then proceeds in a carefully defined sequence, preferably carried out without recourse to either knife or fork:

STEP 1: Place chips in mouth. Chew.

STEP 2: Place piece of pie in mouth. Chew and swallow.

STEP 3: Bite off piece of chip roll. Chew.

STEP 4: Take vast gulp of tea. Swallow, washing down particles of chips, roll and pie.

All of these steps are repeated until the plate is empty. The mug may be refilled if required.

In the most favourable circumstances, the chips will be hot enough to cause the slabs of butter on the rolls to melt, in which case golden rivulets of grease will run down the fingers, to be licked off at leisure. At the end of the meal, plate, fingers, lips and palate should be coated with a layer of white lard which, in the case of the plate, is left to harden. The grease on fingers and lips is left to be absorbed into the skin; the grease on the palate is savoured with the tip of the tongue until it disappears. The feast is rounded off with another cigarette, or maybe two. If the ingredient is thirsty after his meal, he may repair to the nearest public house where he can drink fourteen pints of lager, heavy or Guinness, according to individual taste.

ALEC DOWDESWELL

That morning Alec had decided to walk to work. It was a morning in early spring when the chill of winter still lingered but was dissipated somewhat come ten o'clock under the rays of a new sun. That particular morning was cloudless and held out the promise of a crisp afternoon: feeding the pigeons in George Square after a solid lunch, recharging after the winter hibernation. Alec had been infected with this spirit of renewal and strode briskly along the pavement, throwing out his rolled-up umbrella with each step, swinging his attaché case to the rhythm of his pace. Like many people, Alec planned all sorts of minor adjustments to his lifestyle at this time of year; plans which had been lying dormant during winter came to fruition during spring. Keep a diary: who cares if it's three months into the year? Remember the one you kept for years at school? A regular programme of exercise: *mens sana in corpore sano*. Heart. Diet? Less sugar and animal fats, more natural fibre: 'All Bran' was supposed to be good. This year, without actually realising it yet, Alec had decided to drastically alter the twenty-two-year relationship he had enjoyed with Julia, his wife.

The route between his home and the city centre where his office lay was in some ways a strange one. Starting off at his house in Pollokshields, an area of sandstone villas, Audis for the shopping, and private nurseries, Alec would walk along beautiful tree-lined avenues until he crossed Shields Road. Beyond this junction, Albert Drive was lined with tenements instead of villas, and the trees disappeared as the road descended towards the heavy traffic in the distance. This area had yet to fully decide whether it was up-market or down-market, and a large Indian and Pakistani community had been grafted on to this cultural schizophrenia. At the end of Albert Drive, Alec would turn left, walking along Pollokshaws Road and its extension, Eglinton

Street, towards the city centre. On the right-hand side of Eglinton Street lay the fringes of the Gorbals, the old slums now mostly demolished and replaced with high rise cell blocks riddled with dampness. Around the tower blocks were expanses of waste ground still showing the foundations of the old community, plus a few of the old tenements, isolated now, most of their windows boarded up. Here, as in the rest of Glasgow, the last part of the building to go was always the pub on the corner. Everything above and on every side would be demolished, leaving these life-giving oases stranded incongruously in the middle of waste ground. A drive through Bridgeton or Parkhead on the other side of the river was like a drive through Nagasaki in late 1945. Streets and pavements were laid out geometrically but nothing stood in the blocks between except the occasional corrugated iron pigeon loft and the pub on the corner, heavily fortified with steel shutters and barbed wire. And they were always full. No human habitation could be seen in the vicinity, but the regulars continued to turn up, arriving from God knows where. Eventually, even the pubs would disappear, often seemingly overnight, leaving distraught customers to suffer anxiety attacks as they picked their way over the rubble-strewn landscape looking for the darts they had left behind the bar with Big Charlie.

During Alec's forty-minute walk to the office, he would pass through practically every stratum of Glasgow life. At least he told himself that during his socially aware days. Actually, he passed through only three or four, but that was two or three more than most people saw. This morning, as on other occasions when he had decided to take exercise in this fashion, several cars crept slowly into the kerb as he passed the gravel driveway near his home, and their owners, leaning out from cushioned comfort, offered him a lift, assuming his own car had broken down. They smiled indulgently and wished Alec luck as he declined: they had experienced his fads before.

Retired neighbours and "housewives", walking labradors and setters, nodded in greeting as they carried *The Telegraph* back to the breakfast table where they spun out the morning. Tiny boys and girls in immaculate green and purple and blue uniforms, with little leather satchels on their backs and little caps and berets on their heads, spilled in and out of deep car seats or walked, a line anchored by mummy's hand, towards a cosy classroom and plasticine and poster paints. Older boys stood at bus stops, carrying 'Adidas' bags full of rugger gear, bantering in a mixture of shyness and bravado, trying to engage the attention of schoolgirls whose black-stockinged legs attracted lustful stares of passing sugar daddies. Also at the bus stops were groups of university students. The males stood in rebellious training shoes, faculty scarves swung carelessly round striped rally jackets, bags at their feet bulging with folders and books on sensible subjects, cramming engineering texts. The females, dressed in neat little quilted jackets and dinky dungarees and cute bootees, read D. H. Lawrence paperbacks for the English Lit. class. Peace reigned. All was well with the world. Birds twittered in the trees as the buds reappeared in response to the lengthening days.

Alec narrowly missed stepping on a dog's turd as he halted at the junction of Albert Drive and Shields Road. He crossed at the first break in the traffic and walked down the slight hill towards the railway station, passing tenement blocks, Pakistani grocer shops and elegant women in saris carrying roly-poly children with eyes a million miles deep. Older Pakistani children stood at the bus stops too, some also en route for university, armed with Glasgow accents and frightening ambition, and a new morality which baffled their parents. The first whiff of the emergent middle-class miasma had begun to reach this area, its symptoms being a rash of coffee rooms and "antique" shops, and Swiss cheese plants peering out from weatherseal, up-and-over windows.

As he passed over the railway bridge, Alec saw the Museum of Transport to his right through the passing traffic and resolved for the hundredth time to take Douglas there on a visit. Turning left at the corner after the bus depot, he walked along Pollokshaws Road to Eglinton Toll, then along Eglinton Street towards Jamaica Bridge which led over the Clyde into the city centre.

Passing St Andrew's Cross, he glanced over the vibrant road and saw the first, scarred remnants of the Gorbals of the "razor kings" and of gangster mythology. The grey sandstone walls of the remaining few tenements were pitted with years of exposure to the sulphuric acid in the atmosphere formed by sulphur dioxide fumes being dissolved in rain water. The surface of the stone had peeled off, allowing the softer underlayer to crumble under the attack of wind and rain and frost. Wires connected to television aerials on the high roofs blew in the wind as they dangled aimlessly, only to snake into a kitchen window. Many of the windows showed signs of desertion and dereliction, looking as unlived in as an abandoned shoe, but electric bulbs shone from some in the morning light, the last electro-cardiograph blips in a building marked for death. Below the windows of the flats, the lines of shops flanking the close mouths were succumbing to the pressures of compulsory purchase and declining population. One by one they were raising the shutters for the last time, some owners abandoning a shabby, noble dream to the ravages of vandals, rats and winos. Some of the entrances to the closes themselves were blocked off with sheets of corrugated iron, in a halfhearted attempt to discourage squatters and cowboys on the hunt for lead and copper. The gesture was futile: squatters have their pride. The barriers remained in place, lying askew like drunken sentries.

The inevitable starved mongrels roamed the deserted streets in packs, prowling for bitches and food, abandoned by owners who found themselves in turn abandoned in peripheral housing deserts. Those humans who remained were mostly the very old, postponing their uprooting until the last possible moment. As he walked along Eglinton Street, breathing in the fresh morning air, Alec saw an old woman ahead, legs like drawn bows, contorted by childhood rickets. She walked arm in arm with her diminutive husband, her upper body rocking to and fro to the crippled movement, like a mechanical toy. Her free arm carried a shopping bag which dipped and scraped the ground at the beginning and end of every roll.

Alec took advantage of a red light to cross the main road and entered a deserted side street, being swallowed up immediately by silence and decay. From the mouth of the second close in the street, a pair of trouser legs protruded into the open air. Alec peered down at the prostrate figure, and at the top end of a huge army greatcoat saw a grizzled beard and a mass of matted hair framing a face which seemed like a death mask in the half light. He wondered why tramps never seemed to be bald. Cradled in the lifeless arms was a bottle of 'Eldorado' fortified wine. Perhaps that was the answer. The recumbent figure made a loud spluttering noise to signal his sleep was not his last, and Alec moved on.

Outside of the newsagents which was Alec's destination, a haggard, sparrow-like woman in a headscarf paused to rearrange the bundles of clothes packed in her battered pram, then wheeled the load off to a mysterious destination. Alec halted outside of the tiny, isolated shop and looked into its congested window. Taking up half of the available space was a series of advertisements for a racing tipster's service which relied on spurious claims of past success to entice new clients. The other half of the window was obscured by columns of small ads written on scraps of cardboard, some of them inserted by people who had long left the area. The newsagent, with a mixture of self-interest and fatalism, had failed to remove them, although the insertion fee had long since run out. The shop owner was affected by a mixture of sloth and a vague hope that a crowded window might encourage other potential advertisers.

FOR SALE — baby carriage and baby clothes and cot
ASK INSIDE.

WANTED — Embassy coopons — any amount — best prices
paid — see inside.

FOR SALE — irn, irning board, kitchen table, three chairs.
APPLY LUMSDEN 14 CUMBERLAND STREET
2 UP LEFT.

FOR SALE — Wedding dress, bridesmaids dresses, fur coat,
silver lamy evning gown — OFFERS to
McArthur, 18 Norfolk St.

PLUMBING, JOINERY, PLASTERWORK
ALL UNDERTAKEN REASONABLE PRICE
FREE ESTIMATE PHONE 332 9581 KOMINSKI

TWO ROOM, KITCHEN, INSIDE WC TO LET —
Nice close — 17 Bedford Street
3 up middle — £7.50 p.w. — detales inside.

Alec read all of the advertisements closely, with a kind of hunger. People trying to sell their possessions for a few pounds. Too much pride to be seen sneaking into the pawnbroker. A card in the window could be explained as "clearing out". Pride, amongst the sounds and smells of decay, of the scrapheap, of dead ends.

When he had read every card, Alec entered the crumbling shop through its boarded-up door and bought twenty 'Embassy Regal' and a box of matches from a woman behind the counter who seemed surprised to see any customer whatsoever. Usually, Alec only smoked king-sized cigarettes or his pipe. In the pocket of his suit was a silver cigarette lighter.

Instead of retracing his steps to the main road, as Alec came out of the newsagent's he turned left towards Gorbals Street. The freshness in the air belied the sense of oppression which hung in the area, a malaise born of despair and decay and ghetto building. Alec seemed oblivious to this almost tangible atmosphere as he marched briskly along the pavement, dodging gaping holes in the crumbling concrete, his feet sending dislodged roof tiles spinning and clattering into the gutter. With a brutal disregard of the sensibilities of those who lived in the area, factory walls and windowless, long empty workshops crowded in on people's living space, their bleak, brick facades seeming like the archaeological remains of the outposts of a once vibrant and expansionist capitalism. They had died. Not because the natives were restless: they had died slowly, as if they had been choked to death by the weeds which sprouted from the cracks in the pavement.

The collective spirit of the area had been crushed long ago by a combination of external brutalisation and internal inadequacy.

The skilled, the energetic, the ambitious had left long ago to look for a new life in one of the Central Belt's New Towns, places like Cumbernauld or East Kilbride or Irvine, places where they could forget where they came from in a bright, new home. Or else they had gone to the Midlands of England, where their skills had been soaked up by the car plants and engineering works and steel mills. There, they had joined Corby Rangers Supporters' Club or Birmingham Celtic Supporters' Club, and scanned the results page of the Saturday evening earlies for the football scores, ritually rubbing a club scarf between thumb and forefinger. Or else they were in the "colonies", still believing in the old songs, proud of an unchanged accent after forty years in Toronto or Melbourne or Wellington or Jo'burg, skin like leather and grandchildren who thought you were from Uranus. All of them part of the steady drip, drip, drip which leeched the life from the population, leaving it pale and anaemic, turning those who remained ever inwards in an incestuous, grappling, self-destructive dance which spun in ever-decreasing circles.

On a street corner, next to a church which had been converted into a cash-and-carry warehouse, was the green-painted exterior of an Army Surplus Store. At this relatively early hour it had not yet opened for business, but Alec stopped and stood and stared through a metal grille at the goods displayed for sale behind the window. A few pot and pan sets, and knife-fork-spoon combinations, and khaki balaclavas desultorily scattered over the display area testified to the store's original role as a recycling medium for good quality, second-hand or surplus services' stock. Now it was an outlet for a cross section of the world's shoddiest goods, pathetic, shabby articles which poor people bought under the impression, most probably self-delusory, that they were investing in practical, no-nonsense, hard-wearing outfits. Plastic shoes from Poland with soles you could spit through fought for prominence with Taiwanese nylon shirts looking for the naked flame which would allow them to melt and coat their wearer in an all-weather, water-resistant second skin. Pride of place in the window display was given to a shiny, black coat with a red tartan lining. A large card, hand written with a felt-tipped pen, was attached to the left shoulder:

JUST ARRIVED
"WEATHA-PROOF"
LEATHER-TYPE COATS
FULLY LINED
Only £15.99

Alec looked at his watch. He could cross over the suspension bridge and easily arrive at the office before nine o'clock. He liked to be punctual, despite the fact that, for some time now, there had been no pressure upon him to keep regular hours. Self-discipline was a matter of pride: its exercise gave one a moral and psychological vantage point from which to view the world at large.

Invigorated, Alec pointed himself towards the city centre, whistling a martial air which had lodged in his mind from a black and white television screen. Despite his lack of height and unassuming appearance, he seemed in command of the streets through which he walked, drawing strength from the weakness around him. At his heel, a dog followed, hoping for favour.

FOOTBALL I

Football is Scotland's national sport and it is treated with particular reverence in Glasgow, where five senior teams compete for the allegiance of a population of under 800,000. There are also many junior and amateur teams, and on a Saturday or Sunday morning it's impossible to spit without splashing the boots of a budding star or an ageing veteran on his way to sink in the mud of a local park or skin his knees on the red blaes behind the gasworks.

Every schoolboy dreams of joining his heroes in the Scotland team, and, despite the blandishments of television and 'Space Invaders' machines, the toes of shoes are kicked in on every street corner on every evening of the year, regardless of the weather.

What about the big time, though? Saturday afternoon. The Game. In the north-west of the city you can visit Firhill Park and see Partick Thistle entertain. Just off Maryhill Road, the 'Jags' perform in red and yellow stripes. They are supposed to occupy a special place in the affections of the Glaswegian fan, regardless of his first loyalties. Their happy-go-lucky spirit and erratic form provokes a rueful shake of the head and a whimsical smile as they turn up shock result after shock result: the rogues. Just as long as they lie down and get drubbed by your team. That's the Jags for you: great, isn't it? I fucking hate them.

At Shawfield Stadium, a team called Clyde turn out in white shirts with a wee dab of red to add interest. At least they turn out when there's no dog racing on. Clyde are sometimes known as the 'Bully Wee' or, as some people claim, the 'Billy Wee'. It's said that all the Orangemen in town used to turn out to see them play when the "other ones" weren't playing at home.

A sleepwalk away on the South Side, you can find the home ground of Queen's Park: 'The Spiders'. They received this nickname because of the web of black lines spun through their white tops. The Queens play at Hampden Park, a derelict junk heap which is supposed to be Scotland's national stadium. This coal bing used to be a prestigious venue back in the days when QP were big news in Scottish football. They're strictly small beer now, and every second Saturday during the season you can sit in the ground where Scotland play their international matches, one of only five hundred spectators who have turned out to view a league game against the likes of Cowdenbeath or Stenhousemuir. All this in surroundings which have known the adrenalin flow of one hundred and forty thousand baying, lung-bursting voices, sounding like a thousand of the locomotives their workmates forged in St Rollox, or countless steel hulks slipping down a gravity slipway into the maelstrom Clyde.

The Queens are now the only amateur club in Britain playing the senior game. They pay the bills for the stadium out of the receipts from cup finals and internationals, those feverish occasions when maudlin, tartan-clad sentimentalists cry into their whisky and make believe we're a nation.

Now we come to the big two: Rangers and Celtic, the teams who, between them, have won countless trophies and dominated Scottish football from its inception: the "Old Firm", as brain-cramped journalists call them. The Celts play in green and white hoops, green the colour of the rain-soaked Kerry grass cows grow fat on in April. The 'Tic can be found at Celtic Park, Parkhead, in the east of the city: turn left at the derelict iron foundry and head straight for the Irish tricolour — you can't miss it. The 'Teddy Bears' play in true blue with a dash of red and white and are "Aye Ready" at Ibrox Stadium in the south-west of the town, just up the road from the bomb crater they used to call Govan.

There was another senior football club in Glasgow at one time: Third Lanark — the 'Hi-Hi'. They could be found at Cathkin up until the end of season 1966-67, round about the time Celtic won the European Cup. They died. Just as simple as that. They snuffed it. One day they curled up in a ball and never opened their eyes again. Third Lanark will never come back, although some people who were little boys in 1967 still possess Thirds' scarves, tucked away safely like secret teddy bears.

SAM DUNBAR

"Fucking shite!"

The words rang out in booming tones but few people, if any, paid attention. All around, customers sat or stood or swayed or slumped. Noise erupted from the pub into the street when the swing doors opened to admit another thirsty patron. What was being said? Hundreds of lives were bobbing at random in this confined space, colliding, then moving on. What elements built up this wall of noise? Truths, half truths, lies, confessions, manifestos, boasts, statements of fact, hyperbole, pleas, hypocrisy, whines, demands, jokes, sarcasm, wit, seductions, threats, abuse. True life adventure; suburban melodrama; ghetto violence; boyhood dreams; old men's ravings; kittens' purring; sixties nostalgia; angry young men caught in a time warp. CND duffels on ageing pacifists; crisp black Crombies on pinstriped solicitors; leather-patched tweeds on balding teachers; plastic-shouldered donkeys on nail-chewing dustmen. Urine-soaked trousers stick to old Bobby, the boxer. Poor old cunt. He used to be not bad, you know, 'til he got one too many jabs on the head and had to go to the brain garage. God, I can't stand looking at him. The way he dribbles out of the side of his mouth. The way he dribbles from every hole he's got. Christ, here he comes — why do they let him in here? He always talks to me. I can't understand him. I'm off to the bog. I'll be back when he's gone. Hello, Bobby! How's it going, old son? That's good. See you later.

All around, mirrors and casks and polished wood from another age when the beer was strong and the pies had meat in them. Brass footrail on the floor, rubbed smooth and bright by the soles of countless shoes. Photographs on the wall — not up-market chic in sepia tints, but yellow, curling, faded memories of heroes long gone. Above the gantry, a stiffly posed reminder of a football team now alive only in conversation and middle-aged dreams, commemorated only by a rotting tooth in the gaping mouth of the city and a muffled roar in the recesses of hearts in the geriatric wards.

Lean your back against the bar, raise your eyes above head height, and there are the old customers. The frozen, staring eyes of workers in bunnets standing and sitting in groups, dwarfed by huge link chains or the keel of a ship now rotting at the bottom of the Atlantic. The apprentices sprawl in front, miniatures of their fathers: muffler, boots and flat cap, but as yet no growth on the upper lip. The foremen stand guard at the sides, sprouting bowler hats from the tops of their heads, fingering watch chains which curve across dark waistcoats. They seem to study the men from the corners of their eyes, searching for skivers.

Meanwhile, back in the present, the hungry and the forward planners line their stomachs with pies and peas, preparing delicate tissue for the coming onslaught. The food disappears down countless gullets, for the most part untasted. Ritual need not be appreciated by the sense. Empty packets of salted peanuts and smoky bacon flavoured crisps and KP Rancheros are thrown carelessly over shoulders and trampled underfoot. Fingers are licked and sleeves rolled up. Having searched teeth with tongue for any last morsels of food, a cigarette is lit and the smoke exhaled through flared nostrils. We're off!

Maybe tonight is Friday night. For most, the week is over and life can begin. It's payday. Or yesterday was anyway, and I've still got a wad left in the hip. OK? Even for those on monthly salaries, tradition dies hard. So you went to university and got a degree, and now you're a professional man. But you came from Yoker and your accent changes at five o'clock, and it isn't that long ago you were involved in a wee rammy down in Argyle Street and nearly got lifted. Your old boy used to come rolling in every Friday and Saturday, pissed as a fart, and you like a wee snifter too. Helloooo! Here we go!

A half and a half pint: the old Glasgow special. Half a pint of heavy and a wee goldie — whisky to you, you ignorant bastard. Nectar. I needed that. I could do with another one too. Just a wee drop water: that's it. Whoa! Don't drown it, for God's sake. Cheers. Ahhhh!

And all around there is the noise, even tonight, Monday, start of the week. The noise: incessant; frantic: tongues loosening with ties. Barriers dropped, but tomorrow you'll wake up squirming because you told everyone you screwed your aunt when you were fourteen. In the beginning, few words are spoken. Return to the scene an hour later and arms are flailing, eyes bulging, fingers jabbing, foreheads contoured with veins as the life you've bottled up all week spills on to the floor in an ugly mess, like intestines ripped from your stomach. The mass confessional grinds into gear in a cathartic nightmare. Don't worry: by Monday everything will have been swept out of sight, parcelled up and zipped away until the next time you sniff a cork and have an excuse to bare your soul without fear of derision.

And what is being said? What components make up this sound generation machine? Look at him across there — that baldy bastard who's talking to the bird with the big tits. What's he saying?

"... and then I just told him that as far as I was concerned I was washing my hands of the whole matter. If he expects me to shoulder such responsibility, he can offer me a partnership. In my opinion, the whole thing is ..."

Jesus wept! Well, what about that big blonde bit of stuff in the corner — the one with all the eye make-up on?

"... and then he unzipped his trousers and ..."

What ? What? Christ, see the fucking noise in here! You can't hear a bleeding thing. Well, what about him? The one who's holding the empty pint glass, waiting for someone to buy him a refill. He's a teacher — I'll lay you any money you like. I'm telling you, you can spot them a mile off — I think it's the haircuts. I bet we can hear what he's saying. Boring bastards!

"... standard pretty much the same as usual. you know, wide spread of marks."

"I wanted to talk to you about that, Sam. I had a look at some of the papers you had marked and found your judgement to be, in my opinion ... well, pretty erratic, if you don't mind me saying so."

"Erratic? You don't say? In what respect exactly?"

"Well, to tell you the truth, it looked as if you had allocated some of the marks totally at random. I saw what I considered to be abysmal efforts given sixty, sixty-five, seventy per cent. None of the errors in spelling or punctuation appeared to have been corrected. No comments had been added by you in the margin or at the end of the paper. Some reasonable work seemed to have been rejected by you, totally out of hand. Some seemingly obvious pass work received twenty or thirty per cent. Comfort's essay only got twenty-eight. Again, no explanation for the fail grade was attached to the paper. I know this isn't really the time or place for a serious discussion of marking stratagems, but I was just wondering what your criteria were, if you had discovered some novel marking scheme which I, as your principal teacher, should be made aware of?"

"I thought you might ask that, Bill," said Sam unflinchingly, still cuddling his empty glass.

"Pint, lads," asked a bearded figure in a black leather jacket, putting a hand on each of their shoulders as he peeled off from another group in the direction of the bar.

"Thanks, Gordon. Lager."

"Bill?"

"Not for me, Gordon, I'm driving. Thanks all the same."

As Gordon moved off to try to attract the coy glance of a barman, Sam stood, still nodding his head thoughtfully: "It's funny. I thought you would bring that up."

"And are you going to reveal all?" asked Bill with what he thought was a twinkle in his eye.

"It's actually something I've been working on for some time," explained Sam, nodding as he stretched to accept a new pint of lager from his leather-jacketed colleague: "Cheers, Gordon. Here, give us some of those, eh?"

Bill tapped his foot heavily on the brass rail on the floor as Sam arranged his provender to his satisfaction, crunching a huge handful of 'Golden Wonder' pickled onion flavoured crisps in his mouth, leaving Gordon the dismayed owner of a plastic enclosed vacuum. When he had mashed the mouthful into manageable proportions, he continued:

"It's actually why I was so late delivering the second year

marks." Bill made a face. "I know, I know," said Sam in mock understanding, "you principal teachers have it tough, what with unreasonable deadlines handed out from the top, plus the responsibility of coping with your incompetent underlings."

"You should have been one yourself by this time, Sam; you know that."

"Well, anyway," Sam went on, ignoring this last remark, "I've been working on this new method of assessing essays which tries to make allowances for cultural bias and lack of grammatical skills. Notice I use the word 'assessing' rather than 'marking'. I was trying to arrive at a system which would allow the teacher to make a more objective assessment of the child's creative skills. We don't want to submerge originality in a swamp of grammar and punctuation and spelling, do we?"

"Go on."

"I, or rather 'we' — because I had some help in this from a couple of drama students who were looking for ideas for a workshop — we attacked the problem from a previously unexplored angle. I think we broke new ground."

"Yes?"

"In fact, I think there's enough material there now, generated by our efforts, to justify a short paper on the scheme for *English Now*."

"Sam, could you tell me what you did?"

"We put all of the essays on tape."

"Tape?"

"Tape."

"Sam," asked Bill patiently, his right elbow resting on his left palm, right hand clutching chin, index finger stroking nose pensively. "Sam, why did you put the essays on tape?"

"Don't you see?" demanded Sam, abandoning his pint on the bar, feigning incontrollable excitement. "Lots of these kids come from a background where almost all communication is oral. Some of the parents are illiterate. They heard stories of the old days at granny's knee. Their creative skills are there, untapped, lying dormant just under the surface, clogged with rules about grammar, puncutation, spelling, syntax and everything else which restricts their freedom of expression on paper. We're prejudiced against them even before we've read their efforts because their work looks like something you would find during an autopsy on a nanny-goat. Do you see, Bill?" Bill looked doubtful.

"So, anyway, to escape from the cultural trap — a trap both for us and the pupils — to escape from this trap, I decided to change the medium." Sam paused for dramatic effect, but also to refresh himself from his glass: "With pretty dramatic effects, I can tell you," he went on, foam adhering to his upper lip. "What you might have dismissed as the effort of some half-literate somnambulist on paper suddenly sounded exciting and vibrant and . . . real . . . on tape. Especially when it was spoken in the correct register."

"So that explains the drama students?"

"Exactly!" cried Sam, stabbing the principal with his index finger. "The next stage in the process is to bypass the students and get the kids themselves to speak directly on tape: 'Tales of Childhood', things like that. Or 'Stories from my Granny'."

"Could make a great radio programme," said Bill sarcastically.

"Could do," agreed Sam, choosing to ignore the tone. "I hadn't thought of that," he continued ingenuously.

"And the tapes . . .?" began Bill questioningly.

"Gone," interjected Sam before taking another long draught of lager.

"Gone?"

"Gone: the students took them. Part of the workshop. Remember I told you?"

"Sam," said Bill, looking at his watch, "we'll have to discuss this further tomorrow. I promised I'd take Margaret round to see her parents tonight; her mother complains she never sees her grandchildren. She was asking for you, by the way; Margaret that is. You know, she's been worried about you and Sheila since . . . well, you know."

Sam shrugged his shoulders and took another swig.

"So," said Bill, bending to lift his briefcase from the floor. "I'll see you tomorrow morning. And how about trying to find some of those tapes? Good man. Cheerio all!" This last directed generally to the party from the school grouped round the bar.

123

"Is that you off?"

"Away already?"

"See you . . ."

"Bye, Bill."

"Do you not want . . ."

"Are you . . . ?"

Bill dragged himself away but, as Sam noticed, not before he had a short word in the ear of Martin Wham, the school's assistant principal English teacher. Sam thought he could see Martin glancing at him from the corner of his eye.

"What was all that about?" asked Gordon of Sam as Bill finally left through the swing doors.

"A load of shite!" said Sam with some venom.

"Have you been winding Bill up again?"

"He usually swallows any old mumbo-jumbo I feed him," explained Sam, "but this time I think I've gone too far. He wants evidence."

"Evidence of what?"

"I'll explain later. I can't be bothered talking about it anymore right now. Where's that wee French bit of stuff got to?"

"Now, now, Sam," coaxed Gordon, "remember you're a married man."

"But not for much longer, old son. Not for much longer."

Gordon had forgotten. He looked embarrassed and buried his nose in his glass.

* * *

"Stalin will be rehabilitated."

"Don't talk shite."

"I'm telling you: it's lurking beneath the surface like a dormant plague virus. All that's needed to regenerate it is the correct medium. Any culture will grow given the necessary conditions."

It was now around eight o'clock in the evening. At around six to a quarter past, the crowd in the pub had thinned as people with responsibilities had trickled home for grub and snoozes in front of the fire, leaving the flotsam and jetsam bobbing aimlessly among crumpled evening papers and crisp packets, clutching on to the liferaft of the bar. Now the second shift was beginning to filter into the smoky atmosphere, some of them raising eyebrows as they saw the drink-sodden faces of Sam and his workmates, for here they had remained since five o'clock. Three hours on, voices were slurred and passions aroused. All thoughts of the morning's furry-tongued agony had been firmly tossed to the back of the mind as large and small glasses of dangerous chemicals flooded past gulping tonsils.

Almost an hour previously, the party had repaired to the tables which clung to the walls around the pub, splitting into two groups. Now only six were left, and all of them had forgotten why they were there. The French assistant whose imminent departure they were toasting had left at six o'clock to meet her boyfriend. At seven, Sam had searched the bar for her, intending to whisk her off to his flat, there to spend endless hours listening to Mozart and 'The Rolling Stones Greatest Hits' before making violent love until morning. When he had been unable to find her, he bought another round instead.

Now, Sam was sitting with Gordon, the leather-jacketed art master, and Edgar, a first year teacher from the history department. The table was awash with ash-flecked puddles of drink, and one glass rested on its side. In a separate huddle sat Martin and two female members of the modern languages department. One of them was crying: it was Martin. Both women placed a comforting hand on his arm and looked at one another above his bowed head, shrugging their shoulders. Martin removed his hand from his face and stood up unsteadily.

"Are you coming?" he roared emotionally. Neither women moved nor spoke. Martin kicked over his chair and brushed past several transfixed bystanders, disappearing into the night. One of the women, Angela Damper, slim, blonde, with hair so glossy it dazzled bloodshot eyes, leaned towards Sam, who had been so engrossed in listening to the sound of his own thoughts being born he had missed the excitement.

"He's left his bag again, Sam. Will you take it?"

Sam looked up, his train of thought interrupted: "What? Oh, yea. OK. Leave it. I'll get it to him. Is that you off?"

"Yes, that's us away. See you, boys."
"Are you away?"
"See you, Tricia."
"Where's Martin?"
"Is this it?"
"Whose bag's that? See you, Angela."
"See you."
"You've not finished your drink."
"Angela . . ."
"Tricia . . . stay for another . . ."
"Oh no . . ."
"What's . . ."
"Whose . . ."
"Who's . . ."
"Bye . . ."
"So . . ."
"When . . .?"
"Right . . ."

The women left, wobbling slightly as they felt matchsticks beneath their feet.

"It's always there." Sam was in the mood to dissect the human condition and nothing could stand in his path: "It's in every society."

At times like this he could sense the power in his body: words fell, perfect as raindrops. Matrices of thought gelled, encapsulating all he had ever wished to say. Controlled excitement roared with subdued energy through to his fingertips which darted in every direction, pinning victims to walls of inexorable logic. All the disparate strands of his experience and knowledge could be brought together in a laser beam charged by a million volts of pure reason and truth, lighting up a neon display in his head which would dazzle onlookers, converting the foolish and the mistaken, and illuminating a path through shrouds of superstition, cant and accepted wisdom. That's what he thought anyway, but the next morning he could never remember what he had said.

"Power structures are propagated in blood and it lies at their roots, despite the beautiful blooms they display to the world at large. The Vatican: torture and the rack. The White House: slavery and production lines which grind up bones. The Kremlin: howling Arctic blowing through labour camp clothes. The Houses of Parliament: screaming thumbscrews in darkened rooms and death where the sun never sets."

God, what a load of crap. He talks like a crazy book when he's drunk. Let's listen to a bit more for a laugh:

"Death ran through the Russian system for hundreds of years. It subsisted on it. It swallowed up the bones and blood of offal and grew Tolstoy and Turgenev and Dostoyevsky on its dung heap."

"And Lenin," interrupted Edgar.

"It still swallows up human lives, but now it's Sovietised and the by-product is now millions of coal-dust briquettes instead of westernised prose masters. I suppose that's a worthwhile transformation if you happen to be living in the Siberian wastelands and your balls are dropping off with the cold. *War and Peace* is a big book, but I wouldn't imagine it would burn for long on the stove. If you're a cosy intellectual in Leningrad, I suppose it could be a different story."

Both Edgar and Gordon were swaying wildly on their seats, each desperate to break into Sam's easy, lubricated flow, to destroy him with their own booze-soaked philosophy. Edgar, being younger and more self-obsessed and more drink crazed, managed to leap in first, silencing Gordon with a wave of the hand which unbalanced the art teacher and sent him crashing against the wall: "That's just typical of your crap arguments. You're so cynical it stinks. It's pathetic really. In one part of your mind you think you sympathise with the wee punter who's burning the coal briquettes, but you can't bring yourself to say it out loud in a straightforward way. You've got to wrap it up in an ambiguous package which leaves you in the morally superior position of the anguished intellectual. On the one hand, you want to give the impression that somehow you could organise things so that the peasant could sit with a warm arse at the same time he's soaking in these wonderful cultural riches which only appear in socially unbalanced societies. On the other hand, you're trying to wash your hands of the compromises which allow each objective to be fulfilled."

"That's a big speech for a wee boy," spat Sam viciously, sinking his nose into his glass.

"There you go again!" shouted Edgar, waving his hands wildly and almost disturbing Gordon's dazed equilibrium for a second time. "You can't stand anyone who's emotionally or intellectually committed to a system of thought because it makes you feel guilty."

"Guilty? What the fuck do I have to feel guilty about?"

"You feel guilty because you're inadequate: you're incapable of commitment. You're frightened that if you choose a way of living which requires an outward display of belief, it might later be proved to be false. In which case it's black marks for you on this crazy game you play with the world."

"What?" cried Sam incredulously. "Where did you dig that shit out from? Was it in your catechism, or did you read it in this week's edition of that Marxist *Beano* you always have folded under your arm?"

"Cheap."

"You're correct in one respect: I don't want to soil my hands with any philosophy which is stained with innocent blood. I don't want anything to do with Communism or Capitalism or Christianity."

"OK, Sam: you stay pure. Remain a virgin. Crawl into a hole and watch the world go by as you contemplate the unsullied virtue of Samuel Dunbar. It's easy."

"Easy? Do you think it's easy?"

"Yes. Christ, you don't even fulfil that function. Every morning you go into that school and grind down more bones. You're not as virginal as you think."

"Truth, beauty, love, art: that's all there is in life worth talking about."

Both protagonists stopped in mid arm-waving flow and stared at the source of this profundity. Gordon, having been perched precariously on the edge of a plateau of drunkenness for more than an hour, had now fallen disastrously into the depths of embarrassing semi-incoherence. As he mumbled some more jumbled inanities into his beard, Sam and Edgar, now temporary allies, eyed one another sympathetically. Despite their unbridgeable differences, the pair formed an island of mutually assuring sanity in the midst of this sea of half-digested, crackpot philosophy spewed forth by Gordon whenever he toppled into alcohol-induced delusion. If anyone could be classed as a semi-catatonic hysteric, it was he. Fragments of his former personalities fought for space in his garbled brain. Jumbled thoughts tumbled to and fro in his cranium, emerging as half-formed sentences from two little flabs of flesh in the lower half of his face. Logic was suspended as a random word or idea gained the force of a major philosophical hypothesis, and involuntary sparks from damp tinder stimulated the neural pathways leading to his tongue:

"I've been to Venice. I've been to Florence. Who remembers Joe Cunt, the ice-cream salesman who warmed up Leonardo's chamberpot?"

Both Edgar and Sam sat back, gesturing benevolently, both willing to be diverted for a few moments by this lunatic babbling. Gordon moved both of his hands in a sweeping movement across the table over which he slumped, knocking a full pint glass to the floor with a crash: "Man's history can be viewed only in terms of the heights reached by individuals or small elites. It's worth a thousand years of individual misery if centuries of humanity can appreciate a brushstroke of genius. What would a million years in the lives of a million Melanesians produce for posterity apart from a few mud huts that will disintegrate in the first monsoon?"

"In that case, Gordon," said Sam brightly, "you can volunteer to participate in my latest artistic project." Gordon blinked blearily at his persecutor. "What I plan to do is to insert fourteen three-foot-long acupuncture needles into your head, like the spokes of a wheel, then roll you along an original Model-T assembly line. The work will be called: 'A thinking man's rejection of materialism and his search for natural truth'. Your next of kin will be able to visit the exhibit free of charge until I sell the work to a private collector."

Gordon gave a glazed grin, choosing to ignore Sam's flight of imagination: "Who wants to see the Fiat plant in Turin or a block of workers' flats in Milan? It will all have crumbled to dust in fifty years' time, when people will still be visiting the Coliseum and the Doge's Palace. The Bolsheviks couldn't cope with the latent power of artists they released as a by-product of 1917. So they encased them in concrete because they were shit-scared of what could happen if the ideas they liberated infected the souls of the poor saps their 'Socialist Reconstruction' fed upon. They recognised at a very early stage that free artistic expression couldn't be harnessed to some shabby materialist idea. Real creation was their enemy because it involved spontaneity and a denial of mindless regimentation. They just couldn't handle it, so it was smashed, utterly."

Edgar jerked a thumb in the direction of the bearded drunk: "I can just see Gordon now, dressed up like some Tsarist poof, juggling with Fabergé eggs, tossing Old Masters at the Red Army when they tried to take his original Mozart score away from him."

"Don't come that macho crap with me," sneered Gordon. "Don't you know that homosexuals are attracted towards totalitarian movements? It's the leather, you know."

God, the whole interminable, circuitous argument went on and on and on. Had they forgotten they had discussed all that crap last week, and the week before too? They rabbited on about it every fucking week because it filled in the space between their ears, and convinced them for a brief, drunken interlude that they were sentient beings in charge of their destinies. In truth, all three had cashed in their moral and intellectual chips long ago, and resigned themselves to becoming state pensioners from the time they dusted themselves down after university. And that huge, all-powerful being up above, be he a giant 'Mars Bar' or a super-intelligent cockroach, why he just looked down from his fancy golden throne in amazement and felt a great desire to bite their heads off. He had to restrain himself, however, because he was a Catholic, and felt himself unable to interfere with the free will of his creations.

Suddenly, Sam silenced the others with a wave of his hand: "Shut up a minute, will you? Listen, a bloke's just walked into the bar over there — I want to avoid him. Look round and you'll see him. Slowly! Don't make it obvious. Do you remember him? It's the wee guy who wandered up to me in here a couple of weeks ago. The steamer. Remember? Look, the wee guy with the dark complexion. Do you see him? The one that's just staggered into that Salvation Army punter who's selling the papers. Jesus, he looks pissed again. Listen," continued Sam conspiratorially, drawing closer to his companions, "I'm bolting off to the bog until he disappears. He might just remember you from the last time, so if he comes up and asks where I am, tell him I left half an hour ago." Sam half rose from his seat: "And if he tries to put the bite on you for cash, don't entertain him, OK?"

Having given his instructions and received grunts of agreement, Sam crept from his corner and, none too steadily himself, slunk towards the toilets, taking advantage of every available piece of cover. He made no attempt to rationalise his behaviour. He just didn't want to see the wee guy, that was all, he had decided bumptiously, as if he had more important things to do with his lousy time. As he turned the corner of the bar, now obscured by the central gantry with its old wine casks stacked to ceiling height, he straightened his guilty fugitive's back and rearranged his features to look like the tight-mouthed, self-righteous drunk he was.

It wasn't even the money he would have to fork out. It was just that he couldn't be bothered expending any energy talking to him, trying to decipher his drunken babblings. Because drunk he undoubtedly was. Sam had almost been able to see the red of his eyes from where he had sat. In fact, now he had convinced himself that he had seen it. It was a miracle he hadn't been spotted.

Sam padded round the back of the bar where diners ate midday and early evening, studying himself in the full-length mirrors which lined the walls. As he orbited the central core of drink, he kept one eye, as far as he could, on the progress of the lurcher who was spilling pints and standing on toes as he rebounded from one customer to another, eliciting yelps of protest like the tetchy bell of a touchy pinball machine.

Standing behind a pillar, Sam looked across the vast bar

towards this man who had been his drinking partner a bare twenty-four hours ago: he had been his buddy, his pal. The wee guy he had arranged to slip a few quid to. It was the wee bloke he'd had his arms round two weeks ago when both of them had been as pissed as farts, singing 'Summer in the City' without remembering a quarter of the distant words, almost getting huckled by the police at the bottom of Byres Road. He'd stood guard while the wee guy had gone for a slash up a close in Dumbarton Road.

It was the wee guy he'd always promised to lend books to when he was steamboats, but never quite got round to it when he was sober: the wee fella with big holes in his brain where words should have been poured years ago.

And now Sam was standing, hiding behind a pillar because he couldn't be bothered talking to him. Because the wee man's drunk, that's why. He's jaked out of his nod. He's probably slabbering his words; he might start crying, or shouting and roaring if that's how the mood takes him. Sam Dunbar's lying doggo, skulking behind this pillar, because Sam Dunbar's got enough on his plate, thank you very much, without having Pat McKenna deposited there too. See?

FOOTBALL II

Football is played on a rectangular pitch with two "goals" at opposite ends of the ground, these taking the form of two wooden uprights topped with a wooden horizontal bar. The object of the game is to place a ball, usually with the head or foot, inside your opponent's goal, without infringing a plethora of rules and regulations.

The game is played with eleven men in each team, the modern Scottish game also allowing two substitutes per side. Originally, substitutes were only allowed in the event of injury, but this rule was changed to allow substitutes for any reason, because it was felt that a spirit of duplicity was being introduced into the noble game through unscrupulous managers telling off-form players to feign leg breaks.

The arbiter of this lusty activity is called the referee, a man of unimpeachable impartiality. He in turn is aided by two stalwart assistants called linesmen.

Although the two teams involved can, and do, wear uniforms or "strips" of any colour or combination of colours under the sun, the referee is usually attired in a natty little suit in neutral black, as are his two aids.

The referee's modern day symbols of authority are his book, into which he writes the names of miscreants, and his cards, one in yellow indicating a "booking", i.e. a player's name being written in the book for committing an offence, and one in red indicating an ordering off, i.e. the player being sent from the field of play for committing a serious offence or a series of minor ones. In addition to this, the referee wields a little whistle which he blows every time an offence has been committed, or sometimes, just for the fun of it. The referee is a very important man.

Thousands of years ago, footballers probably used the head of a beaver instead of a ball. No attendance figures are available from those far-off times, but it isn't thought the game was a popular spectator sport. It was a different story in the 1920s, '30s and '50s, however, when hordes of people flocked to every match that was going, and the terraces looked as if they had been paved with bunnets.

The stadiums expanded to cater for this upsurge in interest, a development which wasn't very costly since all you had to do was pile up a big heap of dirt behind the goals and reinforce it with a few railway sleepers. Toilets were provided at the ratio of approximately one per ten thousand spectators, and those fans whose bladders could not cope with the long trek to the urinals or the long wait in a queue once they arrived, why they were lifted by beefy Highland constables as they pissed against walls or into beer cans.

Those were the golden days of Scottish football. The jingling of cash registers and the clicking of turnstiles provided a syncopated accompaniment to the twinkling, dubbined toes and flashing, baggy shorts. Heavy leather bladders caked with mud thudded from bowl haircuts as cigar-smoking haulage contractors struggled to the bank with heavy bags marked "swag".

These days, however, the upstart fan is staying at home. He's pissed off with pies and Bovril, and the rain dripping down the back of his neck, and the urine seeping through his shoes. He's sitting in the living-room in front of the fire, watching 'Grandstand' on the telly, wondering where to go on holiday this summer on the proceeds of his redundancy money. There's a can of Tennent's lager by his side and a packet of 'Castella' in his cardigan pocket. He's waiting for Frank Bough to appear with the teleprinter at 4.40 to see if he's won the pools. His son thinks Third Lanark is the horse which finished behind the first and second in the last race at an old course outside of Glasgow.

The Music Business

Glasgow is the Tin Pan Alley of Christianity. Many of our favourite songs show our strong links with Ireland. They are sometimes merely new words set to old tunes but we are very proud of them. Most can be heard at Ibrox or Celtic Park on alternate Saturdays throughout the football season.

* * *

> Hello, hello, we are the Billy Boys.
> Hello, hello, you'll know us by our noise.
> Up to the knees in Fenian blood,
> Surrender or you'll die,
> We are the Orange Billy Boys.

*

> Jingle bells, jingle bells,
> Jingle all the way,
> Oh what fun it is to fuck
> The Huns on New Year's Day.

*

> Then I looked up to the sky,
> Saw an Irish soldier laddie,
> Who looked at me quite fearlessly and said:
> "Will you stand in the van,
> Like a true Irishman,
> And go to fight the forces of the Crown?
> Will you march with O'Neil,
> To an Irish battlefield,
> For tonight we're going to free old Wexford town."

*

U.D.A.! All the way!
Fuck the Pope and the I.R.A.!
Na na na na, na na na, na na.

*

'Twas on a dreary New Year's Eve,
As the shades of light came down.
A lorry load of volunteers,
Approached a border town.
There were men from Dublin and from Cork,
Fermanagh and Tyrone,
But the leader was a Limerick man:
Sean South of Garry Owen.

*

I.R.A.! All the way!
Fuck the Queen and the U.D.A.!
Na na na na, na na na, na na.

*

The cry was "No Surrender!"
Surrender or you'll die.
With heart and hand,
And sword and shield,
We'll guard old Derry's walls.

*

Singing I'm no' a Billy, I'm a Tim.
Singing I'm no' a Billy, I'm a Tim.
Singing I'm no' a Billy, I'm no' fucking silly,
I'm no' a Billy, I'm a Tim.

*

Follow, follow, we will follow Rangers,
We will fight till the day we die.
Follow, follow, we will follow Rangers,
Up to the knees in Fenian blood,
We'll follow on.

*

Oh there's only one King Billy, that's McNeill.
Oh there's only one King Billy, that's McNeill.
Oh there's only one King Billy,
Only one King Billy,
  Only one King Billy, that's McNeill.

*

It is bright and it is beautiful,
And its colours, they are fine,
It was worn at Derry, Aughrim,
Enniskillin and the Boyne.
My father wore it as a youth,
In the bygone days of yore,
And it's on the 12th I long to wear,
The sash my father wore.

*

You're gonne get your fucking head kicked in!
You're gonne get your fucking head kicked in!
You're gonne get your fucking head kicked in!
You're gonne get your . . .

Pat McKenna

"Where somebody waits for meee,
Sugar's sweet, so is she,
Bye, bye, blackabirda!"

The song could be heard clearly over the din of the line. Pat McKenna was one of the chorus, roaring "Bye, bye, blackbird!" at the end of every stanza, these few being the only words he knew. As Pat sensed his cue approaching he straightened, raised his arms and wiggled the fingers of his gloved hands like a Christie Minstrel with only half a black face.

The leading chorister was a spark, perched high above the overhead track, his legs dangling in mid-air from the edge of a steel crossbeam:

"Make my beda, light the lighta,
I'll be homea, late tonighta,
Blackabiiiiirdaa — byyyyye, byyyyyaaa!"

Prompted by this rather dramatic finale, designed to milk the last drops of theatricality from the lyric, those within earshot broke into applause, and some even removed a glove to insert fingers in their mouths, emitting piercing whistles:

"More, more!"

Pat felt a finger tap him on the shoulder as he joined in the show of appreciation: "Spell."

He turned round: "Billy, you wee beauty!" he cried. "Just as I was dying for a piss too." Pat grabbed Billy Paterson by the ears and drew his face closer, planting a wet kiss on his nose.

"Get to fuck!" Billy cried, breaking Pat's grip with an upward sweep of his arms: "Are you some sort of poof or something?"

"If only I was, Billy. We could make beautiful music together."

"Fuck off. Just make sure you're back here in half an hour to take over again."

"I'll be there, Bill. I wouldn't miss it for a keek at your wife's drawers."

"Oh aye, I've heard it all before. You've been late twice today already. No wonder Stewart's talking about giving you your jotters."

"Billy," said Pat after a slight pause, pointing towards Paterson's feet, "do you see that mash hammer down there? Well, going to do me a favour? Grab a hold of it and ram it up your arse."

Pat jumped from the platform at his station and kicked an empty milk carton high into the air, splashing the toecap of his boot with pasteurised flecks of white. In the toilet he relieved his straining bladder at the urinal, pissing the money he had borrowed that morning against the cold tiles, watching steam rise from the yellow stream. From behind him he heard a rushing flood as one of the water closets was flushed. There was a sharp "snick" as the bolt was pulled back from the door. Pat glances over his shoulder as Archie Campbell emerged into view, adjusting his overall with old man's fingers, the other hand clutching a tattered paperback.

"We meet again, old-timer!" shouted Pat, buttoning his fly. The grey-haired maintenance man nodded in greeting, slipping the book into one of the many capacious pockets on his chest, arms and legs:

"Pat, I see from the rolling eyeballs that you've been hitting the bevvy again. Would I be right, now?"

"Too true, Archie," agreed Pat, rubbing a hand over his face. "I'd a skinful down in the 'Castle Vaults' at dinner time. And talking about bevvy . . ." Here, Pat glanced conspiratorially over his left shoulder, seeing only his own reflection in the cracked mirror. ". . . Are you holding any?"

"You know me, Pat. I'm always holding. But do you think you should bother? You're beginning to look a bit the worse for wear."

"It's the drink from last night, Archie: it's still in my system. It'll soon wear off." Pat chuckled and placed a hand on the old man's shoulder: "That's what I'm frightened of."

"Have you eaten anything?" queried the old man.

"I had a bit of breakfast this morning."

"Did you get hold of a pie down at the 'Vaults'?"

"No time, Archie. It was pandemonium down there. You know these twelve o'clock sessions."

"Aye," said Archie reflectively, hands deep in his pockets, "I used to be in there myself. Not any more, though," he continued, suddenly straightening and patting his belly with his hand. "The old gut won't stand for it. I've got to relax with my drink now."

"Aye, well you've got plenty of opportunity in here, Archie."

"Come back with me, son, and I'll give you something to eat. The wife's always making me up too many chits these days. I think she's trying to make me grow back into my old suits. She's hoping I'll live until I'm sixty-five so she can keep on getting the wage packet.." Both men left the toilet and strolled back towards the old engineer's sanctum.

"Do you mean to say that you hand your wage packet over to the wife?" asked Pat incredulously.

"Certainly," replied Archie. "Don't you?"

"Do I fuck. She doesn't even know how much I earn."

Archie looked at Pat quizzically: "And how's the money situation?"

"Chronic."

"Exactly!" exclaimed Archie triumphantly. "That's what I mean, son. Mine used to be too. Now I hand all the money over to her: she pays all the bills and buys my socks and tobacco, then she slips me a few bob for a punt and a wee drink."

"For fuck's sake, Archie, you never struck me like that: handing over the wages; the wife doling you out pocket money."

Archie stopped and looked straight at Pat: "Son, I'm sixty-one. I've had my fling. When I was younger I stayed in Calton and I was tossed out of every pub and whorehouse round the Gallowgate. Now all I want is a bit of peace and quiet. I want mince and tatties and a big bottle of 'Guinness' when I get home at night. I want a full pouch of tobacco in my jacket every morning. I want tinned salmon on my pieces. I want to sit back and watch the racing on the box every Saturday and not have to worry about the electricity being cut off. Come the Fair, I want two weeks at Saltcoats with a few quid in my hip." Here he paused for a few seconds, seemed to think, then continued walking: "Maybe you should be thinking along these lines too."

"Me?" asked Pat in amazement, stopping dead in his tracks, finger pointing at his own breast. "Me?" he repeated, now addressing Archie's back, the old man having advanced five or six paces in front of him. "She'd drop dead if I came in on a Friday night and plonked the pay packet on the table. Me?"

"It comes to us all, son," replied Archie without turning round. "It comes to us all."

"Anyway," shouted Pat, now hurrying after the old man, "what about the horses? Do you tell the wife you're running a book in here?"

"What?" asked Archie, it being his turn to feign incredulity. "The book? I don't get involved in her hobbies, she doesn't get involved in mine. Anyway, it's pure recreation. You know me — I don't run about in a big flashy car." Here Archie stopped and winked at Pat: "I'm only in it for the entertainment — I like to meet people."

"Oh aye," said Pat, again addressing Archie's retreating back. "Oh aye. You can pull the other one now, Archie. You can pull the other one now."

Archie's cave was furnished with two benches, a table, and a one-bar electric fire, an addition since Pat's last visit. On a steel girder behind Archie's seat — that area of the bench which was distinguished by the presence of a piece of worn foam rubber filched from the upholstery shop — was a photograph of the Third Lanark team of season 1954-55 which had succumbed to Glasgow Rangers 2-3 in the third round of the Scottish Cup after a 4-4 epic struggle which in turn had followed a 0-0 draw. This was possibly the only photograph in the entire plant which was not in any way defaced.

On the wooden table was a copy of the *Daily Record*, opened at the Racing Section, a *Sporting Chronicle*, two pencils, a pair of spectacles, a spectacles case, a handkerchief, an ashtray containing cigarette ends and pipe dottle, a pipe, a box of matches, a pouch of tobacco, two paperback books bearing the titles *Dusty Trail to Abilene* and *Duel at Devil's Canyon*, several sandwiches wrapped in a 'Mother's Pride' wrapper, a thermos flask, and a packet of obscene playing cards. As Pat squeezed between racks of components, following Archie into the hide, the old man shoved the packet of sandwiches across the pockmarked table towards him:

"Eat."

"I'm not hungry, Archie. You know how you get yon way." Pat flopped down on a bench: "I've got a hell of a drouth, though."

"I'll tell you what," said Archie, leaning towards him, tapping the food with a yellow nail. "You eat one of those and I'll give you a drink."

"Archie, are you trying to be my mammie again?"

"That's it, I've stated my terms: you decide."

"OK," agreed Pat with a sigh. "Pass them here," he continued, gesturing with his index finger. As Pat unwrapped the sandwiches, Archie fumbled in a storage bin, producing a bottle of 'El Dorado' fortified wine and a half-pint glass:

"Eat," he repeated, pouring a small measure before returning the bottle to its hiding place. Pat took a bite from a cheese and tomato doorstep and made a grab for the glass, feigning a tremble in his hand as he moved it to his lips. Archie laughed: "I don't think you're as bad as that yet, Pat. But there again, I don't think you're far off it."

"How are the kids?" asked Pat, ignoring this last comment. "Any news?" he continued through a mouthful of bread.

"We heard from Jeanette a couple of weeks ago."

"Is that the one in Toronto."

"No, she's in Rhodesia: Bulaweyo. It's Jack who's in Canada. We haven't heard from him in a wee while. Anyway, Jeanette says it's getting rough out there, so they're thinking of moving to South Africa, for the sake of the kids."

"Not back here?"

"Are you kidding? What's for them here? I reckon this place'll just about see me out then it'll fold. And it's the same story all over. What's there to come back to?"

"True enough. Things seem to be going from bad to worse."

"I'm telling you, Pat," said Archie resignedly, "I can't make head nor tail of it, I really can't. Across there they've got a swimming pool."

"Is that right?" Pat took another swig of wine. "Someone was just talking to me about that the other night. Have you ever thought about going out there yourself?"

"Well, Jack once said that he'd send us the money for the trip out to Canada, so we'll maybe make it one of these days."

"Archie!" The cry came from outside of the cave walls. A few seconds later the face of an apprentice engineer appeared round the corner of a storage rack: "Arthur says you're wanted on the phone in the supervisors' room."

"Who me?"

"That's what he said." The apprentice glanced sideways at Pat and peered into his glass before disappearing.

"Oh well," said Archie, stretching. "Must be my stockbroker. OK, son," he shouted after the vanishing boy, "tell him I'll be there. It'll be the wife again," he explained to Pat. "She phoned last week to tell me there was a leak under the sink in the kitchen. What the fuck was I supposed to do about it, I ask you? It's these old tenements: falling to bits. Eat those pieces," he warned as he left, pointing a warning finger at Pat.

"OK, Archie, see you."

"See you, Pat. Look after yourself."

As Archie slipped through the gap in the barricade, Pat tossed his half-eaten sandwich on the floor and moved to the storage bin, fumbling for, then finding the old man's bottle of 'El Dorado'. He poured a quarter pint into his glass then replaced the bottle. Reseating himself on the bench, he flicked through the *Sporting Chronicle* while he sipped the wine, its syrupy sweetness cloying his palate. A sharp nose appeared round the corner of the racks:

"Archie not here?"

"No, he's away on the phone. Hey, Tam!" shouted Pat, calling back the nose as it sniffed away to find another bookie. "How did Ragusa Imp do in the 1.30 at Fontwell, any idea?"

"Still running," said Tam with a sneer.

"Wait a minute, what about Swordsman in the 2.00?"

"Binger. Three legs. When will you ever learn, Pat?" asked

Tam with a mock sigh. "Leave it to the experts — like me. Twenty-three pound win on Friday — not bad, eh? See you later."

Pat did not reply as the sharp nose disappeared, nostrils twitching. Instead he lifted the glass of wine to his lips and drained the contents. Fucking horses. He moved again to the cabinet and poured what remained of the wine, just less than half a pint, into his glass, replacing the empty bottle among the voltmeters. Old Archie would understand. He'd buy him another one tomorrow.

As he rolled the drink round in his mouth with his tongue, gargling with small amounts, he glanced at Archie's books. Beneath the title *Duel at Devil's Canyon* was the author's name: Clint Whitby. On the cover where two desperados, hands poised dramatically over holsters. On the ground, holding on to the leg of an 'ornery dude in a black stetson, stretched a buxom saloon gal, weeping copious tears as she bared a thigh and seemingly fingered the tough hombre's member. Pat turned the foxed, musty pages at random, looking for dirty bits but meeting with no success. The *Duel* was a boy scout tale of sanitised good overcoming cardboard evil, with not an orgasm in sight. The cover, in bright reds, yellows and blues, was a tease, tempting gulls like Pat to buy it furtively, keeping it steaming in a brown paper bag until they reached home. Archie himself was past all that: he bought the books for the stories. He had read sixty-seven out of the seventy-three titles in the 'Pecos Western' series.

Suddenly, the nose reappeared: "Pat, there's a man with veins bulging out of his head looking for you."

"Who?"

"Billy Paterson. He says you were due back five minutes ago."

"Fuck him," said Pat carelessly. "Hey, Tam, any news on the 2.15 at Plumpton?"

"Hold on, let me guess what you picked: was it Good Intent?"

"That's right," agreed Pat, raising himself slightly on his seat.

"Fell at the first. I just saw it on Hughie Brown's portable TV. What did I tell you, Pat?"

"Fuck off!"

"Hey, have you been hitting the bevvy? You look half smugged."

"I've had a wee nip."

"A wee nip? Your eyes are like 'Jelly Tots'."

"Christ, can a man not have a wee drink anymore?" whined Pat.

"Drink on, old son, drink on," said the nose on leaving. "At least if you're unconscious you can't bet any more."

"Fuck off!"

Pat tossed the paperback onto the bench and slammed his now empty glass on the table, dislodging several dog-eared playing cards which fluttered to the floor, some revealing suits, others showing breasts and luscious lips. As he stood up, he swayed slightly, holding on to the edge of a storage bin with outstretched fingertips. That bevvy from last night must still be doing the business in there right enough. That wine's hitting right down where it counts. Fucking horses.

Outside of the barricade, life flowed sedately on upon its normal course, oblivious of the presence of a little drunk man swaying along the passageway of 'L' Block of a motor vehicle plant in the West of Scotland. A horn sounded close by, making Pat start. He staggered into the wall as a fork-lift truck roared by, its driver wearing a Nazi stormtrooper's helmet. The machine pulled into the side of the passageway a little ahead of Pat and the driver jumped from his seat, looked round twice, and disappeared from view through a door leading to the outside world.

The truck was parked next to a solid wall of boxes. Stacked on pallets, they reached about sixteen or seventeen feet into the air. These boxes, all of them sealed with brown sticky tape and bound with wire, contained little metal components which did not appear to bear any meaningful relationship to any model of car constructed in the factory. They were made of pressed steel, being roughly kidney shaped and approximately six inches across at their broadest point. Four holes had been punched in each component, each hole being of a different diameter. On the bottom of the component, or was it the top, a small metal lug protruded, seeking a home.

Pat reached the truck and climbed into the driver's seat. Searching for the controls, he pulled the lever operating the front forks and raised the two metal prongs about six feet into the air.

He tried to stand up, but knocked his head on the protective canopy above the seat, the blow causing him to wince and hunch his shoulders protectively. Stooping, he placed his left hand on one of the two front struts supporting the canopy, and swung his upper body outwards. His right hand grasped the vehicle's roof, preventing himself crashing to the floor as he pivoted wildly on one leg. Now, leaning slightly backwards, both feet on the floor of the cab, his head was raised above the level of the canopy. He inched towards the front end of the truck, moving sideways with tiny steps, facing the blank wall of brown boxes.

As he made his slow progress, Pat was oblivious to his growing fascination for a slowly swelling group of onlookers who stared in astonishment at the wild man's latest antics, whispering, nudging, winking and giggling. Engrossed in his task, he reached the front of the cab and rested his right elbow on the top of the canopy. Grasping one of the upright fork tracks with his left hand, he flicked a leg to the nearest prong and hauled himself out of the cab.

After a desperate scramble, Pat found himself on his knees, perched on the left fork of the machine. With the exaggerated precision of the slow-motion drunk, he raised himself to his feet and stood, swaying, towering above the crowd of spectators, holding on to the fork tracks for support as he gazed glassily at the blank surface of the wall of boxes two feet from his face. The next stage in his ascent involved the relatively simple task of moving from the forks to stand on top of the canopy, a step accomplished with a degree of drunken grace. Once established at this new height, Pat found the top of the cardboard wall reached the level of his throat. Placing both forearms and elbows on the boxes, he gave a small leap and raised himself by pressing down on the horizontal plane with his palms, his whole upper torso now creeping above the highest level. Holding himself in this position with elbows locked and muscles quivering, he swung first his left knee than his whole leg on to the top of the mountain, rolling his whole body on to the four-box-wide upper platform.

As he momentarily disappeared from sight, the gathering assembled below let out the breath they had collectively held they had seen the cardboard box Pat rested his weight on teeter on its edge, momentarily seem to lose its equilibrium, then settle back into place as the full pressure of Pat's prone body rested upon it. The crowd, now numbering around a dozen, rippled with pleasure, appreciative of this dangerous stunt. Pat's face reappeared over the precipice.

"Night, night, Pat!" shouted one wag.

Pat replied with a glazed grin and a short wave before vanishing again as the fork-lift truck driver came back in from the cold.

* * *

A passer-by would see only an apparently lifeless shell and lines of varicoloured, unsold cars lined up next to the railway siding. An almost imperceptible hum filled the air, the sprawling power lines leading to the plant seemingly quivering with exertion as they pumped the life blood into the many cells which made up the organism. It lies like a beached whale on the outskirts of the dying city, washed up by a sea too polluted to sustain life. Some perverted voyeur keeps it alive, shovelling flesh and steel and sweat into its stinking mouth, making his living from the steaming shit which the beast ejects from the other end. Occasionally, the system seizes up, because the whale is gasping for fresh air, nerve ends crying out for the bite of salt sea breakers crashing over its bulbous head. And so the sideshow speiler throws a bucket of piped piss over the prize exhibit of his tap-room joke, sometimes prodding its belly with a sharp stick to hurry its digestive processes.

And if the beast dies through neglect or despair, why there are plenty of other beaches with space for new carcasses, the area pegged out, viewing stands already erected. You pack your suitcase and move on, leaving the stinking mess to breed plague cells which infect those left behind. The last few diarrhoea dribbles stain the soil as the hulk evacuates itself for the last time. The skin wrinkles and the organs shrink in the sun as decay sets in, the slow, natural cleansing process which after a hundred years will produce only a brown stain on green grass to show the beast ever existed.

Those last death throes are the worst as violent spasms send shockwaves through the earth. That and the all-pervading stink of the first rotting days when the death-bringing odour causes cuts to fester, and the noisome air lingers like a death shroud over the dupes who kept the show on the road.

But while the stranded whale survives, all seems well. Cosmetic skills bring an illusion of health. Just enough sustenance is provided to keep the leviathan alive — but spare the expense. And, almost imperceptibly, the giant is crushing itself to death beneath its own weight. Its very magnificence is its own undoing. It cannot survive in this alien environment — but its own no longer exists: it too has been appropriated by the showman and turned into a charnel house.

Pat sleeps and the world grinds on. Five thousand men gnashing their teeth in the biggest beaver lodge ever seen, assembling jigsaw kits of little wheeled boxes nobody really wants.

But *I* want one. I need a shiny, yellow job with head-rests and a digital clock and a cassette-radio and a hatchback and those wheels with the perforation in them. I want to go "vroom, vroom!" along the motorway and pick up French hitchhikers with long, black, shiny hair who will unzip my trousers and fondle my cock as I roar through green fields in my driving gloves.

I need one to impress my twelve-year-old classmates whose eyes glaze at petrol smells, who lie deep in padded rear seats, protected from the wind and rain and the nasty men with smelly drawers who travel on the Corporation buses. I want to hear a reassuring "kerlunk!" as my door closes me in and I can relax in my own purring shell. It even has fold-down seats so I can curl up and close my eyes when it gets dark.

I want to smell my own smells and brush cigarette ash from the plastic protective cover on the seat, and drum preoccupied, exasperated fingers on the dashboard as — damn it! — another light changes to red. But then slip in the clutch — first — quick foot on the accelerator — second — third — top — bowling along — wet outside — warm within. Hummmmmmm . . . Heater on, feet like toast. Sneakers and T-shirt while outside, umbrellas blow inside out and collar-up coats soak up rain.

Blow air slowly through my teeth at a scratch, complain over petrol, talk of MOTs and services, jingle car keys, file route maps. Shake, shake, shake my head over pedestrians as they scurry pathetically to safety past snarling, no-time-to-lose bonnets. A novice in the esoteric language of the manual — enjoy the camaraderie of the road! Wave on oncoming traffic and learn little twists of the wheel and pressures on the brake which bring you miraculously out of skids. Park smoothly in a bare car space with a no-nonsense flick of the wrists; flash my new hazard lights on a corner. Aid damsels in distress: a knight of the road sucking in his belly as he leans into the engine, studying the little fluffs of hair behind her ear instead of the spark plugs. Thumb idly through car accessory catalogues, although I don't go in for that sort of thing, really. Put on my seatbelt until I forget that programme on the telly. Do you know you can increase fuel consumption dramatically if you travel at a steady twelve and a half miles an hour?

Holiday time and the luggage fits neatly into the boot. Is that all? For God's sake, don't forget anything. No hitchhikers now, what with the wife beside you reading the map and Julie playing 'I-Spy' and Billy puking up 'Smarties' into a plastic bag. Jesus, the car gets so sticky. It should be a one-man machine, really, its contours moulded to fit your body. But you can dream on the route as the motorway signs fly overhead and late 1960s West Coast music plays on the cassette. Put if off — it's making the kids sick! But you're there at last: you've made it, even though you're 200 sleepless miles away from your destination.

Our little man has unplugged himself from the system. He's up there — can you see? Up on top of all those boxes, recharging the old batteries. If the noise of the plant would stop, if the whole world could stand to attention, everyone would be able to hear a gentle snore as Pat dribbled from his mouth, curled up in the foetus position. What a laugh! What a joke! What a piss! Wee Billy Paterson's back there tearing his hair out, what's left of it. How long's he been out for now? Fuck knows! If no one wakes him up, he'll come to in the middle of the nightshift. What a cracker! Imagine Paddy boy's face when he knows he's been putting in some unpaid overtime!

Has anyone tried to wake him? No, old Archie Campbell says it's probably better to leave him where he is. If he starts staggering about the block he'll get nabbed by one of the Gestapo in five minutes flat. Watch it! Here comes Stewart! Jesus, look what he's got with him!

* * *

Dry mouth, eyes glued, cramped muscles, nose blocked. Pat's addled brain was trying to assimilate some confusing input information. A whining, whirring noise was coming from close by. Whine . . . click . . . silence. Silence apart from the background roar of the factory. Whirr . . . click . . . silence. One of Pat's eyes opened. His head was resting on a curled arm, knees tucked up close to his chest. He felt a crick in his neck and pins and needles in his left leg. Whine . . . click . . . silence. Pat managed to open a second eye. Moving only his head, he surveyed the scene. From where he lay, all that was visible was a mattress of boxes and, on the horizon twenty feet away, the whitewashed bricks of the block wall, unrelieved by windows.

Suddenly, a hand appeared on the edge of the boxes, about nine inches from Pat's head. It was a right hand, and on the pinky was a black signet ring. With a minimum of effort, Pat could have covered it with his own loose hand. Whirr . . . click . . . silence. The hand jerked, and hair could now be seen above the line of boxes. Pat's eyes opened wide with horror as the hand which had rested on the cartons was raised, palm upwards: down then up; then down then up — a gesture which seemed to indicate that the head of hair wished to be lifted higher into the air by whatever device was being used to achieve such elevation. Whine . . . click . . . silence.

Pat was paralysed. Only his sphincter muscle made any concession to movement. The last whine, the last click, had brought a full head and shoulders and chest into view as the prongs of another fork-lift truck duplicated Pat's climbing exploit. Silence again reigned, broken only by a noise like the clanging of a cell door in Pat's head as he stared into the eyes of Stewart, and felt the searing force of the grin which stretched across a face like a death mask.

BUSY, BUSY

Glasgow was once considered to be the "Second City" of the British Empire. It held its position proudly behind London in that conglomerate of races and nations over which the sun never set. Day and night, the whole place clanked and buzzed and sweated and strained. Steam rose everywhere, and smoke, billowing into the grey sky. The River Clyde, pulsing through to the sea, was viscous with sludge and chemicals and slime, but people were proud of it: they were Clydesiders. People in frock coats called them "men of steel and rivets": hands calloused, skin disfigured with the burns from molten pig iron.

All along the banks of the river came the ringing hammers on steel as pieces of metal were shaped into ocean-going dreams. The men could send pieces of themselves down slipways where the bow wake slap and the rattle of chains would be drowned by the sound of hoarse cheering. The whole world relied on wee men in bunnets who got drunk on Friday nights. They scratched their names on the keels and travelled to Shanghai and Montevideo and New York and South Sea Islands in the sun.

You could touch every part of the globe from Wood's of Port Glasgow and Stephen's of Linthouse and Elder's of Govan and Denny's of Dumbarton and Scott's of Greenock and Brown's of Clydebank and Barclay Curle of Whiteinch.

You could sail the seven seas on the *Comet* or the *Albion* or the *Columba* or the *Servia*. Or the *Aquitania* or the *Normandia* or the *Hantonia* or the *Jutlandia*. Or the *Paris* or the *Aberdeen* or the *Buenos Ayrean*. Or the *Royal Sovereign* or the *Royal George*. Or the *Queens, Elizabeth* and *Mary*.

In the summer sun, the sweat tricled from every pore in your body, soaking the shirt on your back, plastering the hair across your forehead, running in your eyes, leaving a salt taste on your lips. In winter you worked in rain, snow, sleet, hail and frost, your hands blue and stiff, cracking the ice on the water barrel with a spike, white ghost touches peppering your eyebrows.

You swung your hammer in a relentless, vengeful rhythm, pounding your body into exhaustion and your mind into coma. Men in bowler hats with watch chains strung across their bellies eyed you suspiciously, and you cursed under your breath with every muscle-jarring ring. Faces behind glass peered at your efforts, measuring progress, counting profits, cutting costs. And sometimes the cost they cut was you. You would lay away your tools for the last time and walk out of the gate without looking back at the skeleton stocks. Until there was a war. Then you could return and build once more but you built coffins which did not sail through the Spice Islands but now lie, hulls resting, creaking silently in mid-Atlantic or halfway to Archangel under an empty sky.

But now there are no wars either. And anyway, it is too late for you: you are dead. You fell sixty feet from a scaffolding; a red-hot rivet crushed your skull; your leg came off under a girder and you died, screaming, pumping blood in a slow ambulance. You read of Napoleon and the Crimea, the Sudan and the Boers, and the Hun and the Nazis, but you had spilled your blood closer to home where no one won any medals.

THEATRE

Orangemen wear dark suits, white shirts, dark ties, bowler hats, white gloves, orange sashes, sombre faces, and sometimes they carry tightly rolled umbrellas. Orangewomen wear summer frocks, high-heeled shoes, white floppy hats, orange sashes, handbags, and have small, collapsible umbrellas concealed on their person. Neither the men nor the women are really orange; their complexions are perfectly normal, unless, of course, one of them has had jaundice recently, in which case he or she might have a yellowish or even a slightly orange tinge.

No, they are Orange in the sense that they belong to the Orange Order, an organisation whose main function is to march in public to display fidelity to the Protestant truth and hostility towards Catholicism and the intrigues of the Pope and his Jesuit spies in Rome. They march at specific times of the year, like the Twelfth of July which is the date in 1690 when the troops of King William of Orange defeated the troops of King James at the Battle of the Boyne, near Drogheda in Ireland. According to present-day mythology, King William, or King Billy as he is fondly known as, represented the Protestant faith, King James the Catholic. In fact, the Pope sent a letter to Billy congratulating him on his victory, but since this fact does not conform with contemporary prejudice, it is forgotten about. All the fighting was about who was going to succeed to the English throne: Billy won.

There are three other regular celebrations, like the Black Walk and the Apprentice Boys of Derry Walk, and there are various practice walks too, which take up a lot of time. In fact some lodges (the Order is split into Lodges: like beavers) seem to march every fucking week, including the one down the road from me which regularly wakens me up early on a Saturday morning when I have a hangover.

The reason they wake me up is because they don't just march

quietly in some courtyard or park secluded from public view: they march along the main roads and they make a lot of noise. They have bands playing: flute bands; noisy flute bands with big drums. The music is actually rather catchy, as long as you forget what the words are. This act of forgetfulness is rather difficult if you're a Catholic because the songs are usually about battering fuck out of us.

When a Walk is in progress, the traffic stops. The marchers are in files stretching along the road, all in their Sunday best, eyes forward, squarely and confidently marching towards the Truth, huge banners depicting bloody victories blowing in the wind. At their side march the stewards, supported by the boys in blue, our faithful bobbies, ensuring that no lunatic commits suicide by attempting to walk through the ranks. In front of each lodge contingent marches the flute band, dressed in rather ropey uniforms, with little hats on their heads. Younger than the body of marchers, the band is composed of drummers, flautists, and the man who is the centre of attention, the Titan who plays the Lambeg drum, a huge bass instrument which beats out the rhythm with a mind-numbing boom. The marchers progress sedately along the route at a leisurely pace. In contrast, the members of the band tend to become rather excited. Some start to gyrate to the rhythm of the music, the flautists weaving their upper bodies like Indian snake charmers, their elbows protruding like fins, the drummers spinning like tops without breaking beat, the Lambeg drummer, imprisoned by his burden, shaking any limb which is free. At the very front, the mace carrier tosses his rod high into the air, twirling, lost in the sky; he cartwheels in the road, regains his balance, spins round, dances from side to side in time with the music, extends his arm without glancing upwards, and the mace slots back into his outstretched hand.

In this way, the band cocky, the body of marchers solid, surfeited with mutual reassurance as to divine will, faces glazed with certainty, conscious of approval from raucous onlookers, smugly walking the march of the chosen people, in this way the Walk progresses through the city. Shoppers are imprisoned in cars and buses as a throng of camp followers run from street corner to street corner to watch the bands pass by, some marching behind, skipping to the music as they make their way to the rallying point in Glasgow Green, Bellahouston Park, or elsewhere. Like Red Guards in Peking, they ignore traffic signals: nothing can stop their inexorable progress towards the rally: a flood, it gains in size and momentum as it sweeps through the streets.

Once at the meeting point, things calm down a little. Refreshments are produced; sashed families picnic on the grass; young children play at the edges of the gathering; infants, dressed in orange for the occasion, are comforted in mothers' arms; youths show off in front of the girls in the band. On stage, the political message is conveyed: Ulster ... Papists ... Majority Rule ... Stormont ... Rome ... Army ... Queen ... Faith ... Dublin ... God ... No Surrender ... Loyal ... True ... Danger ... Betrayal ... Alert ... Conspiracy ... Ready ... Defend ... Ours ... Power.

***

If you want to see an Orange Walk, go to Ulster, or Liverpool, or come to Glasgow. If you want to see lots of them, I'll sell you my house.

ALEC DOWDESWELL

Outside of the bingo hall, colour photographs stared at potential customers beneath a circus line of red, orange and purple light bulbs. Under scratched glass, four round, off-white blobs presented unchanging grins to the world, Paul, Derek, Doris, Rita. "Your 'Mecca' Staff." Always at your service behind the paint-starved doors where cosy lighting tempted the shivering housewives into the warmth. "We Are Here To Serve You." In frozen poses, always smart and attentive: shirts spruce, armpits odourless; hair chiselled into lacquered earmuffs; belying reality which presented a yawning, shabby face.

Dinner jacket with leg stripe, lilac ruffled shirt, frayed cuffs, grey neck, withered collar below which a Tom Jones bowtie attempted a limping impression of decade-old sophistication. Paul and Derek bore identical epicine faces framed by pageboy hair covering ears and collar. Derek guided arms and handed over tickets with fingers which bore the lingering evidence of a hasty meal. White grease had hardened under his fingernails: the pads of his fingers left greasy dabs on flesh and paper. On the smooth skin of his cheek, a last crumb clung stubbornly in view, despite random searches made by a nervously flickering iguana-tongue. Occasionally his fingers swept the fringe of hair from his eyes, revealing a white, spotted forehead. When he thought no one was looking, he would raise his fingers to his nostrils and sniff the strange combination of odours which lingered there.

From his vantage point on the pavement before the entrance to the hall, Alec, shoulders hunched against the autumn rain, compared the boy's image with reality and debated which was preferable. A woman carrying a huge handbag nudged him from behind as she stared in through the glass doors at the jostling crowd gathered round the ticket box in the foyer. A bus-load of waddling grannies had toppled out of a nearby coach and were now struggling with one another to be first into the welcoming warmth. Steam rose from damp cloth as the herd panted, stood on toes, strained necks, shouted: "Aggie! Over here!"; launched handbags like bolas; said it was just like the war. Vast thighs and arses, squeezed like suet in tweed coats, wobbled with effort as ten tons of flesh flowed around and over Alec, marooned in a tidal wave of high-pitched laughter and pebble glasses. Hysteria was only a false call away as this single-minded juggernaut, fuelled with brandy and 'Babycham', and vodka and blackcurrant, belied its superficially multiform personality and marched with unity of purpose towards its goal. "House!"

Oblivious to everything in its path. Sweeping aside Alec, and the newsboy selling the *Evening Times*, and the old boy in the red polo-necked sweater and tartan tammy who sold cheap ink markers from a cardboard box. Even the experienced 'Mecca' handlers seemed to flinch in the face of the column, familiar though they must have been with this swirling tide of monomaniacs: "Well, I've cut it down to Tuesday and Thursday nights. And my Saturday afternoon too, right enough. And then I usually manage along on Mondays as well, unless my daughter-in-law — you know, Joanne — unless Joanne comes round with the kiddies. I can't very well leave them in the house themselves while I go to the bingo now, can I? Last Monday I just pretended I wasn't in when she knocked. I mean to say, we've got to have our wee pleasures now and again, haven't we? I mean to say, what would life be like without them?"

Not totally unwillingly, Alec found himself swept along by a group of laughing pensioners and washed inside the swing doors into the foyer. He pretended to dust himself down as the women tossed some ribald remarks in his direction while fumbling in their purses for money. A whispered comment from one sent the others into fits of mouth-gaping laughter which gashed the hall.

Alec half grinned, not knowing how to respond. He made a move towards the door but as he did so stopped and gazed around at what had once been familiar surroundings. He had been in the building several times before, in that no man's land between the child and the man, when the building had functioned in its original capacity, that of a cinema. He had taken a half pretty girl through those doors over twenty-five years ago: what he often called his first romance, although he had never even kissed her on any of the four outings he had enjoyed before his mother put a stop to the relationship. Class conflict. They had met by chance when she had spectated, or rather jeered, at a football match he had played in at a local pitch. He could remember the agony of the game: hacked and scythed by boys who had long before recognised the brutal reality of their social position. Then outplayed and humiliated by tiny geniuses who recognised football along with boxing and crime as one of the few safety hatches available to escape from painful oblivion.

She had belonged here, living close to the furnace of proletarian dreams, fuelled by the very films he took her to see. He, having sprung from the nouveau riche of Pollokshields, was bound by stricter codes of propriety than those whose longer tenure in the upper echelons of society might have encouraged more genuinely held delusions of their being members of the elect.

"Member, sir?"

"What?"

"Are you a member of the club, sir?"

"Club?" stammered Alec, bemusedly looking into the round face of Derek which appeared, fully animated, before him. "Oh, yes. Or rather, no. I'm not a member. Actually, I didn't really intend to . . ."

"Step this way, sir, if you please. It'll only take a few seconds to jot down your particulars, then you can go in and enjoy yourself. It's just a formality, really."

Alec followed the boy to a small trestle table where membership cards could be seen, stacked neatly in a tray. By now, the wave from the charabanc had subsided and customers were entering the hall in pairs and threes, more subdued, but still emitting the occasional knicker-wetting rip of laughter. As one woman entered, shrew faced, with silver tips to short black hair, she popped a last chip into her mouth before crumpling up the white wrapping paper and throwing it vaguely in the direction of a litter bin near the table where Alec and Derek were now standing. The ball missed its intended target by a good three feet, rebounded from the wall, knocked over a pile of membership cards and fell, its malevolent energy expended, at Derek's shining feet. Derek looked at Alec with an expression which mutely spoke of the trials, the strains, the pressures, the pain a man in his position was subjected to in performing his thankless task. He put his faith in his tailor to the test as he bent to pick up the offending object, and he sighed deeply as he straightened, red faced, to deposit it in the bin with a petulant flick of his wrist.

"Now," he said, brushing imaginary contamination from his hands as he addressed himself once more with a smiling, if strained countenance to this, as yet, innocent customer. "Could I have your name please, sir?"

"Cameron," stated Alec in reply, feeling, despite himself, a certain sense of camaraderie with this little fat fellow who was transgressed against rather than transgressor. "Cameron," he said in a friendly tone, imbued, so he thought, with a note of sympathy for the boy's tribulations. His own efforts were sometimes not appreciated — he knew what it felt like. He suppressed an urge to slap Derek on his rounded shoulders and declare his colours in the battle to elicit gestures of appreciation for unsung heroism. "Alexander," Alec added as he saw Derek write down the first piece of information.

"What's your address, Mr Alexander?" asked the fat boy, pen poised above paper as he glanced up at his new client.

"No," corrected Alec gently. "Alexander is my first name. It's 'Alexander Cameron' not 'Cameron Alexander'."

"But you said your name was 'Cameron'."

"Yes, that's my surname," explained Alec.

"Why did you give it to me first, then?" demanded the boy incredulously.

"I always do — it's the done thing, isn't it?"

"Not in here, it's not," said Derek contemptuously, tearing the card into four pieces and throwing them with a flourish on top of the chip paper in the bin. He glanced sharply at Alec before reaching for another card, a psychic stab which told Alec he had been consigned to the ranks of those formless anarchists who plagued the fat boy remorselessly, attempting to dislocate his ordered constellation of ideas.

"Alexander Cameron." The dinner-jacketed Job spoke the syllables aloud as he wrote them on the fresh card, as if pointing out a key concept to a dyslexic child. When he had finished, he darted another glance towards Alec as if daring to be challenged: "Address?" All pretence of servility or even civility seemed to have been abandoned. Alec had to pause for a moment as he adjusted to his altered circumstances:

"17 Bedford Street."

"That's 'Bedford Street' is it?" asked the boy, his voice iron clad with sarcasm. "It's not 'Street Bedford'?" Alec managed to grin weakly. "Twenty-five pence, please. Thank you." Derek tore the card along its perforated dividing line, handing Alec the smaller of two pieces: "You are now a member of the 'Bonanza Bingo Club'," he chanted mechanically. "Fill in your personal details on the back of your half of the card, if you will. Bingo cards may be purchased at the ticket booth. Enjoy your evening, sir."

With these words, Alec was dismissed by the sweating juvenile, forever consigned to that category of species classified as "Awkward Customers".

* * *

"House!"

The call rang out for perhaps the tenth time since Alec had been inside the hall. It had sounded in a variety of female voices: harsh, triumphant, timid, excited. As each cry came, there was an immediate release of tension as the other gamblers enviously watched the winning card being sent to the stage to be checked for accuracy. Conversations restarted: the reverent hush was broken as cards were compared, heads shaken and hard luck stories swapped. One number! That's all I was waiting on: one number! Do you know, Jessie, that that's the third time that's happened to me tonight. without a word of a lie: the third time! I ask you: is that not awful? Here, do you want an Everton mint?

Paul, the second male flunkey, identical to Derek in all but the colour of his ruffled shirt, pink as opposed to mauve, leant forward to accept the card from a nervous claimant. He marched in a businesslike manner to the front of the hall where the bingo caller, a plastic god on the pedestal which was the apron of the cinema stage, pronounced his verdict.

The caller, a figure of some charisma to the audience, holding a position of status in the greasy hierarchy of the bingo empire, checked the numbers on the card against the numbers which had been chosen in the previous game by the random selection apparatus. The call was good. New game on.

All idle chatter in the hall was extinguished by the words: "Eyes down." Heads bowed, pens twitched. Each participant retreated into an obsessive pose, blinkered to all by the numbers before their eyes which promised to pay the gas bill. Alec chewed his pencil and studied his card, caught in the tension.

"Key of the door: 21. Legs 11. Five and four: 54. On its own: number 8. Four and two: 42. All the sevens: 77."

And so it continued: the ritual of the bingo hall. Alec scratched out numbers on his card as he heard them called. His neighbour to the right was marking two cards simultaneously. Two tables in front of where he sat was a hugely inflated woman facing the caller with a tea tray on her lap. Spread on the tray were five cards, each of which the woman was marking with breathtaking speed and accuracy. Her dough-like hand travelled in a circle over the display, sometimes darting with deceptive speed to obliterate another number with an ink marker. As she sat, her figure was motionless except for the roving hand and the rhythmic heaving of her vast shoulders as her frame made unreasonable demands on lungs strained to capacity.

All around Alec, the crowd was singlemindedly concentrating on one task to the exclusion of all other thought and awareness, packed like the linked circuits of a silent computer in the carcase of the former cinema. If anyone's attention strayed from their numbers, it was to snatch a brief glimpse of their neighbour's card, or to glance momentarily towards the caller in his pulpit. By his side was a large plastic globe which contained dozens of little coloured ping-pong balls numbered from one to ninety, bobbing around aimlessly, agitated by a stream of air which shot into the enclosed space from below. Some of the balls were sucked at random into a tube which led to the caller's left hand. He picked them up, one at a time, and transferred them to his right hand before holding the number up to his eye. Having completed this practised, flowing movement, he leant towards the microphone and announced the number with little smacking explosions of his lips, the metallic, hollow ring carrying to the furthest reaches of the hall. He brought the word; they awaited his call.

"Doctor's orders: number nine. On its own: number four. Six and seven: sixty-seven. Four O: blind forty."

"House!"

At the precise moment this shout was heard, most of the crowd in the hall rose to their feet and thundered into the aisles, jostling, bumping and boring, seemingly frantic in their attempts to leave. Women had abandoned coats, and were packing like frenzied rugby league second row forwards in blancmange hats and brooches, heads lowered like rutting water buffalo. For a brief, panic-stricken moment Alec thought he had misheard the shout. It must have been a cry of warning from someone who had glimpsed a snake of smoke beneath the fire doors. Or a shriek of terror as a body slumped, lifeless, over a half-filled bingo card, laid low by a jealous stiletto. Had the cry been "mouse!"? Memories of manic scenes from the *Beezer* and the *Topper* flooded back into garish, technicolour view. Alec squirmed restlessly on his seat, card and pencil slipping to the floor. He rose to his feet, craning his neck in an attempt to see what was going on.

"Is this your first time?" The question came in a calm voice from below and to his right, from the neighbour who had been filling in two cards at once. "Is this your first time at the bingo?" The question was rephrased as Alec stared down blankly.

"What? Oh yes, it's my first time. Listen, just what is going on here?" As Alec asked this question, much of the scrum had broken up. Some women had obviously left the hall, others were shaking heads, but for the most part returning docilely to their seats.

"Oh that?" asked Alec's neighbour rhetorically. "It's the machines."

"Machines?"

"Fruit machines. You know: one-armed bandits they used to be called. Now they haven't got any arms at all."

"But why..."

"It's just that when it reaches time for the break, they all rush out to try to be first in the queue to play one of them, you see? Did you not notice them when you came in? They'll be standing ten deep in front of them now."

"Is that right?" Alec sat down again, chuckling softly. "And here was me thinking there was a fire or something."

"I suppose it did look like that," said the woman, tilting her head towards Alec and smiling so marvellously he thought she was acknowledging someone behind him. He glanced round at an empty seat. "I just thought I'd ask you," the woman went on sweetly as Alec turned again to face her. "You seemed a bit worried, so I thought to myself: I bet he's not been to the bingo before." And then with some concern: "I hope you don't mind?"

"Not at all," reassured Alec. "For goodness sake, no. Thanks for telling me." And as he listened and talked, Alec studied this woman who had spoken to him.

Mid-thirties, he thought. Probably three stones overweight. Pretty face, despite the excess flesh. No jewellery, very little make-up. Just some delicate shading around green eyes. Sparkling eyes. Eyes alive. Smiling.

Her clothes were of that unflattering design opted for by most heavy women: shapeless, anonymous drapes concealing shameful bumps and bulges. Alec's eyes flicked over them, drawn by breasts which sagged despondently towards her lap, drooped as if her brassiere had given up the struggle in the face of overwhelming odds.

Her blonde hair was piled high on her head in a confusion of coils and braids and curls and clasps, with little wisps escaping behind her ears and on her neck. As she sensed Alec examining her, she made a vain effort to pat it into shape with surprisingly delicate hands.

"Terrible weather we're having," she started. Then, rummaging the capacious bag at her side: "Sweet?" She held a packet of 'Opal Fruits' towards him.

"No thanks," he said regretfully, pointing towards his mouth. "They go for my teeth."

"Oh, I know," his neighbour agreed as she unwrapped a strawberry-flavoured chew and popped it into her mouth. "They gum up all the wee spaces, don't they? I'll have to go to the dentist myself, but I'm just a big scaredy."

"You should try mine," suggested Alec. "He's really good. Even I go, and I'm a confirmed coward." His new friend gave a short laugh and gently pushed Alec with the back of her hand:

"Well," she went on after a pause, "I'll have to go soon or else I'll end up with a big set of wallies, that's for sure. Look!" She opened her mouth, tongue stained with sweets, and pointed vaguely towards her molars. "Look at that one. Look!" Alec knew he had no choice — he leant towards her mouth. The woman continued, attempting to speak while her mouth gaped wide open for Alec to peer inside: "The ng h ha ow a ay ingit."

"Pardon?"

She closed her mouth, unwrapped another chew, and launched it at the offending tooth: "I said: 'it's going to fall out at any minute'. Did you see it?"

As it looked as if she was going to display her champers again, Alec hastily concurred: "Oh yes, I saw it; it looks in bad shape."

"Did you think so? Is it really as bad as that?" She looked worried and placed her hand on his arm.

"Oh well, maybe it's not too bad." Alec and the woman looked at one another straight faced for a moment, then both burst out laughing. His neighbour again gave him a gentle push with her hand. "My name's Alec, by the way," said the newly self-aware jokester, surprising himself with his boldness in proffering his hand. "Alec Cameron."

"Betty Russell," said his new friend, introducing herself as she accepted the greeting. "Very pleased to meet you. Is this really your first time here?"

"Yes it is."

"We don't get many men at the bingo, you know."

"I wouldn't know about that. This is my first time here, remember?" Both gave broad grins.

"I've not seen you about before," observed Betty. "Do you come from round here?"

"Yes. As a matter of fact, I live just round the corner in Bedford Street."

"Bedford Street?" Betty screamed this so loudly that several people spun round in their seats to see if anything interesting was going on. "Bedford Street?" she repeated in amazement, but this time with more restraint. "I live in Bedford Street too. Number eighteen. Which number do you stay in?"

"Seventeen."

"Seventeen? Just across the road from the wee dairy?"

"That's it. We're nearly neighbours."

"But you must have just moved in. I know nearly everyone in the street, especially now it's getting shorter all the time."

"Yes, I only got the place a few weeks ago."

"Wait a minute," questioned Betty suspiciously. "You don't stay three up the middle, do you?"

"Yes, that's right. How did you . . .?"

Just at that moment their conversation was interrupted by the return of an old woman who shuffled along the row to sit down next to Betty, having entered with the other slot machine players who were trickling back for the next session. Betty turned round to acknowledge her:

"Any luck, mammie?"

The old woman, who looked seventy but was probably sixty or less, shook her head bitterly: "They're fixed these machines. Fixed." She complained. "Mrs Marley nearly had four bars three times. Three times! Anyway, that's me finished. I'm having no more." Betty turned to Alec and jerked her head in the direction of the old woman:

"Every time she comes she says that. Don't you, mammie?" This last question was accompanied by a swivel of the head in the direction of the snivelling old woman, a movement that was to be repeated. "Except last week when she won twenty pounds. Isn't that right?" The old woman sat tight lipped, trying to ignore this gentle ribbing from her daughter. Betty turned to Alec again: "She says she doesn't want anyone to know about that. Judging by the noise the money made coming out of the machine, half of Glasgow must have heard it. Is that not right, mammie?" Betty turned to make a face at Alec, bringing him into the conspiracy to tease the old woman, who sat with both hands firmly hanging on to her handbag.

"Mammie, this is a new neighbour of ours: Mr Cameron." Mrs Russell unfroze enough to give Alec a nod of recognition. "He's moved into number seventeen." At this, the old woman became more animated. "Three up, middle." On hearing this, old Mrs Russell's nose wrinkled in disgust:

"Three up middle?" she repeated, and in doing so shook her shoulders as if affected by a chill.

"Look," pled Alec, "could you tell me what's so terrible about my flat? What's so special about it?"

"Well . . . Betty looked away. "It used to be . . . You know."

"What?"

"Well, before you came, a woman used it."

"Yes?"

"Well, you know. She *used* it."

"What do you mean, she . . . Oh, that?" Comprehension dawned on Alec's face. "You meant it was a . . ." He was silenced by an unmistakable look on Betty's face. He gave a light chuckle.

By now, everyone had begun to settle back into their seats, in preparation for the final session. Calmly, the bingo hall patrons readied themselves: arranging cards, testing pens, placing rows of Everton mints and other assorted jube-jubes on laps. Crazy, bouffant hairdos were patted into place by geriatric hands, and bums wriggled as creaking bones were rearranged into the most comfortable positions. Shoes were picked off again underneath the seats and relieved toes wriggled, raised from the floor to steer clear of fag ends and rogue pieces of 'Butterkist'.

The bingo caller walked back on to the stage and switched on his microphone, testing it was fully operational by tapping it lightly with a fingernail. A concealed button reactivated the stream of air which sent coloured ping-pong balls into tireless movement, each bobbing seductively, teasing the audience with a brief flash of the number which would fill a card.

"Final session, ladies and gentlemen," announced the caller in a syrupy voice which had been lubricated during the break by a pint bottle of 'Guinness'. "Eyes down for a full house."

Before his eyeballs revolved on command to stare at his number grid, Alec glanced briefly towards Betty. She darted a look in his direction, frightened lest she failed to catch his gaze. Meeting his eyes, she smiled and raised crossed fingers into his line of sight. Alec grinned in turn and replied with a similar gesture, lifting his chin in a nodding movement to reinforce his unspoken thoughts.

"Six and nine: sixty-nine."

Alec crossed the number off his card. Good start! But that surely did not explain the half-excited, half-contented warmth which suffused his body.

POLITICS

Who started it? That's what I want to know. The Scots or the Irish, the Irish or the Scots? We've always been mixed up — for hundreds of years. The Scots were just a tribe from Ireland anyway — but don't tell anyone.

Look at Cromwell, a warty bastard who really messed things up. He sent Scottish Presbyterians to Ireland, planted them there as a bulwark against the papish hordes. And they're still there — in Ulster. See what I mean?

Then in the nineteenth century, hordes of Irishmen came to Scotland — the navvies — building the railways and the canals. Most of them were Catholics, but a fair proportion were Protestants, many of whom were Orangemen. Alright? The Catholics made the biggest impression, though, because before they came, why, there were hardly any Papes here at all, at all.

So now we've got Orangemen in Ulster, Orangemen in Scotland; Micks in Ireland, Micks in Scotland. Now, the Micks in Ireland wanted Home Rule, and a British political party called the Liberals said they could have it. The Orangemen in Ireland wanted to stay part of Great Britain, and a party called the Unionists said they could. So when they held elections in Scotland, the Irish Catholic Home Rulers voted Liberal, the Orangemen voted Unionist. Now, neither of these political parties gave two fucks about Ireland, Scotland, Billies or Dans, or anything remotely concerning the poor saps in their bunnets filing into the polling booths. All they wanted was votes, and the Scots delivered millions. Do you follow?

When the Anti-Christ in the form of Socialism first timidly showed its nose in Scotland, led by Keir Hardie and the Scottish Labour Party, it made little headway. Most working people put their faith in the Liberals, except in Glasgow where the Orange vote meant the Unionists held sway.

But — Socialism was making progress. After the election of 1906, many working people swung to Labour and the Independent Labour Party. Except — guess who?

NUMBER 1: The hard core, working-class Irish Catholics who voted Liberal.

NUMBER 2: The working-class Orangemen who voted Unionist.

Jesus, it's a miracle! A man called John Wheatley, a Lanarkshire miner, changed NUMBER 1. He formed a Catholic Socialist Society which, despite apoplexy from the pulpit, led the Mick vote into the arms of the good old Labour Party, where it snuggles comfortably to this very day. Indeed, one of my first political lessons was to overhear a conversation on a bus in the course of which an amateur political analyst advised his friend not to vote Labour because the party was "hoatching with Catholics".

The Pope wears red socks!

The Orange vote was not to be moved. No surrender! They voted Unionist and they still do, in the guise of the Conservative Party. So what? Well, how the fuck do I know? Why do you always want me to explain everything?

SAM DUNBAR

Believe it or not, if you push open that swing door and glance up to the back of the pub, you'll find the three of them still drinking. No joke. There they are: the three bears, the three steamers. Steamer number one, Samuel Dunbar: aged thirty-five; married, but not for much longer; two kids, aged eleven and twelve; profession: crackpot philosopher and teacher of English in a school for hottentots. Number two steamer, Gordon Mauchle: aged twenty-eight; married, with as yet no offspring; profession: pain in the arse and teacher of Art in a school for cataleptics. Steamer number three, Edgar Shaver: aged twenty-three, single, but going steady with his sister's brother-in-law; profession: cardboard revolutionary and teacher of History in a school for those born yesterday. Now, what is their common denominator? Their common denominator is that they're all as drunk as vat rats, that's what their common denominator is.

Mauchle is resting his head on the table, his eyes closed, small bubbles popping from his mouth as he breathes. Shaver is having an animated conversation with Mauchle's head, jabbing his index finger down towards his hair, which is floating in a pool of lager. Dunbar is at the bar and is being told, none too politely, that he is not going to be served with any more drink. He has retained enough sanity to realise it is useless to argue with sober people.

"The bastards aren't going to serve us."

"What?"

"The bastards aren't going to serve us."

"What?"

"The chargehand says we're too drunk."

Receiving this information, Shaver snorted and raised himself to his feet like a slow motion hydraulic lift: "I'll talk to them. I'll sort this out."

"Hold it, hold it," pleaded Sam, restraining him by the arm. "You'll get us barred. I drink in here all the time, you know."

"Fuck that!" shouted Shaver, throwing off Sam's grip, nearly unbalancing in the process. At the bar, the pair were being eyed by the chargehand and another member of the pub staff. They were muttering and nodding their heads in Shaver's direction.

"For fuck's sake," hissed Sam between clenched teeth, "keep the noise down. We'll be out on our ears."

"They're papping us out anyway, so what's the difference?"

"Come on," coaxed Sam, "let's make tracks. I know a brilliant wee pub in Govanhill where they don't even throw out corpses." Shaver still showed signs of aggression. "Come on," wheedled Sam. "This pub's shite, anyway." On hearing this rationalisation, Edgar brightened and indicated his assent with a sharp nod of the head.

"Come on, Gordon."

"On you come."

"That's it."

"Up you get."

"We're off, Gordon."

"This pub's shite."

The three left in a line, Gordon being shakily supported in the centre, mute and unknowing. The bar staff visibly relaxed as they saw the trio heading for the door, sweeping through the crowd. As they paused on the threshold, Shaver turned and roared at the top of his voice: "Your pub's . . ." Before he could complete his sentence, Sam somehow bundled both him and Gordon out into the night, and the barmen were never to learn the details of Ed's objective assessment.

"Are we going for a bus?"

"No, we can walk it; it's not far. Over the bridge, then along Eglinton Street to Victoria Road. Come on."

"Come on, Gordon."

"Uuhh."

The trio walked towards the Clyde past flocks of couples arm in arm, and hunting packs of boys, and giggling whirlpools of girls. The centre of the city was alive and vibrant, and energy, excitement, laughter and simmering danger splashed wildly from the chasm-like walls of the streets to mix in a restless movement of colour and sound. At the bottom of Jamaica Street, just before the bridge, it was quieter, and here they paused for a rest, depositing Gordon on a low wall beside a public toilet. The two fumbled for cigarettes, Sam producing his battered packet before Edgar, who felt for his matches. As they smoked, they stared at the artery water of the Clyde, watching the Christmas lights reflect on its oily surface. Neither spoke, both lost in blurred thoughts, impervious to the chill wind which blew up from the river, freezing the snow ruts on the pavement. With a last exhalation of smoke, Sam flicked his cigarette behind his shoulder into the gutter, staggering slightly through the Newtonian reaction. As his head turned, his eyes dimly discerned a bus pulling in to a stop fifty yards back in the city centre.

"Fifty-seven!" he shouted, punching Edgar's arm. "Run for it!"

The two made a crazy rush across the road towards the store lights, legs and arms windmilling through the air like a flock of pelicans. Gasping, they threw themselves at the automatic doors just as they were closing and pushed their way into the warmth. Sam thrust a grubby pound note into the ticket machine:

"Three thirties," he wheezed at the driver, who was already accelerating his vehicle away from the stop.

"Three? Who's the three for?" the driver queried, glancing sideways as he changed gear.

Dunbar looked at Shaver. Shaver looked at Dunbar. Both of them spun round to look through the doors as the bus roared on to the bridge. They were in time to catch a glimpse of Gordon hauling himself to his feet, holding on to the iron railings which topped the low wall where he had been abandoned. His body shaped a triangle with the wall being the base. His legs formed one side, his body and outstretched arms the other, while his arse was the apex. Slowly, the angle at the apex was becoming less acute as he pulled himself into a vertical position fist over fist.

Dunbar and Shaver, the new comedy duo, burst into fits of laughter as they realised their mistake. Through watering eyes, Sam helplessly gestured towards the driver: "Just make it two," he gasped. "The other one didn't manage it." This last witticism brought further choking laughter from the pair as the tickets clicked out and they staggered inside past other smiling passengers.

"He'd never have been served, anyway."

"No. Best thing that could have happened to him."

"He'll get home all right, won't he?"

"Sure, no problem."

"Missing in action."

The two roared again as the bus bumped off the bridge past an amber light.

* * *

The pub was crowded with customers when they arrived and it was impossible to find a seat. In any case, chairs and tables were few in number in the 'Afton Glen', serving as they did to cause only further obstruction in the already cramped drinking area. On the right-hand side as customers entered the front door, the bar extended half the length of the wall. Behind it, wooden shelves packed with bottles, cans and packets of cigarettes stretched from ground level to above head height. In the middle of this display sat an antiquated till, and above this was positioned a gantry holding bottles of whisky, gin, vodka and dark rum, their necks pointing towards the floor. Behind the formica counter which supported six beer pumps, three barmen toiled, pulling pints and squeezing spirit measures from optics. All three smoked; all three had dirty dish towels thrown over their shoulders. One drank tea from a half-pint glass, standing, head back, with one hand on his hip, a curl of smoke rising from his waist. Above the barmen's heads, resting upon one of the green-painted shelves, was a framed photograph of some of the regulars engaged in rather ambiguous activity with a large cod-like fish and a gigantic trophy which seemed to be full of liquid. The snap bore the legend: "Afton Glen Sea Angling Club 1976".

The narrow space between the bar and the opposite wall widened at the back of the pub, and here the few tables were spread, surrounding a barely smoking open fire. Here could be found the handful of female customers to be found in the 'Afton Glen': tired old women in nylon leopard coats and wrinkled tights. To the right of the fireplace at head height was a decrepit dartboard and a blackboard divided into two sections, one headed "Home", the other, "Visitors". A notice beside it gave details of darts and dominoes tournaments, and a warning that last games were to begin not later than 10.45 p.m.

The floor, which seemed to be covered in a linoleum-like substance, was swimming with spilled drink, and shoals of cigarette ends confusedly schooled in the wake of shuffling feet. In front of the grate, an old man sat alone, clutching an empty glass, serenading the moving shapes he saw on the floor with toothless songs. A youth leant over one of the tables and whispered some words in the ear of a woman, sentiments which caused her to throw her head back and point a black mouth at the ceiling, cackling like a cracked chamberpot. A man in concertina trousers rested his hands on another's shoulders, head bowed then violently lifting as he spat out incoherent spasms of death and life and despair and watery bonhomie. A bell sounded with a deafening ring.

"Last orders now, paleezze!" a barman shouted into the air while scraping the head from a pint of 'Guinness' with the steady stroke of a blade.

"We'd better get a move on," slurred Edgar as the pair pushed their way towards the counter.

"No problem," reassured Sam over his shoulder as he wedged forward. "Drinking-up time in here's endless. Pint of lager?"

"Right."

With two drinks held high above his head, Sam edged his way in towards the dartboard where a small expanse of floor could be seen. The old woman screeched again. The singer looked up at Sam and Edgar as they squeezed towards him: "All right, boys?" he asked the pair, raising his head to peer at them through misty eyes, scratching his forehead, tilting his bunnet at a crazy angle.

"All right, pop."

"Jesus, it's a hard life, isn't it?"

"Too true," agreed Sam, splashing lager over his coat sleeve as an elbow nudged him from behind.

"Aye, it's a bastard." The old man sighed as he bent his head to the floor once more, rolling his empty glass between leathery hands.

The pub was becoming more congested. The original customers, none of whom were willing to venture out into the snow, were being joined by others crowding in for a final snifter, having been ejected from nearby pubs whose interpretation of the licensing laws were less liberal. The door at the back, which opened on to the wider area of the pub where Sam and Edgar stood, wheezed to and fro, bringing a draught of cold air as crowds elbowed their way in. A second, longer ring of the bell pierced the tumult:

"Drink up now, paleezze!" called the barman halfheartedly as he continued to serve customers, stuffing money into the bulging till.

Sam and Edgar danced an involuntary jig as they were elbowed from all sides, moving their arms in a meaningless rhythm as they attempted to maintain the equilibrium of their drinks. There was a spluttering thud behind them as a pint was knocked over on a table, eliciting a chorus of violent abuse. An old man wearing tartan trews under a splaying coat was bending and unbending at the knees and waist like a drunken jack-in-the-box as he spilled disjointed syllables out of a spastic mouth, jabbing his finger into space as he righted the world's wrongs with an aphasic spasm, blasting out gobs of air, addressing people who no longer existed or had never been, drawing raucous comments from a band of junior hard men who were pretending to be drunker than they felt. Edgar gasped his lager down and made a vague gesture towards Sam through a rumbling belch:

"Again?"

"Why not?" asked Sam rhetorically, raising his glass in agreement. "You'd better speed it up, though."

"Come on now, gents, paleezze!"

Sam was left alone as Edgar slid towards the bar. He was being forced further and further towards the door by the increasing pressure of the ever-swelling crowd. Still they rolled in, and the blast of icy air from outside began to slit Sam's body with a sobering knife. A man with very short, red hair peered into the warmth, bringing a flurry of snow blowing on to the pub floor. The drunken youths began to abuse him, flapping their arms in exaggerated gestures to show their displeasure at the draught of winter reality.

"Shut that fucking door!"

"Come in or get out, you fucking prick!"

"Come on to fuck!"

Still holding the door ajar, the man turned to address someone behind him, then stepped inside. He was followed by a square-shaped man with long, scything sideboards, who in turn preceded a giant with black, shining hair greased straight back from a lumpy forehead. As the door closed behind them the three, dressed in identical black Crombies, stood for a moment looking at everyone and no one, then silently rearranged themselves, the giant taking up the lead position as they began to wedge their way towards the bar. As they passed, the huge man knocked Sam aside and he momentarily mouthed a protest until the words stuck in his throat when he saw the look of the red-haired man as he scanned the crowd, staring Sam in the eye for a fraction of a second.

The three seemed to move more purposefully than the other drinkers, like policemen at the scene of an accident, and a pathway magically opened before them as they strode forward in single file. The group of young hard men were momentarily stilled, and they buried their noses in their pints as the trio marched past them, not giving them the dignity of being noticed. The ranks of drinkers closed up almost organically behind their black backs as they pushed forwards, until Sam could see only the heads of red hair and sideboards, and the powerful shoulders of the giant, topped by a swivelling black dome which revolved as he searched the faces around him with his astonishingly small eyes. Suddenly, the huge man's arm swung through the air and a finger on the end of a fist pointed accusingly in the direction of someone Sam could not see. A cry split the night:

"You're claimed, Cameron!"

The roar came from the giant, and for a tiny moment of time, it froze the scene. Conversation stopped, drinks were suspended in mid-air, throats gagged in the act of swallowing. Sam's eyes bulged as he stared open mouthed at the crystallised tableau of aggression. In an instant, it dissolved into chaos as a woman's scream pierced a mad percussion of breaking glass. A hand pushed Sam in the chest and he was sent crashing backwards on to a table top, smashing bottles and glasses as the surface tipped to the floor, taking him with it. He lay spreadeagled among the debris, facing the ceiling, as the pub erupted. People were climbing over him in their panic to reach the door, standing on his legs and chest, grinding his back into broken shards, and for several horrifying seconds Sam thought he would be crushed to death. One of the leopard-skinned women lost her footing on a rolling bottle and toppled on to him, deafening him as she yelled gin-soaked hysteria into his face, a dangling earring stinging his eye as it shook like a chandelier in an earthquake.

The bar was emptying from both ends as people fled from the violence in the centre. Almost gibbering, Sam flung the woman aside with strength he did not know he possessed and looked up to see one of the drunken youths grab the old man in tartan trews by his lapels, arcing his arm to smash a beer bottle over his head before dropping him, pumping blood, as he turned to fight his way through the door. As Sam sat up, the woman still draped over his knees, someone kicked him on the head and he smelled the concussion taste of blood and bone at the back of his throat. Uncaringly thrusting the woman aside, he scrambled on to his hands and knees towards the mahogany bar, dodging stampeding feet. A boot crushed the fingers of one hand as a space opened in front of him and, looking up, he saw the whole scene being played out in unreal clarity.

Everyone behind the trio led by the huge man was mobbing towards the back door beside the dartboard, everyone in front of them was trying to flee through the door Sam and Edgar had used when they had arrived less than twenty minutes previously. Because the pub was narrower at the front, the crowd was log-jammed, ribs cracking as they fought their way to safety. In the middle of this group was a little man who was distinguished from the rest by the fact that he had his back to the door, his face turned towards those who, judging by the look of terror on his face, were his pursuers. He had a large, swelling bruise on the side of his face, too far advanced to have been the result of this melee, and was dressed in a dark blue donkey jacket with plastic shoulder pads. Holding his hands out, palms beseeching, he screamed a name in a voice which was no longer human:

"Tam!"

Tam, for this was the huge man's name, was peeling people from the pressed, panic-stricken crowd which jammed the space between himself and his quarry, passing the bodies to his underlings, red hair and sideboards, who propelled them with maximum force in the direction of the rear door near where Sam crouched, transfixed behind the curve of the bar. The mob at the back of the pub had almost all escaped, and the remainder were fighting their way out, except that is for the old man in tartan trews who lay gurgling in his own blood, and the woman who had fallen on Sam. She lay cowering under the remnants of a broken table, jabbering hysterically, in full view of Sam who was turning his knuckles white as he dug his nails into the stained wood he hid behind.

The bar, pumps abandoned, barricaded Sam from further violence as he waited for the crush at the door to clear, allowing him to make a dash and escape unseen. Suddenly, as he crouched, Sam recognised the body which was being peeled from the jam at the front of the pub: it was Edgar, face chalk, still holding two quarter full pints of lager. Tam spun him to his henchmen and Edgar, fearing the worst, raised his hands in a supplicant gesture, forgetting what was in them. Red hair, seeing two glasses being brandished threateningly, bobbed to one side as Edgar staggered towards him then raised his boot in a mighty swing, catching Edgar full in the groin. The effect of this awesome blow was delayed for fully half a second before Edgar doubled up, the glasses splintering to the floor. Sideboards raised him by the collar then transferred his other hand to Edgar's throat, lining the patient up to his satisfaction before jack-knifing his neck muscles to butt him full on the face.

Despite the sounds of chaos in the bar, Sam heard the crunch as bone met bone, and saw Edgar's face explode as Sideboards dropped him to the floor. A surge of animal panic swamped Sam's body, a spasm of terror mixed with disbelief which loosened his bowels and sent a strangled cry of horror to catch in his throat where it was constricted to a low moan of pain. At that moment, the exit at the rear of the pub cleared and Sam was further panicked by a streaking blur as one of the barmen, towel still draped over his shoulder, bolted for the empty night. On supercharged legs, Sam followed close on his heels, bursting through the door and nearly slipping to the ground as he skidded on the ice, eyes staring in shock. His arms slid round a lamp post as he spun round, attempting to regain his balance. Almost doubled up, legs flailing, he made a mad dash towards anywhere.

He found himself running across the site of a demolished tenement towards the civilising lights of the main road, around him a bomb burst of fugitives scattering like shrapnel, stumbling and falling over bricks and chunks of masonry concealed under the snow. Sam tripped over a sheet of corrugated iron and thumped down, winded, bruising his chest on a lump of concrete. As he lay gasping for breath, arms thrown forward, desperately trying to rise, a figure leapt over him and he realised with horror it was the small man with the bruise on his face, jumping like a mountain goat in adrenalin terror; somehow, he must have escaped. But if he was running in this direction, so too were his pursuers. Sam scrambled to his feet and looked desperately around him, seeing shadowy figures running everywhere. He felt a choking sensation in his throat. The fall had made rubber of his legs. A green, white and orange Corporation bus had halted at a stop on the main road some fifty yards distant, disgorging passengers; no one queued to enter. He could not make it. Running blindly, leaning forward, almost overbalancing as his feet slapped down crazily, arms outstretched, flailing, he summoned his lungs to burst, careering ever nearer. A figure in front launched himself through the disembarking passengers. The bus was pulling away. He could not reach it. For the second time that night he burst through closing doors, on this occasion collapsing on the platform below the driver who roared through the gears.

"Jesus, that must have been some battle," the driver said wonderingly as he steered his vehicle through the still scattering crowd, some of whom appeared to be flagging the bus down. The passengers who had alighted at the stop were now swelling the panic, scattering into close mouths for shelter. What sounded like a bottle smashed against the automatic doors as the bus accelerated, and a loud anonymous thump sounded at the back as a second object thudded from the panelling. Sam crawled a few yards along the aisle, fumbling in his pockets for his fare, one fraction of his brain even now ordering his response as if this were the bright, lawful world he had slipped from. On his knees, supported by an outstretched arm, one hand still entangled in his trousers, he retched, and a violent stream of liquid gushed from his mouth as his protesting stomach emptied itself. Gasping for breath, he retched twice more, then again, finally bringing forth a trickle of bile from his straining abdomen.

Police sirens shrieked in the air, blue lights revolve as cars raced past the bus towards the pub, empty now apart from a few unconscious bodies and two pools of blood.

"Sorry, lads," the driver called cheerily over his shoulder: "I'm only going as far as the garage. That should see you out of trouble, anyway." And again, with a suggestion of awe: "Jesus, that must have been some barney."

Sam managed to haul himself to his feet, hands sticky with vomit, and with one fist gripping an upright pole he swung into a seat, his head slumped sideways on to the cool window. About a third of a mile along the road, the driver cut through the gears and swung off into a side street, coming to a halt at a bus stop just outside of the gates of Larkfield Garage.

"That's it, boys," shouted the driver as he detached his ticket machine from the side of the cab. "You're on your own now." Sam heard footsteps behind his back and he opened one eye to see a small figure passing hurriedly down the aisle, a figure clad in a donkey jacket with plastic shoulder pads:

"Hey, you!" Sam shouted as he stumbled to his feet. The small figure spun round briefly in an instant of panic before scrambling through the doors. "Hey, you!" Sam shouted again more loudly, his throat raw with retching. He dashed after the fugitive and saw him skid to the ground as he attempted to run on the road which was packed with hard snow. Sam, anger conquering fear, threw himself on top of the man, pinning him to the ground. The prisoner made frantic swimming movements as he attempted to free himself, and Sam sensed his weakness: "Oh no you don't," he cautioned the man, tatters of authority returning to his battered ego. "I want to have a word with you."

The figure on the ground ceased to struggle, instead, pressing his face against the snow in resignation. Sam rolled from his back and placed a restraining hand on his collar, gingerly raising himself and his captive to the vertical. He looked at the small man under the sodium glare of the street lights and winced as he again saw the angry bruise on his face. Despite this shaft of compassion, he talked tough: "Come on, you. You're not getting off as lightly as that. My mate's back there, you know."

"Please," the little man said in supplication, "just let me go, please." Sam stood back a little in surprise as he heard his cultured voice, examining the man more closely. "Don't bring the police into this, please. I had nothing to do with it, really."

"Nothing to do with it?" asked Sam, his voice raised in anger. "Nothing to do with it? From what I could see, you had everything to do with it. Those bears were after you, weren't they?" The man remained silent. "And my mate got in the way of it, didn't he? And the pub's wrecked and my suit's ripped and there's an old guy lying back there with his head caved in. And you've got nothing to do with it?" Sam's questioning was becoming hysterical, and he shook the little man to and fro to emphasise his words.

"Look, I can explain everything," pleaded Sam's captive. "You can't blame me for your friend being hurt. Those men were trying to kill me. I had nothing to do with it."

Sam released his grip on the man's collar and looked him up and down, noting the incongruity of the clothes and the voice: "What were you doing in there, anyway? And dressed like that? You're no workie. Were you up there trying to pick up a bit of fanny, is that it? Did you pick up someone's bit of stuff, is that what happened?"

The small man glanced at the remnants of Sam's respectability: "I suppose I could ask you the same questions, couldn't I?" he chirped in a surprisingly confident voice. Sam made a threatening movement towards him. "Wait a second, wait," the man pleaded, the tone of his voice changing instantly. He held the palms of his hands splayed in front of himself to fend Sam off: "I think we've seen enough violence for one night, have we not?"

Sam untensed his body and let his fists unclench. "Come on," he ordered, gripping the sleeve of the man's coat. "I've not finished with you yet." Sam dragged him towards a pair of telephone boxes which stood at the corner of the main road. "You're going to wait in here until I've phoned the pub to see about my mate." He pulled open the heavy door of one of the booths and released his grip on the man: "Wait here." Seeing the man's eyes darting along the road towards an approaching bus, he had second thoughts: "Get in there; I don't trust you outside."

The two crammed into the box and Sam lifted the receiver: "Christ, what's the number?" A tattered telephone directory lay in a puddle at their feet and somehow Sam stretched for it, standing on tiptoe, arse in the air as he raised the heavy book with the ends of his fingers. Fumbling in his pockets, he cursed: "Give me 5p; all my money's fallen out of my pockets." He dialled the number and the tone rang out. He tapped his fingers on the window, glancing suspiciously at the man beside him, prepared to blame him if there was no reply. Rapid pips sounded and Sam pressed the money into the slot. A voice broke through:

"Yes?"

"Hello?"

"Yes, hello?"

"Hello?"

"For fuck's sake, hello! What do you want?"

"I was in the pub tonight . . ."

"Oh were you? I hope you had a nice time. We're having a wee party here now: there's some boys in checkerboard hats might want a wee word with you if you drop by."

"Listen . . ."

"I'm listening."

"I'm phoning up about my mate. He was in there too."

"Oh was he? That's great."

"I think he might have been hurt. I'm phoning up to check that he's all right."

"Are you? That's fine and considerate of you."

"Is he OK?"

"How the fuck do I know if he's OK? I don't even know who you are, never mind your mate."

"He was wearing a dark blue rally jacket. With a white stripe over the shoulders."

The man on the other end of the line was silent for a moment: "Young bloke?" he asked.

"That's right," said Sam eagerly.

"Young bloke with no teeth?"

"No, that's not him."

"Well it is now: his teeth are all over the floor."

"Jesus Christ, where is he now?" asked Sam frantically.

"Hospital."

"Which one?"

"How the fuck do I know? The Victoria, I think."

"Christ!" hissed Sam through clenched teeth, his free hand squeezing his temples. He was silent for a moment, hearing a muffled voice then laughter on the other end of the line: "OK, thanks," he ended dejectedly.

"Hey, listen, pal," the voice called: "Tell your mate he can come back for his teeth any time: we'll keep them for him." Click. Sam gently replaced the receiver and stood, silent.

"Bad news?" the small man enquired. Sam bundled him from the box:

"Out, you."

"Is your friend all right?"

Sam pushed the man in front of him and stood staring at the sky, black apart from a single star. "I've got to get to the Victoria," he said as the small man turned towards him, "and you're going to give me the money for a taxi."

"I can't," said Sam's captive with a sigh, patting the pockets of his donkey jacket. "I left all of my money in the pub."

"What do you mean, you left all of your money in the pub?" asked Sam threateningly. "What did you leave all of your money in the pub for?"

"I had to," explained the man, stepping a pace backwards. "I had to leave the money for someone. I had to. I left it behind the bar just before . . . He paused. "Just before it happened."

"Listen, I'm going to get the taxi fare out of you if I have to ram my fist down your throat."

"But I haven't got any money," protested the man in a half scream.

"Come here." Sam grabbed the man by the lapels of his coat and spun him round, thrusting his hands into his pockets. The man struggled, and Sam nudged him far enough forward to boot him in the arse: "Don't make it difficult." He dragged the man forward again and fumbled in his pockets, bringing out wads of used paper tissues, and bus tickets, and crumpled stationery.

"What the fuck's this?" Sam asked as he examined several tattered envelopes. "Are you two different people or something?" He read the typewritten addresses: "Mr Alexander Dowdeswell; Mr Alec Cameron. Who the fuck are you, anyway? Dowdeswell or Cameron?"

"I can explain . . ."

"Look, I'm not interested in your explanation. All I want is my taxi fare. Your Dowdeswell address is the nearest; we'll go there for the money."

"No, we can't," said the man in some panic.

"OK, we'll go to your Cameron address; that's not much further."

"No, we can't," repeated the man in the same tone as before.

"Listen, Dowdeswell or Cameron, or whatever your fucking name is: we're going somewhere, and I'll give you two seconds to make up your mind where. Either that or I'll flag down a police car and they can take us."

The man twisted this way and that, his breath coming in anxious sobs: "But I can't; I can't go to either house. You don't understand: I can't. Betty . . . My wife thinks . . . We . . . I don't know . . . We . . . I can't . . . You don't know what . . ."

"I'm waiting," said Sam impatiently, folding his arms. "You must have been heading for some fucking place tonight, unless you were going to kip in the streets. Decide."

"But I had nowhere to go. You don't understand . . ."

"Listen, I don't want to fucking understand. All I want's the money." A police car approached them from the direction of Shawlands. The small man noticed it with a start and began to pull Sam across the road:

"I'll get you your money."

Sam observed they were heading towards Pollokshields: "So it's," he paused to consult the envelopes: "Mr Alexander Dowdeswell, is it? Pleased to meet you, Alex. Have you seen Alec Cameron recently?" The man remained silent as they walked along Albert Drive.

* * *

Alec paused before the driveway of a large red sandstone villa and turned to Sam: "Wait here; I'll be out shortly with the money."

"Are you kidding?" asked Sam incredulously. "I'm not letting you out of my sight."

"For pity's sake, I live here. You've seen the envelope with my name on it. Where am I going to run to?"

"But according to this other envelope," Sam held it up to the glow of the street light: "You also live at 17 Bedford Street. How do I know you live here? You might be a stamp collector for all I know."

Alec clenched his teeth: "Then for goodness sake, be quiet. that's all I ask: be quiet." Sam grinned as they crunched up the driveway.

Alec clicked the mortice lock then turned the Yale in the half-glazed door behind the storm shutters. Through the gloom Sam could make out marble pillars in the entrance hall. "Jesus," he muttered, half to himself, "this is the size of my entire flat." At the right-hand side, a broad stairway ascended into darkness. All was silent apart from the faint hiss of car tyres muffled by the trees which edged the garden, and the metronome tick of an invisible clock.

"Quiet," hissed Alec as he padded towards the first door on his left which gave on to a room lined with books. He carefully searched his keyring and slid directly to a bureau which stood in the bay window, unlocked the roll top and rummaged in a pigeon-hole. He withdrew an envelope and took from it a crisp £5 note which he handed to Sam. "There," he whispered. "Are you satisfied now?"

"Oh yes, I'm satisfied," replied Sam in a voice louder than necessary. "I'm a man of simple needs."

"Quiet!" mouthed Alec. He guided Sam back through the furniture to the entrance hall and the front door.

"What the fuck is your name, anyway?" asked Sam as he stood, about to leave.

"I thought you weren't interested?"

"That's right; I said that, didn't I?" replied Sam with an empty grin. "You've got off pretty lightly tonight, haven't you?" Alec fingered his swollen cheek. "My mate's in hospital, the old guy in the tartan trews is probably dead, and here you are: paying off the last witness before you creep back to your castle." Alec shrugged his shoulders then shivered in the cold air. Sam laughed lightly as he turned to leave: "Give my regards to Mr Cameron if you bump into him." Alec shivered once more.

The man in the donkey jacket, seemingly even smaller now, closed the front door with a barely perceptible click and softly tiptoed back to his study, feeling curiously deflated. A floorboard creaked slightly and the offending foot sprang up automatically. He held his breath and listened, but the house remained still apart from the tick, tick of the clock, oblivious to all things. Alec's heartbeat was returning to normal for the first time in what seemed like many hours.

Suddenly a sound like the Alcatraz escape siren tore the night to tatters. An extended shriek split the silence as the front door bell rang and rang and rang, and a dog began to bark. After endless seconds the vengeful noise stopped and Alec could hear swift footsteps as someone ran down the driveway towards the main road. Alec froze in horror as noises stirred from upstairs. A light clicked on. He heard a female voice drift down from above:

"Jennifer, stay in bed." Then a pause as if someone was replying, speaking too low to be heard. Then the first voice again: "No, *I'll* see what's going on . . . Oh my goodness, a man's running about at the bottom of the garden, waving something at the house. Look, he's gone out of the gate now . . . He's running down the road. It must be one of those drunken football fans again. Was there some sort of game on tonight?"

There was another silence and Alec could hear his heart beating as he stood perfectly still. The first voice continued: "Don't worry; you go back to sleep. I'll check to make sure everything's all right."

Alec's mind went blank and his limbs became paralysed. His mouth gaped open and a hard lump burst in his chest. He looked towards the front door, then to the study, then again towards the front door, but his legs could not carry him in either direction. The light on the stairs clicked on and he could hear the swish of a dressing-gown as slippered feet descended.

NEMAS

Names mean a lot to me, did I ever tell you? There's a lot in them. You can tell things about a person by what he's called. I don't mean to say I believe all that crap about people's lives and personalities being shaped by their names, like people are supposed to grow to resemble their pet dogs. No, not that — although I suppose there might be something in it. After all, do you know any professional football players called "Claude" or "Percy"? There again, I suppose you could ask if you've ever heard of *anyone* called "Claude" or "Percy" outside of the pages of the *Beano*.

John Wayne's real first name was "Marion". Now, he would never have made it as a film star if he'd stuck with that handle, especially as a rough, tough, baccy-chewing desperado with one eye. So he changed it: Bingo! — a star is born. If he had remained true to himself and retained his old name, no one would have heard of him (who wants to know a guy called "Marion"?). He would have joined the police force, reached the rank of sergeant, and died, a broken-down alcoholic, at the age of fifty-three, leaving a shabby wife, three kids he didn't know, and a lot of debts.

The point I'm trying to make is that names can affect your life. They can open doors, or close them. Look at Germany in the 1930s: someone with a name like "Aaron Gluckstein" didn't stand much of a chance of making a success of himself. He would have been better changing his name to "Marion Something". There were lots and lots of people in Europe at that time with names like "Aaron Gluckstein": the Old Testament part of the telephone directory. There aren't so many of them now. Most of them were killed. Millions of them. Do you see what I mean?

Just imagine you have arrived in Birmingham, desperate for a place to stay. You phone round a few numbers, looking for a flat to rent. The people seem agreeable. They ask you your name. You say:

1. Ian Smith.
2. Hastings Banda.

Which one, 1 or 2, is the key of the door marked, "yes, the flat's yours"? Come on now, honestly. It's not a difficult one.

Thumb through the phone book in Glasgow; hundreds of thousands of names: Colin Adamson, Andrew McFarlane, Patrick Quinn, Cameron McGregor, Michael O'Rourke, Gordon McIntyre, Sean Doyle, James Miller, Campbell Munro, Francis Boyle, Alexander Hermiston, Dominic Kelly. A mixture. As you can see, there are names of Irish origin here: the Paddys, the Micks, the Seans, the Franks, the Doms. There are also some good old Scottish names: the Colins, the Andrews, the Camerons, the Gordons, the Jameses, the Campbells, the Alexanders. "So what?" you might say; or at any rate, you might say if you come from the backwoods of London, or New York, or Milan, or Brussels. The thing is, speaking as a Glaswegian, you can lay pretty secure odds that all of the Pats and Franks are Catholics, and that all of the Alexanders and Campbells are Protestants. Clever, eh?

Now, years ago in Glasgow, things went much better for you if you were a Gordon than if you were a Dominic — if you went for a job, many firms would hire Gordie before Dom. In fact, some firms would prefer to take on no one at all rather than hire the man with the shamrock stamped on his forehead. On the job-hunting scene, especially when the teagues were advancing from their proletarian beginnings in search of that bourgeoise nirvana enshrined in the words "lawyer" and "accountant", the name was like a number tattooed on the arm. So much so that when the prayers had been said and the examinations passed, many started their own professional practices, and, in turn, transformed them into new sectarian backwaters. Anxious lawbreakers looking for a gown to represent them would scan the brass plates: "O'Reilly, Quinn & O'Hara"; "Meikle, Maxwell & Findlay". Take your pick. Rosary beads to be lodged at reception.

Another way of separating the sheep from the goats was to casually ask which school the prospective employee attended: "The Sacred Heart of Jesus of the Bloody Way to Calvary." "OK, son, we'll let you know. Next!"

Names like mine present a problem: "Ian" is Scottish, "McGinness" is Irish. "What the fuck is he? Is he one of us? What school did you go to?" "I forget." "Oh."

Of course, all of this was back in the bad old days, when all of us Catholics wore wellie boots and never washed under our oxters. We're civilised now; integrated; well, a bit. Anyway, we know our place: we've carved our own niches with ample room for advancement; we've built a parallel system. We're happy; we're OK. No complaints. It's over . . . And then I pick up my *Daily Record* and I look at the sports pages, at the team lists from last Saturday's football matches, and I study the team selection fielded by Glasgow Rangers for the game against Celtic on August 24th 1980: McCloy, Jardine, Forsyth, Jackson, Miller, Russell, Bett, Redford, McDonald, McAdam, Johnston. Wait a minute. What happened to the Connollys and Donnollys, the Doyles and Boyles? Wait another minute: I'm now looking through my "Wee Red Book" 80/81, the *Evening Times* football annual, price 25p, on sale at your newsagent NOW! In this little volume, all of the Scottish international players of the past are listed, together with the names of the clubs they played for. Going through this list, I can't find any *former* Teddy Bear players with Irish names either. It's a constant litany of Duncansons and McColls and Hamiltons and McKinnons, names redolent with covenanting, stiff collars, Presbyterianism. "Pat, me bhoy, sure 'n' wasn't oi after tellin' ye to stick to de football now? Bejesus, you'll never grow up and play for de Loit Blues."

It's got to be said. I can't keep it in any longer: IT'S STILL GOING ON. Honest. You don't believe me? Well, there are only two alternatives to explain the policy of Glasgow Rangers Football club towards signing players:

Alternative number 1: In their entire history of over 100 years, Rangers F.C. have never found a Pape, a Fenian, a left footer, who could reach a sufficiently high standard of football skill to be considered worthy of the honour of pulling on the light blue jersey. Pat's only got one foot; Eusebio can't head the ball; Keegan's too lazy.

Alternative number 2: "We don't like *you* and we don't like darkies either, so fuck off, Paddy. What school did you go to, Mr Beckenbauer?"

SPECTRUM

Glasgow's colours are orange and green. Even the Corporation buses carry this colour scheme, two broad bands being separated by a non-mans-land of cowardly white. Some of the inhabitants of Glasgow even call themselves "Orangemen", and on spring and summer weekends they march to and fro in the streets of the city wearing silk sashes of this colour, banging big drums to scare the living daylights out of wee men who wear green underwear.

One football team in Glasgow plays in green: they're supported by people called O'Reilly and O'Malley and O'Flaherty, rosy-cheeked men with shamrocks in their memory banks who recognise the "thwack!" of a caman. The Orangemen in the city don't support the green team: they'd rather be seen dressed in their wives' clothes, or even dead. They support a team who play in — no, not orange, but — blue. Jesus, where's the symmetry in that?

Although they support the wee blue men, however, the colour orange is very close to their hearts. For example, problems arise when the blue team plays against Dundee United, a team who turn out in *orange* strips. Usually the blue fans would vilify the United players by shouting such comments as; "Get to fuck, you orange bastards!" You see: *orange* strip, *orange* bastards. But the blue men are *Orange* too. How can anyone *orange* be a *bastard*? Puzzle. Dilemma. Rationalisation: For *Orange* read *tangerine*. Now: *Orangeman* to *orange* clad players: "Get to fuck, you *tangerine* bastard!" Problem solved.

And then we have the little men in green, the little leprechauns who prance about the terracing watching the team in the green and white hoops. Many of them carry flags which have three stripes, one each of green, white, and . . . *orange*. But that's another story. Under no circumstances can the green men be seen buying a bottle of *orange* soft drink. Even vodka and *orange* is out. Limeade is in. If only crême de menthe was freely available in the Second City. Jelly Babies are popular sweets among green children because you can bite the heads off the wee *orange* men, or slice their feet off, or puncture their bellybuttons with sharp, canine teeth.

Some people in Scotland even have "Green" as their surname, but the only one I've ever been acquainted with was Jewish, so he doesn't count. I've yet to hear of anyone called "Orange", apart from William of Orange who must, I suppose, be blamed for a lot of this shite. There are, however, babies who have been christened with the surnames of the entire green football team, or the surnames of the entire blue (Orange) football team, a fine weight to carry through life.

As you might imagine, wardrobes are fairly unbalanced too. The Orangemen, for example, cannot wear any shade of green. The green men, however, are even more awkwardly placed: not only is *orange* taboo, but red, white and blue, especially when combined, are out too, an aesthetic disadvantage which is a clear case of discrimination.

PAT MCKENNA

Pat sat in the ante room, staring at his nicotine-stained fingers. Above the door a barefaced clock made a loud, double ratchet click every sixty seconds to signal the passing of another minute. Sixty of them made up a single hour.

The room was a narrow one, like a guillotined corridor. Above his head was a panel of frosted glass behind which a light had just gone out. Beneath this panel was a wooden bench, and upon this Pat sat. Opposite him was a narrow trestle table on which was positioned a defaced blotting pad. Next to the pad was an empty plastic tray, burned in several places by the tips of cigarettes, and dangling below this was a chain which had once secured a ballpoint pen.

Above the table, the wall was painted a dingy cream colour — or was it white which had seen better days? The blankness was enlivened by two posters stuck to the wall with sellotape, both urging the casual reader to adhere to safety regulations. One showed a lighted cigarette end smouldering amidst a bundle of what seemed to be highly inflammable rags: "Fire Bugs Kill!". the second poster showed an anthropomorphic spark flying into the face of a cartoon welder who was working without the benefit of a pair of safety goggles which sat conspicuously in the foreground: "Eyes Can't Be Replaced! Watch Out! There's Sparks About!"

Pat rubbed his face with his hand. He felt numb. A shiver ran through his body. He seemed to be drained of all energy. Try as he might he could not organise any logical structures in his brain. Any sequential thought stream broke down almost at the second it was formed. Amidst this chaos, he sought the familiar. Touch, smell, taste. Slowly, tangled memories unfolded, seeded, took vague, impressionistic root, breathed a healing perfume which dulled his senses.

He felt the sun on his face as it beat down with unaccustomed heat in a Scottish June, walking hand in hand along the beach at Troon, toes gouging the hard-packed sea sand. Talking wildly, he had gestured once too often with his free hand and the ice-cream had dropped from the top of his cone to fall with an excruciatingly icy touch on his outstretched foot. He had turned to her with an anguished expression, cone and foot outstretched as evidence, and both of them had doubled in helpless, arm-entwining laughter which ended with a kiss.

He heard the laboured pants of his own lungs as an old bread board was transported to Kelvingrove Park one winter a hundred years ago, early in the morning when the previous night's snowfall crunched underfoot like a bite into hard chocolate, and the world stood back, muffled and calm. He had held the back end, his brother Frank the front, and they marched in step, calling out time: "Hup, one, two, three. Hup, one, two, three." They marched with back straight and chins high, and Pat studied Frank's ears from behind, red with cold, flowering from a cropped head.

Once at the park, they had climbed to the top of the hill and arranged themselves on the board: Frank taking up the rear, Pat, squeezed between his brother's knees, hunched in front. With a crab-like movement of his legs, Frank had propelled them from the crown of the hill down the steep slope and the board had picked up speed quickly, carrying the two featherweights faster and faster, hurtling downwards, careering past trees and statues, over paths, anonymous under the ghost robe, whizzing past the nose of a startled early-morning dog walker and his equally startled dog, and with every second devouring the distance between themselves and the river, half frozen, with blobs of ice clogging the weed beds. Pat, his eyes wider and wider as disaster loomed, clung to Frank's ankles and couldn't remember a prayer.

Suddenly, the makeshift sledge hit a bump, lifted in the air and, landing on its edge, pitched the brothers into the snow where they rolled over and over before coming to rest as the bread board slewed into the iron railing which lined the Kelvin. Pat, regarding the world through snow-flecked eyelashes, could not decide whether to laugh or cry. He looked to Frank for guidance, and five minutes later the pair had regained the summit, prepared for launching.

The click-clack of steel tackets on the marbled aisle of the church as he left the confessional, head down, studying the pattern in the stone. Feeling elated as he left the church after saying his penance, relieved of the burden of guilt. Perhaps he had stolen some money from his mammy's purse; maybe he had smoked one of his Uncle Dan's fags. He could not remember details of the offences, only the feeling of euphoria: it was all out, off his bony little chest, forgiven then forgotten by the Big Man. He had walked sedately as far as the outside doors, blessing himself with holy water from the greening font, depositing a penny in the Black Baby box. Regaining the outside world, he had raced down the wide steps leading to the street, jumping the last three to land with a loud slap as his feet hit the pavement, then leaping into the air with tireless limbs. Behind him, Frank was proceeding at a much slower pace, descending one step at a time, his sharp face grim. As his brother, four years his senior, reached the pavement, Pat grinned up at him, his eyes alive and bright with the knowledge of the innocent. Frank, the victim of a more adult chastisement, turned viciously on this deluded fool who painfully reminded him of simpler times: "What are you so happy about?" he snapped ferociously, and Pat was instantly subdued. Deprived of the opportunity of sharing his contentment, he wondered what sins might make him feel like that when he was Frank's age.

The pain inside his skull, much like the one he suffered from now, as he stood before the altar with another she, the sun splitting into a hundred colours as it passed through a stained glass window. Best suit, tie choking, hair greased and swept. Not listening to Father Gilmartin's Irish brogue, oblivious to the fire in the stare of his new bride as she burned into the side of his newly shaven face. In his nostrils and at the back of his throat was the stink and the taste of incense another priest had shaken over Frank's coffin five months before. Inside were the bits and pieces of his brother the fire brigade had pulled from under the juggernaut his car had sliced into. Later, during Frank's wake, as he desperately tried to dull the pain which racked his emotions, as he attempted to still that alien, unmanly, silent howl which filled his chest, he had begun the new life which now stirred beside him in his bride's womb.

Every sense in Pat's body strained for memories. The taste of his semen as he licked a finger smeared with the stuff after one of the first mysterious ejaculations. The rough, cardboard feel of a host as it stuck to the back of his tongue after communion. Waiting until it melted, sensing the touch of the nuns who had prepared the unleavened bread. As the strange, unfood taste rose in the back of his throat, trying not to chew and so torment the tortured body. The lights of the Christmas tree at the Kelvin Hall: elephant dung steaming under chained mountains; candy floss dissolving like a dream in the mouth; toffee apples sour underneath a sticky crunch. The feel of his father's razored stubble on his cheek as he nuzzled in his lap. His mother's hand absentmindedly stroking his hair as she stared from their high window, waiting for no one to arrive. The acrid smell of a match and the first choking gasp of a primary school cigarette. The rub of a girl's pubic hair, not soft as he had imagined, but harsh and wiry like his own in the enveloping blackness. An accordion wheezing out the old tunes. Granny Mullen's cracked voice quaking as she sang songs of guns and blood and grieving mothers. The ache in his toes as he strained over adult shoulders to see heroes acting out a drama on the football field. People looming gigantically above him as he lived his life unnoticed, powerless, at the mercy of strong adult arms; fearful, eyes darting, looking for burrows under the covers, peering silently out at a hostile world. Then, blue skies above green fields as the clanking gate swung to and fro. Perched on the bottom rung. Silence, then a bird rustle: "Prince! Here boy, here boy!"

A door opened.

"Pat, could you come in now?" Pat looked up, half drugged with memories and stale booze, a small dribble of saliva at the corner of his mouth. Reality smashed its way into his consciousness; a chill of air blew away the addictive fumes from the soothing balm which had masked his psyche. His nerves were stripped: he became aware of a dry mouth and a somersaulting stomach. A sickening realisation dawned that his time had come.

Pat raised himself to his feet and entered the office beyond the ante room. He entered through a door held open for him by a balding man in his mid-forties: small, stocky, with a full black moustache and a growth on his chin which would have benefited from a shave. The man was dressed in a dark blue suit, baggy at the knees, and as he closed the door behind Pat he hitched the trousers up over a burgeoning belly, clear of scuffed suede shoes.

"Take a pew, Pat," the man said, gesturing towards the chair in front of a desk inches deep in paper, folders and charts. Pat obeyed these instructions and watched as the man briskly moved round to sit in the chair opposite him across the table. There, the man slumped as if exhausted. He let out a deep sigh, loosened his tie and top shirt button, and made a sweeping movement over the desk with his free hand: "Look at this stuff." Pat looked. "Just look at it," the man urged again. He picked up a bundle of papers in both hands and dropped it back on the desk where it landed with a slapping noise. A loose sheet slid to the ground and Pat stooped to pick it up, the blood surging to his head as he did so, until he thought his eyes would explode. Straightening, he placed the sheet on the top of the skewed folder.

"There's enough work here to keep me going for the next six months," the man continued, ignoring Pat's service. "And there's more of it coming in every day: unfair dismissal, injury claims, victimisation, bonus problems, overtime disputes, union elections, health and safety inspections, resolutions to conference, management cock-ups, national policy statements, redundancy rumours, action committees . . ." The litany folded as the last drop of air was exhaled from his lungs. "You name it, I've got it," the man went on, rising from his chair and moving from behind his desk, again hitching his trousers, absentmindedly feeling his fly to check it was secure. "Enough work for six months," he mused, staring vacantly into space as he perched on the edge of the desk, one foot swinging in mid-air. "Six months," he repeated softly, fingering his moustache. Suddenly, he brought his hand down violently on top of a pile of documents with a crash which jolted Pat bolt upright in his chair like a chastised schoolboy: "And then fucking pricks like you come along and screw the whole thing up!"

The colour drained from Pat's face and despite himself he felt a slight movement in his bowels. His mouth clenched tight and a mist formed over his eyes. He glanced timidly at the man who was roaring at him, who was staring at him with bulging eyes, whose veins suddenly formed a streep map at his temples. The man stood up again, rehitching his trousers. He turned his back towards Pat as he returned to his seat. Pat knew that broad back. Hundreds and Hundreds of years ago. It belonged to a man called Michael Moran. He had been best man at Frank's wedding. He had cried at Frank's funeral, still bearing the scars of the car crash. And he had asked Pat why *he* hadn't cried. Pat had told him to fuck off.

Michael Moran sat down again behind his desk and opened a cardboard folder which lay on one side: "Latecoming: verbal warning. Latecoming: written warning. Days off: verbal warning. Days off: written warning. Drinking during working hours: sent home with a written warning." He closed the file with a flick of his wrist. "And it's my job to make a case for you?" he asked incredulously, lowering his head like a turtle, staring at Pat's blotched face. "There's five thousand men outside there whose jobs are on the line," he said slowly, emphasising each word with a jab of his index finger towards the shop floor. "And I've got to waste my time with this shit." Moran sat back in his chair, arms dangling limply at his side, silent.

The whole office was still, cocooned from the roaring turmoil of the plant. The silence grew oppressive and Pat could hear the ticking of his watch. He felt himself shrink in size. His head grew heavy and seemed to sink into his shoulders. He could not meet Moran's persistent gaze, and lead weights dragged his eyes down to floor level. He felt a leap and flutter in his heart, and a tightness crept over his scalp. Seconds passed; minutes seemed an eternity away. Pat tried to swallow, but alcohol had dried up his saliva leaving his tongue huge and bloated, adhering to the top of his mouth. He tried to lick his lips.

Moran stood up abruptly and left the office by a door to the side of his desk. The door had almost closed behind him when he reappeared, head and neck peering behind the frosted glass: "Wait here," he ordered. "Don't move."

As the door closed with a loose shake, Pat passed a hand over his face, drawing the skin above his eyes together in folds with his fingers: he needed a drink. Michael Moran. When Pat had started work at the factory, Moran had been shop steward for the maintenance workers on his block. One day, as he made his way round the section with notebook and pencil, Moran had suddenly spotted him at work on the line, had stopped dead in his tracks, his face pale. Exchanging a brief word with the person whose grievance he was listening to at the time, he had walked towards Pat with his hand outstretched, welcoming him to the plant with appropriate words of condolence for a man who had entered the "steel hamster cage" as he described it. He later explained that as he glanced across at Pat, he thought for a brief moment that he was looking once more at poor, dead Frank, who had been under the sods for over six years. Moran had not seen him or any of his family since the funeral, and the intervening years had seen Pat grow more like his brother as the sharp McKenna features had leaned out of the last vestiges of youthful padding.

Moran had been civility itself, asking after the health of his mother and sister, chuckling as he learned of the expansion of Pat's brood. He had heard Pat had married, learned of it from a mutual acquaintance in Manchester where he had lived until three years previously. That explained Moran's disappearance from the district: he had left no friends or relations to reveal his whereabouts. He too had "taken the plunge": a Liverpool girl who had stayed down south when Moran had decided to come home. Scotland was the place for him; he couldn't understand the English.

Pat had known as he spoke that Moran only talked to him because he was Frank's brother. They had never "seen eye to eye", and the final barrier had dropped between them at the funeral. Pat had mocked the political work Frank and Moran had been involved in, being more interested in more direct pleasures. Frank had taken his brother's jibes in good part, sometimes gently chiding him but understanding what he saw as his state of confusion, always turning the conversation to less contentious topics. He had once told Pat that he would never try to convert him, but instead would rely on Pat's growing experience of the world to convince him of the need for change and action. Frank would occasionally invite him to Labour Party socials, making excuses for his brother when he got drunk or started fights or abused people, sneering at their seriousness and their intense discussions. But Pat had seen Moran's jaw clench each time they met, as if he was trying to restrain himself from revealing the disdain he felt for a man who scorned his roots, his class. Occasionally, Pat would see the two arguing, and he knew that he was the topic under discussion. Frank would reason with Moran, trying to excuse his brother's behaviour, laughing at his rough edges, because he could remember leading a small, runny-nosed boy by the hand as they climbed a snow-draped mountain in winter. He understood the fear which hid beneath the defiance in Pat's eyes; Moran saw only the violence of tongue and fist, the wild, uncaring energy which tormented him as he spun from pole to pole with an uncomprehending and directionless fury.

It was Frank who, on several occasions, appeared with enough money to bail Pat from gaol when the law had caught up with him after nights which led to blank-faced mornings in echoing, piss-soaked cells. He would slap Pat on the back, laughing with sadness-soaked eyes as he hugged him with the open, undemanding love of the unthinkingly generous. He would take Pat into Deeley's Café and force cups of tea and sausage on rolls into his protesting belly, stuffing a pound note into his empty pocket. He would defend him in front of maternal courts: "He's only a boy", and quietly help him to pay his fines.

Pat shrank from his kind words: they tortured him more than any blows he had received in the mad, spinning fights he had been caught up in around George Square or Sauchiehall Street. Sometimes he hated Frank: he did not want to be understood or to listen to someone pleading on his behalf. He did not want to be forced to love this man who lifted him up by the armpits and supported him against the world. He wanted to run on headlong towards the wall which held the whole stinking edifice aloft, to bring it down around his ears, burying himself, Frank, Moran, and everyone else who inhabited the entire poxy city. He would look at

Frank, tears of anger and frustration in his eyes, burning with uncomprehending resentment. But Frank would laugh his big, natural laugh and punch him on the shoulder, or wrestle with him as if they were kids again. And as Pat struggled to free himself from the arms which held him pinned, once or twice he would see the brief look in Frank's eyes which told him all neither of them could say, and tears of a different kind would threaten him as he longed to throw down the mask, to dissolve in a sea of self-pity and sob-choked words.

But all of the time Moran was in the background. No longer trying to poison Frank against his brother, because that had proved to be impossible, but revealing to the world with every gesture, every shoulder slightly turned, every nuance of irony, how much he despised Pat and the whole lumpen stratum he was lodged in. However, Pat was not defenceless: he was not a helpless victim. He learned how to bait Moran, how to taunt him with effortless ease, until his face became whiter and whiter with impotent fury. Seeing him trying to impress a political contact in the pub, Pat would approach him, slapping him on the back like a long-lost friend, then noisily draw gobs of green phlegm from his throat, depositing on the floor between their feet before extending a mock apology, signalling the joke to his friends with a movement of his eyes. He knew that Moran longed to assault him, not only verbally but physically. Experience had taught him to recognise the moment an adversary contemplated attack, but he could relax in the knowledge that Moran would not choose a battleground where he held none of the advantages. In those days, Pat had been aware of and glorified in his own strength, his own narrow certainties. Moran could not touch him. His only avenue of attack was through Frank, and that was swiftly revealed to be a dead end.

With Frank's death, the only link between them was severed, and their orbits quickly separated. Before Moran had "gone south", their paths had occasionally crossed in pubs or in the local streets, but they had acknowledged one another with only the barest of nods, although sometimes Pat had been aware of Moran glancing at him from the corner of his eye, quickly averting his gaze if he realised Pat had become aware of his attention.

When the two men met that morning in the factory, six years later, both seemed to have changed, at any rate physically. Moran was paunchier and had lost hair from the crown of his head, although he had made no attempt to disguise it. On Pat's thinning cheeks were starting to appear the first broken red veins which signalled his drinking habits, and his eyes had lost the hardness that Moran remembered so well, being now lost in pools of moisture which threatened to spill over at any moment. On examining him closer, Moran saw his resemblance to Frank as only a fleeting impression. Here was a plasticine figure of the genuine article.

Seemingly, time had also changed both men's attitudes. Pat no longer had the energy for sustained aggression: he was in the process of being worn down. Moran had apparently mellowed over the years, and when the two men's paths crossed he would always stop for a brief word, keeping track of the progress of Pat's kids. When Pat's mother died, Moran sent a mass card to the house. His politics too seemed to have softened with age, indeed, on occasion, Pat found himself defending him against the attacks of the militants in the plant who hungered for a tougher line to be shown towards management. This friend of Frank the sad idealist had become a gradualist, a manipulator of the system, abandoning the rhetoric of dialectics for a more comfortable stance which reflected the relative affluence of his constituency of car workers. It appeared to have been a successful transformation, because Moran rose swiftly in the unofficial trade union hierarchy until he had reached his present position of sub-convener of the engineering union.

Almost without realising it, Pat had begun to respect him. He was sensitive of Moran's friendship and followed his success with a strange feeling of pride. At mass meetings he would manoeuvre himself to the front ranks of the crowd, and would shove his way forward to greet Moran as he climbed down from the podium having finished a speech. Moran would always snatch a moment from his busy schedule to briefly pass the time of day: "Hello, Pat. How's things?" Pat, his own lights dimming, would momentarily bask in reflected glory. One local election, Pat had almost canvassed for Moran in his bid to win a ward near the plant for Labour. He had offered to help out when Moran had mentioned his candidacy, but somehow other things had "cropped up" and he "couldn't manage it". Sorry.

Now, Pat was sitting in Moran's office staring at the wall, and his right eye was beginning to twitch. Moran seemed to have gone for hours, but Pat couldn't really tell: time had become a feather pillow wrapped round his head. He heard muffled voices from behind the frosted glass door through which Moran had disappeared. One voice was male, the other female, and Pat heard the female dissolve into tinkling laughter as the deeper tones crept nearer. There came the rattle of crockery and the sound of a handle being fumbled as a shadow patched itself together behind the knuckles of glass.

"Get this down you," ordered Moran as he invaded the room, thrusting a cup and saucer towards Pat. "You look as if you could do with it."

Pat accepted the tea and took a sip: it was hot and very sweet. He gagged slightly as it went down, but it massaged his stomach and cleared the alcohol dryness from his mouth.

"Now," pondered Moran, again flicking through Pat's personnel file as he eased into his chair. "What are we going to do about this?" He looked Pat straight in the eye, man to man: "If you ask me, the best we can do is to ensure you don't get sacked for industrial misconduct. That means you might not be suspended from receipt of unemployment benefit for the statutory six weeks. The problem is," he mused, making a wigwam of his fingers, "what reason are we going to give for your dismissal?"

"Dismissal?" queried Pat, half dazed, speaking for the first time since he had entered the room. "Do you mean I'm going to get my jotters?"

"Are you joking?" asked Moran incredulously. "With this record you would have been bagged from any normal firm years ago."

"You mean I'm getting paid off?"

"Too fucking right you are getting paid off. Your services are no longer required. The only reasons I'm going through this rigmarole is that management don't want any problems union-wise with this big Iranian order coming up." Moran leaned across the desk to confront Pat: "And neither do I. So you're going, Pat, it's as simple as that. The only point at issue is how you go: heels kicking, or out the back door. And believe me, if you go out heels kicking you'll get a report from here that'll mean you'll never get another job in Scotland outside of the Bar-L mailbag room."

"Hold on, hold on," protested Pat, galvanised by the hot tea and a reawakening sense of injustice. "You're my union rep, not some management bastard. You're here to protect my rights, and I want them protected."

"You don't get any protection with a record like this," stated Moran calmly, tapping a fingernail on the file. "You get the bullet."

"Fuck this," cried Pat rising to his feet, waving a hand in the air. "I've been victimised."

"Victimised?"

"And I've got plenty of witnesses to prove it."

"Sit down!" shouted Moran, his face again showing anger. "You're not going to use my office to exhibit your paranoia." Pat stared at him for a moment before averting his gaze. He sat down. "OK," continued Moran with overstated patience, barely holding his emotions in check. He spoke to Pat as if he was a child: "You tell me all about being victimised."

"Give us a break. You know what goes on in here."

"No, come on; you can enlighten me."

"You know the score: you've been here long enough." Pat gestured vaguely behind himself. "You can ask anyone out there if you're still not sure."

"No," said Moran patiently, like a slaughterman coaxing a beast towards the poleaxe, "I want you to tell me what I've been missing all these years."

"Listen," said Pat, talking as if to an imbecile, "you know as well as I do that if you're a pape in here your card's marked as soon as you walk in through the door. We've got no fucking chance in this place because the whole shebang's run by Orangemen and fucking Masons. If you don't tie your boots the right way, you're out the door as soon as you sneeze. Ever since I came to this section, Stewart's been up my arse as soon as I turn round. As soon as he clocked my name, the cunt had it in for me. Why is it always me who gets it in the neck for coming in a bit late, or for having a wee drink in me? Half the fucking plant's doing the same."

Moran slowly rose to his feet, placing his hands on the deck, looking down towards the still gesticulating Pat: "I'll tell you why everyone's got it in for you — it's because you're a lazy, incompetent bastard. You're a fucking waster. You're a danger, not only to yourself but to your workmates, and, along with a number of other cretinous cunts, both Catholic and Protestant, a danger to the future of the whole plant. The biggest joke is that the system's so corrupt it actually tolerated you for so many years. You don't give a fuck, management doesn't give a fuck, the owners don't give a fuck. If we'd left it up to you, the whole fucking abortion would have rolled over and died years ago. The whole shower of you are parasites, feeding off the sweat of decent men, people who're trying to make some semblance of a future for themselves and their kids."

"Future? Do you call working in this shitehole a future?"

"Put it this way — it certainly doesn't figure anywhere in your horoscope. Do you think I don't know the place stinks? Do you think I enjoy seeing men being chewed up and spat out? The difference is that I'm trying to change it, along with hundreds of other committed people in the plant, while you're skulking in corners, howling about your persecution mania, wondering where your next drink's coming from. You're not getting sacked because you're green and someone else is orange — you're going because even this poxed-up system can stomach only so much poison." Moran sat down and there was a moment's silence as both men breathed deeply. "Who do you think covered your shift while you were sleeping it off in your bed in the sky?"

"Oh, so that's it," said Pat slowly, comprehension dawning on his face. "It was that wee shite Billy Paterson who put the knife in, was it? I've covered for that wee cunt plenty of times."

"Billy Paterson's got fuck all to do with this. He hasn't stuck the knife into anyone."

"Well who was it then? Someone must have grassed. Who was it? Who turned me in? If it wasn't Patterson it must have been Whitby, that money-lending leech. Did he think I was going to run away with the cash?"

"Whitby's got nothing to do with this either. If I had my way, he'd be out the door along with you."

"If I had my way." Pat repeated Moran's words slowly. "That's what it boils down to, doesn't it? Since you got this wee office you've gone power fucking mad. You've always been a jumped-up Hitler, ever since you knocked about with Frank. I could never understand what he saw in you."

"I'm telling you," spat Moran, his anger rising once more, "if Frank was in this office now he'd be telling you the same things I'm telling you. How you two could have been brothers escapes me. Frank had more integrity in his little finger than you've got in your entire carcass. He used to tell me you'd grow out of it, but I knew better — I knew you were rotten to the core. You've never done anything unselfish in your life — it's been take, take, take ever since you were a wee boy. Take from Frank, take from your mother, take from your workmates. Well, I'll tell you, your days of taking in this factory are over. We're getting rid of you and that'll make my job a hell of a lot easier, I'll tell you that for nothing.

"Oh, I see," said Pat in mock comprehension: "We're all here to make your job easier, is that it? What do you think we voted you in for? So you could have an easy life? So you could sit in your cosy wee den, cutting your toenails? You're supposed to be here defending my interests: I've seen fuck all evidence of that so far."

"I'll tell you what I was voted in for; I'll tell you what my job is: it's to defend the interests of the workforce at this plant. And as far as I'm concerned, that involves getting rid of you with the minimum of fuss."

"So much for the old Socialism, eh? So much for the old workers' power. I always knew that was a load of shite, now I know you thought the same way too."

"Workers? What are you talking about workers for? You're a dosser, a leadswinger, not a worker. The most exertion you put in of a day is going for a crap. If there was workers' power in here, you'd probably be put against a wall."

"Oh yes, you'd like to see that, wouldn't you? Everyone who stands in your way: bump! Problem solved. Just tell me one thing, though: when was the last time you were out there, soiling your hands on the shop floor? Talk about parasites! You jump about the factory in that wee monkey suit of yours with all your hangers-on trooping behind you. Christ, you all look like managers now. And here you are, doing their dirty work for them."

"Listen, you wee bastard, I do a bloody sight more work than you do, monkey suit or no monkey suit."

"Oh yes, you work hard all right, but who's it for? Is it for Joe Cunt out there on the floor, or is it for M. Moran Esquire? Ask anyone in this place and they'll tell you that at the first whiff of a full-time union job you'll be out that door before your notebook hits the ground."

"Wait a minute, just let me get this straight: who are you trying to compare me with? I'm no saint, but at least I can sleep easily at night. I'm not denying I've got personal ambition, but at least I'm channelling it in the right way. Are you comparing me with you? You've got nothing: no ambition, no beliefs, no guts, no faith, no friends, nothing."

"What do you mean, no friends? I've got more mates in this plant than you've ever known."

"Mates!" Moran sneered.

"You've always been hated, you bastard: it's you who never had any friends. Even Frank thought you were an oddball — he told me."

"Try again, Pat. You're not going to get me that way. I knew Frank better than you ever could. Mates!" Moran sneered again.

"What are you trying to get at, eh?" demanded Pat, growing visibly agitated. Moran said nothing. "I'm telling you, if my mates got the bastard who shopped me, there wouldn't be much left of him. I could step out there right now and pull this whole section out, and say 'bugger' to the shop steward." Moran remained silent, turning a pencil on its end, then on its point, then on its end. Pat's breathing grew sharper as he tried to elicit some response:

"My old dear thought there was something funny about you too. She used to tell Frank to steer clear of you."

Moran raised his eyes from the pencil to confront Pat: "Fact number one: your mother used to invite me round to the house when you were out, to ask my advice about what she could do with you. Fact number two: Frank told me that the next time you ended up in the cells, he was going to leave you there. Fact number three: the two of them, Frank and your mother, reached a decision just before Frank was killed: they were going to give you your marching orders. They were going to throw you out of the house, just like I'm throwing you out of this plant now. They'd had enough of you, just like I've had enough of you. Frank told me the night of the crash."

"You and Frank, you and Frank!" repeated Pat through tight lips. "Do you know what I think? Do you? I think you wanted up Frank's arse. I think you're a bender. You're a fucking poof, that's what your problem is." Moran's pencil broke with a dry snap as his face grew whiter. "That's what we couldn't put our finger on," spat Pat, the veins in his forehead standing out in relief as he leant forward, gesticulating wildly, years of accumulated bile spilling out. "You're a fucking queer, that's why you left your wife down south — she tumbled to you. If Frank had got wise to you, he would've stuck one on you, I'll tell you that for nothing."

Moran calmly laid the two broken halves of the pencil on the table before him and straightened an already neat file: "I think it's about time that this interview drew to a close." He spoke softly, carefully enunciating every word. "But first of all, I'll put you out of your misery, OK? You want to know who shopped you, right? You want to know who grassed? Well, I'll tell you." Moran leaned slightly towards Pat, squaring his head on his shoulders to stare into his face. "Archie Campbell turned you in, boyo. That's right, don't look so shocked. Old Archie: your 'mate'. He managed to crawl out from his bolt hole long enough to make it to the supervisors' office."

"That's a fucking lie!"

"And will I tell you why? will I?"

"That's a fucking lie!" repeated Pat, slamming the palm of his hand down on the arm of the chair.

"Archie Campbell turned you in because he was sick of you, like everyone else in here's sick of you, like all your 'mates' are sick of you. They're fed up lending you money, they're fed up covering up for you, they're fed up hearing you whine all of the time, they're fed up with you putting their jobs on the line, even old Archie, who hasn't done a hand's turn in fifteen years. You're bad news: trouble follows you like the plague. Everyone wants to get back to a quiet life: they want you out the door. And if you go out on to the floor now to try to pull the men out on strike, even the lavvy cleaner will spit in your eye."

"That's a fucking lie," repeated Pat, but weaker now as a confusion of thoughts and emotions fought in his brain. Moran rose slowly to his feet, his face impassive, and he picked up Pat's file, letting the contents slide into the metal waste bin at the side of his desk:

"Close the door behind you," he said over his shoulder as he left Pat rigid in his seat. "And by the way," he added, as if as an afterthought, standing with the door half open, allowing the muffled sounds of machinery to enter the room. "Archie wants his bottle of wine back; you won't forget now, will you?" The door clicked shut behind him and Pat was left alone. He placed his hands under his thighs and began to rock to and fro, seeking comfort from the movement.

He could not have said how much later it was when he hauled himself to his feet and left the office, again passing through the narrow anteroom. Outside on the factory floor the roaring and crashing and sparking and grinding continued as if nothing had happened. Some people looked oddly at him as they passed by but he was oblivious to their stares and nods and whispered comments. Raising his eye from ground level, he scanned the section for what would be the last time and in a sudden flash recognised a face peering at him through a gap in a shelf fifty yards away.

"Pop!" he cried, suddenly reanimated, waving his hands wildly, causing more people to stare. The face disappeared and there was silence despite the noise.

Sculpture

Glasgow is full of statues. They're everywhere, even in the most unlikely places, although most can be found in parks, surrounded by iron railings and neatly trimmed grass. Many of them carry long lists of dead people, citizens of the Second City who are buried miles and miles away from where they were born. Most of the names are very ordinary, and some of them are familiar to me, names like Thomas Mulhern and John McAndrew. I used to know people called Thomas Mulhern and John McAndrew but it is not my former acquaintances who have been honoured. It's their grandfathers or great uncles, who died years and years ago. Or at least everyone assumed they died; sometimes, no one really knew for certain. Sometimes the people who cleared up found little bits and pieces of limbs and skulls lying around so they gathered them up, put them in canvas bags, and attached a label on which they wrote the names of people who hadn't been seen for some time. My grandfather, a miner from Steppes, was nearly put into a canvas bag on a beach in Turkey. After that he hated big fat men who smoked cigars.

Other statues in Glasgow bear only one name, usually that of a hero of capitalist contruction. My favourite can be found at Govan Cross, just along the road from the shipyards. It says:

SIR WILLIAM PEARCE

BART M.P.

DIED

18th DECEMBER 1888

AGED 55 YEARS

The sandstone colum which supports the statue is covered with chiselled writing. You can stand back and admire this bronzed, frock-coated Victorian, then close in for a good read:

asashipbuilderandengineerhisoriginalityofthoughtandmarvellous
skillinexecutioncontributedlargelytothedevelopmentoftheNaval
MerchantileMarineintokenofhiseminenceinhisprofessionhewas
createdabaronetin1887hisextensiveandaccurateknowledgeledto
hisappointmenttoserveontheRoyalCommissionsontonnagelossof
lifeatseaanddepressionoftradehiscareerfurnishedastriking
exampleofwhatgeniuscombinedwithenergyinindustryand
indomitablecouragemayaccomplisheveninashortlifetime

ERECTED

BY

PUBLIC SUBSCRIPTION

IN GRATEFUL RECOGNITION

OF HIS NUMEROUS NOBLE

QUALITIES AS A MAN AND EMPLOYER OF LABOUR

1894

foratimeheservedasaCommissionerofPoliceoftheBurghofGovan
hewasalsohonouraryColoneloftheSecondVolunteerBattalion
HighlandLightInfantryProvincialGrandMasterofGlasgowa
CommissionerofSupplyJusticeofthePeaceandDeputyLieutenant
oftheCountyofLanarkwhenGovanwasmadeaParliamentary
Divisionin1885hewasreturnedasitsfirstrepresentativeandwas
reelectedin1886

One of the first statues I remember noticing with any great interest was the imposing figure of King William of Orange in Townhead, near where I attended school. I didn't really know who he was at the time, only that he was a "bad man" in Catholic street mythology. I used to walk through the little park where his statue stands, on my way to the school dining hall, and I would see fathers out for a walk with their tiny children point a finger at this laurel-wreathed figure on his stallion, bending as they whispered orange and green half truths into wriggling ears. And on the base, there are again words etched, on one side in Latin, on the other in the King's English. Words like SOVEREIGN, PIOUS, VALIANT, INVINCIBLE, COURAGE, DANGER, SAFETY, IRELAND, PURER,

RELIGION, LIBERTY, POSTERITY, JUST, PATRIOTIC, YOKE, SLAVERY, FAITHFUL.

Erecting statues was, of course, the great Victorian pastime, and the practice petered out in Glasgow, as in other cities, after the post-1945 "roll of honour" building boom. Recently, however, two additions have been made to the catalogue of the city's treasures. Down on Custom House Quay on the edge of the Clyde is a small memorial to "La Passionara", a tangible reference to the city's socialist roots rather than a reminder of another distant war. Dolores stands on top of a ten-foot-high steel girder, her hands reaching up to the sky, rather as if she is about to dive into the river. The memorial has been given a few licks of paint since it was erected, none of them part of any official refurbishing programme, and several anonymous telephone calls to the City Chambers have threatened to tip this symbol of the Anti-Christ over the edge of the dock unless it is removed, if not completely then to a less public and hence less corrupting site.

The second addition to Glasgow's tourist trail can be found in Buchanan Street pedestrian precinct, and it too aroused passions when first revealed to the public gaze, although this time the objections were of an aesthetic rather than a political nature. The statue in question is a modern work cast in bronze and it is called "Dream of Kentigern". It is supposed to represent the spirit of Glasgow, but detractors say it resembles a dog turd with wings.

ALEC DOWDESWELL

FROM THE BRAINWAVES OF A SLUG

Two months after our conversation about dentists, I was standing with her at the edge of a graveside. I held one of her elbows, her brother Thomas, or "Tam" as he liked to be known as, held the other. As she stopped down to pick up some earth to drop on her mother's coffin, we took most of her weight, and I could feel my legs shaking beneath me as we took the strain.

Previously, at every funeral I attended, whether it was a family or a business affair, the rain fell, either in a cold drizzle which chilled the bones, or in torrents which made the grass, ploughed up by so many hard-shod feet, disappear in a carnage of mud. That day, however, the sky was blue, the sun shone, warming bodies seeking a respite from winter, and birds sang on the branches of trees which were coming into bud. Around our sombre funeral party, daffodils and crocuses burst into colour. An aerial photograph taken at that moment would have shown us as a cancerous black blot in a joyous landscape. I was sure that at one stage in the proceedings I caught sight of the scut of a rabbit as it raced for cover behind a tombstone in a flash of white.

The season, not the ceremony, reflected my mood. I savoured the warmth of the body beside me as my fingers sank into the ample flesh beneath the mourning coat. Despite the tragic occasion, she had dabbed on some of the perfume I had given her some weeks previously after our first near intimacy. I breathed in its odour, mixed with the smell of damp earth and the all-pervading fumes of mothballs from clothes worn only to funeral breakfasts.

Her mother had long been a widow, so I calculated that, technically speaking, Betty was now an orphan. I stood upright beside her, shoulders straight, looking every inch the perfect means of support in my plastic shoes and nylon shirt.

There was no lack of mourners. Apart from Betty, myself and "Tam", assembled round the graveside were assorted ageing brothers and sisters, and nieces and nephews of the deceased. They in turn were outnumbered by hordes of toothless old age pensioners from the immediate neighbourhood who stood shaking their heads and sighing over the mysteries of the life/death cycle, and wondering when it would be their turn to be "laid to rest". One old codger was so affected by this philosophical nightmare he forgot whose funeral he was attending and approached me to offer his condolences on the loss of "your father". I was feeling so cheered with the whole affair that I could not bring myself to correct him.

I, of course, was paying for the whole show. The old girl's insurance policy had only realised around £120: it had been cashed and recashed in former years to tide the family over the recurring crises which plagued them. This, of course, was not enough to cater for the needs of so many hungry and thirsty mourners, without taking into account the general funeral expenses: coffin, flowers, etc. I had hired four cars, not counting the hearse, and involved myself in allocating seats to those of the old woman's former cronies who seemed most infirm. The others would have to walk.

The minister, seeing my prominent role in organising the logistics of the operation, formed the impression I was a grieving son and displayed his most soulful face when he shook my hand outside of the church before setting off for the cemetery. I informed him I was only a "close friend of the family", information which did not deter him from delivering a eulogy on the old harridan's finer points. I began to suspect we were burying the wrong body.

All in all, I seemed to be on the receiving end of more expressions of grief than was "Tam", whose face, blotched with my drink, was growing more and more feverish as he saw his laundry and catering service disappear beneath the sods. He, of course, could not contribute towards the funeral expenses, being in a more or less permanent state of unemployment. I did not expect, nor indeed desire, gratitude from him for my act of generosity which was, however — and here I must pause to give myself some credit — an act of goodwill not demanded by any protocol. Neither, however, did I expect to witness the display of unveiled hostility with which he treated me while both alone and before the world.

Let us look at the facts: despite calling regularly on his sister during the previous two months, I had seen very little of him. When we had met, our relations, while hardly cordial, had not been overtly antagonistic. In the days leading up to the funeral, however, in those three short days since his mother had keeled over with a thud while carrying groceries home from the corner shop, his attitude towards me had changed out of all recognition. It was as if the artery which had exploded in his mother's brain had burst a dam of resentment within him.

Perhaps I am over-simplifying the situation. It seemed as if, having seen one meal ticket vanish with a silent gurgle, he immediately cast his net for a replacement: Betty fitted the bill nicely. Unfortunately, I did not slot into his warped jigsaw of priorities. I had suddenly been transformed from an annoying blot in the background to being a rival, an enemy to be taken care of by any means at his disposal.

Already vague murmurings were stirring: "who was I anyway?"; "where had I sprung from?"; "who did I think I was, interfering with their family affairs?"; "who needed my money?". I must, however, give him some credit: he restrained his attacks until his "ma" was tucked away underground, seemingly affected by a sense of decorum, an artefact from the early days of his family life. Who can tell? Perhaps he was sensitive to Betty's feelings: she was certainly distraught, more upset than I could have imagined. I myself felt a strange conflict grow within me: on the one hand tenderness and a protective urge towards this woman of more than thirty years who was in many ways still like a child, in others imbued with the wisdom of centuries. On the other hand, a surge of joy due to the elimination of a stumbling block between myself and my goal, which I was then beginning to perceive clearly.

But to return to "Tam". A man of thirty-seven years, physically huge, unmarried apart from a disastrous six-month period in his early twenties, uneducated, lacking in culture and awareness, with no knowledge of the world outside of his universe of a dozen streets in the Gorbals, most of which had been knocked down. An artefact: belonging to another place and time; a meaningless relic exposed during an archaeological dig. Unheeding of politics, science and the arts. Baffled by the complex mystery of simple societal functions. A meaningless dot on the edge of the universe. A stone dropped in a pool which caused no ripple, no change, however transient. He came, he lives, he will go, affecting nothing, changing no one: a noxious wisp of an existence. Betty told me that, in the nights following her mother's death, he would whimper and cry in his sleep, like a lost kitten. I am sure these raw emotions were not tapped by grief but by a slowly creeping, gnawing awareness that his last tenuous link with the world had been severed. He would wake up alone, in silence, in a vacuum. He could find drinking partners and "lads" to have a laugh and a joke with down at the bookmaker's, but who could he empty himself to? A sense of horror was engulfing him, creeping up in a black shroud while his back was turned. Panic and anxiety were burrowing their roots into his system. The anchor had been cut. Betty was now the only person who could tell him who he was. Eventually, he too would be beneath the earth, and he could feel its clammy touch. It was a cold place where no man knew him, where his name was forgotten, even by himself. Who was he? He was "Tam". Who is "Tam"? He is Mrs Russell's boy. But she is dead. Who is "Tam"? He is Betty Russell's brother. But Betty has gone. Who is "Tam"? He is a thirty-seven-year-old "boy" who died in a flat, and no one even noticed he had disappeared.

And so "Tam" clung desperately to Betty's elbow at the Graveside as she bent to throw earth on her mother's coffin. Betty the foundation, the rock he could leech on to. Betty, who could give his tenuous existence substance. She would breathe life into him again. She would give him a position: "I'm Betty's brother." without her reflected light, he was a panic-stricken, shadowy figure with no presence, scuttling into the corners of derelict tenements, avoiding the horrible, revealing glare of reality which would strip him naked and reveal only a curl of smoke spiralling skywards. I'm "Tam". who is "Tam"? One morning he would wake up and he would no longer exist.

***

The funeral and the first deadening period of mourning passed. For several weeks after the death of her mother Betty wore black, and I kept a respectful, or perhaps a wary distance as brother and sister consoled one another in their respective forms of grief. Then one afternoon when I called at the house, I was greeted with a tearful hug and, my head clasped to a substantial shoulder, I noticed that Betty had discarded the black weeds in favour of the very fetching, pastel yellow two-piece suit I had bought her shortly before her mother's demise. Half sobbing, she apologised for her behaviour of the previous few weeks when, she explained, she had been too involved in her own suffering to devote to me the attention I deserved. Pooh-poohing this suggestion, I caressed her back consolingly, whispering "there, there" into her ear as if she was a distraught child. Eventually, still clinging together, I felt the sobbing stop. I stood back from her, still holding her by the waist, and stared into her eyes until we moved together simultaneously. My lips touched hers and my chest pressed against her breasts. My tongue darted into her mouth and her legs moved against mine, causing the beginnings of an erection. My body collapsed into hers and I squirmed my belly, thighs and chest against her, trying to burrow deep into folds of flesh, seeking warmth and steamy-damp comfort. I bent at the knees, then straightened, rubbing my length against her as I rose, my shape finding a ready mould. I wanted to crawl all over this woman, to explore that vast frame, hide under mounds of flesh, sniff orifices, lie within her, be possessed.

Suddenly, at the height of my delirium, a key sounded in the lock. We broke apart immediately, and Betty jumped to one side to greet Tam as he came through the door carrying a white plastic bag, the contents of which made a clinking noise. His sharp eyes darted towards both of us and Betty flushed slightly as she smoothed down her skirt. As her brother grunted a greeting and turned to remove the Yale from the lock, she mouthed some words at me over his shoulder, pointing to her watch then towards the door. She raised four fingers, tucking the thumb against her palm, to indicate the time we would meet at my flat, a signal we had arranged while her mother had still been alive, playing her chaperone role. Tam brushed past me, avoiding my eyes, leaving an alcohol wake, and with his back towards her asked Betty what she had bought for his dinner. Still standing at the door, I enquired as to his health, but was met only with silence as he disappeared into the kitchen. Betty pressed against me briefly and whispered "four" into my ear before pointing me towards the close. I left, my now flaccid penis leaving a drop of fluid which felt cold on my skin, and as I descended the stairs I could hear voices being raised, one gruff, one shrill. As I left the close mouth there was only silence.

Later that evening, when Betty came to me, she was again in tears, and showed me a map of bruises on her left upper arm where Tam had gripped her viciously, trying to shake all knowledge of me from her head. She had been unable to keep our arrangement to meet at four because her brother had refused to let her leave the house. Only after he had eaten and drank himself into a stupor could she creep away, clutching a battered suitcase into which she had thrown some of her treasures. It could not go on: she had to leave. But where was she to go? I held her in my arms and licked little areas of her face where tears had splashed, whispering in her ear the words she wanted to hear.

That night I truly broke into my new life, an awesome experience as I floundered in the rippling sea which was her body, now swimming rhythmically, now struggling desperately for breath as a breaker smashed over my head. Finally, a wave crash threw a needle spray of pleasure over my being as I leapt spasmodically like a struggling salmon until, mouth gasping, fingers clutching, I braced my feet against the bottom of the bed and yelled as I emptied, my testicles twitching between her legs.

We lay there together, within a third skin, each movement making a slurping sound as our sweat mingled and cooled. I fell asleep in her arms, head cushioned on floating breasts, mouth twitching unconsciously for a nipple, but when I awoke, who knows how much later, she was gone and I was dribbling on the pillow. I looked up and saw a mammoth white shape looming towards me in the half darkness; crockery rattled. She thought I might fancy a cup of tea. I rolled into the still warm depression she had left in the bed and stretched my arms, untensing the muscles of my face with a grimace, slowly bringing one hand round to grasp a mug. She deposited the tray on the floor by the side of the bed and climbed in beside me, breasts swinging as she stooped. her frame, dominating mine, crept into my side and she lay there silently, her nose under my arm. She had had a boyfriend before, she told me — a boy friend — she who was past thirty — but it had never been like that. This pleased yet surprised me, since she had lain passive and mute throughout the whole proceedings, while I had concentrated on my own pleasures, glorying in an orgasmic fantasy made flesh. I laid my cup on the floor and almost purred, exploring my new domain at leisure, running my hands at will over this compliant estate, lifting and probing, running my fingers into crevices, scratching ownership with sharp nails, caressing and being caressed until I reawoke and launched myself once more on these now charted waters.

***

The days and weeks and months following my breakthrough filled me with a rising awe, as if an inner sun climbed and flooded every sinew with light and warmth. My whole existence poured like sand in an egg-timer, but from the narrow spout of a constricting bowl into an open field where the air blew particles with an anarchic breath. Occasionally, I had to re-form, to force myself upwards, back into the tightly packed glass sphere, but as I did so, fewer and fewer of the grains of my former personality could be recalled from the strange vantage points where they had lodged. A new constellation of simple, sensual pleasures flickered briefly in the darkness and grew ever stronger with the passing days and nights, feeding on my liberated spirit, occasionally faltering but then waxing, becoming more confident in their light, dispelling the gloom which had haunted me until they became fixed points masked only by the greater magnitude of the false light which starkly examined me as I attempted to feign my previous orbits.

On those days when I plunged and plunged again into my new life, I would remove my constricting clothes and tense my muscles, feeling reborn pleasure in my body, making wild gestures of delight as I grunted my satisfaction. I allowed myself to float where the meandering stream would take me, bobbing contentedly, thoughtless, without will, relying on the animal force which welled up within me to magically guide me where it would.

Laughter, wild, foolish laughter became my constant companion as I abandoned my past, daubing paint on my skin, dressing in animal pelts and feathers, eating raw flesh, hunting, hands gory with hot blood, brute sex, the roar of the spring stag. I was free and gloried in my liberation. Obsessed with visions of what I perceived as true nature-rites, naked desire, I dreamed constantly of possessing the power of flight, casting off the final convention. I was Ug, brute-faced Neanderthal, disembowelling literary classics, smashing small boys' pianos, screaming to the wild air as I pounded philosophers' skulls with the thigh bone of an ox. I grimaced and revealed my teeth, buried my first in hair, drawing a body closer with the movement of an arm. I threw off control and so controlled myself for the first time; anaesthetised myself and so drank in the passions and pleasures which had been drugged into sleep.

And yet who would have glanced at me in those heady days and guess the magnitude of the change which had occurred? On the surface I seemed to have exchanged one sleepwalking existence for another, cruder mode. Yet each banal new experience sent explosions of pleasure through my senses as I broke wind in the face of the old world, brayed with derision at the flabby, self-congratulatory culture which paraded its self-righteousness in Sunday Supplements and soft, padded, first class commuter trains. I had plumbed hidden depths, struck the lode-bearing rock, crumbling its oily texture in grasping fingers, immersing myself, smoothing its touch over a straining body. I revelled in new filth, defiling my sensibilities, amputating that which I had formerly believed to be precious, to allow stronger, more vital growths to sprout. I spat on the holy places, dredged thick sludge from forgotten recesses to muddy the crystal waters of reason and civilisation and decorum and expectation and received culture and good form and good taste and objective criticism and tact and clean fingernails.

I found myself on "trips" along with Betty. Outings; explorations. She, enjoying them on her own individual level, I, seeing them as odysseys of discovery, drinking in detail, saturating my senses with garish colour and the rub of cut-price nylon against my skin; the smell of cheap tobacco and the whine of fairground organs.

Bobbing in Central Station among the multicoloured flotsam and jetsam of a holiday weekend: plastic carrier bags clutched, the handles stretching and narrowing in sweating palms; huge straw holdalls crammed with copies of *Weekend* and 'Andrex' toilet tissues, scratching bare white legs. Craning necks scan the departure boards: TROON — PLATFORM 12. Stampeding feet, sweating armpits, children begging to be thrown under the wheels of a quivering train.

Rip-top cans explode on the formica tops of British Rail tables: lubrication begins. The first ear is warmed. A huge woman hitches her floral tent over insolent knees, splaying her blotched legs, wheezing with exhaustion as she fans the air with a paperback Mills and Boon. Silence is unknown, but instead of wrinkling my nose in disgust, I positively revel in the chaos, laughing spontaneously, giggling without cause, provoking suspicious stares: I am still outside.

A purple-faced toddler attempts to swallow the world as he searches for the sound which will do justice to the misery he feels in this uncomprehending adult world. I squeeze in beside a trousered Betty, rubbing my thigh against hers, feeling the warmth through two layers of cloth. Trickles of sweat ooze from my body, running beneath my shirt which is a damp, clammy skin as I lean back against the seat. The sun bursts through the grimy window as we lurch out from under the Victorian glass canopy of the station on to the bridge which spans the Clyde. Below us, the light is reflected on the empty, low-water river, sluggish in the heat.

Swiftly through the warehouse jumble to Paisley where more day-trippers cram into carriages, outstretched bags forming a prow as they cut through the crush. Garnock, then a vista of green and the glint of the sea behind swelling dunes. Sandwiches cut the previous night exhaustedly curl towards the centre, the mobile breakfast washed down with lukewarm 'Coca-Cola'. Everything is vibrant and loud as laughter falls easily. A brief moment of panic as the train pulls into Troon: TICKETS — back, no, inside pocket; relief. Fumbling with bags on the rack and a log jam as we shuffle past a bored ticket collector, yawning in peaked cap and shirt sleeves.

Head for the briny smell and feel sand beneath liberated toes, not yet burning as the sun arcs towards the centre of the sky. Skidding and sliding down dunes and I fall to my knees, gasping, sand gritting under my fingernails. Foot prints on the hard sand flash a contrast of light as water is temporarily squeezed from the packed surface, only to seep down again when we leave them behind. The first, clear ripples of warm water, growing colder as it reaches ankle bones. Bend down to roll up trouser legs another few notches, and a gnawing ache as the cold grips my calfless legs in a cramp. Race out, race in: easier now. Kick a fireworks display in the air as Betty shrieks for cover. Taste the sweat salt and sea salt on my lips and chase a tiny crab along the foreshore: nature vainly attempting to reassert itself.

Lunch in a jolting pub, appetites whetted by country air: pork pies, crisps, beer, salted peanuts disappear, swelling girths, straining buttons. The afternoon is more leisurely, the initial euphoria giving way to a calmer appreciation of the day of freedom. A walk along the promenade, the pavement burning through thin plastic soles, and above, dirty seagulls circle in the blue sky, aping vultures in their forage for the crusts and cores of picnic lunches.

In a mired field behind the dunes, revolving space capsules tear screams from children and adults, shrieking above the tinny music of fairground engines. Sticky candy floss harvests hair and wool, and ice-cream melts down cones on to hot fingers which are licked deliciously. Packs of boys prowl before herds of girls, feigning disinterest as eyes flick longingly amidst horseplay camouflage. We wander from stall to stall, testing dart throwing and rifle shooting and rubber ball launching, accumulating trash as money is spilled on to wooden counters, china dolls and miniature teddy bears stuffed into swag bags.

High tea in a restaurant where the ageing waitresses dress in black festooned with white lace, a feeble gesture of longing for the languorous past. A corner full of youths in stiff leather jerkins spit chips on to the starched tablecloth and the staff dream of stiff, dainty pinkies and nice families. Haddock and chips, and bread and butter, and tea and cakes: two each with guilty giggles as Betty prods me with her toe under the table.

The sun is sinking when we return to the station, silent now but grunting with contentment as our weary bodies mould into the train seats. As the engine throbs into life, my head nods and I am dreaming of nothing, only vaguely aware of the tightening skin on my nose and the sand in my shoes. Children are still, curled up on laps, clutching slowly deflating balloons. A pack of cards sits on one table, abandoned, spreading out with the movement of the carriage. The smell of suntan lotion hangs over reddened bodies, and a young man rests his head on his girlfriend's shoulder. The unknowing train pulls its load back to the real world.

Glorious months passed, spring turning to summer then to a golden autumn. Whenever I could, I would escape to my new world — touching, tasting, looking; absorbing new experiences which stimulated raw nerves and reached a part of my being which I could not fully comprehend. I revelled almost orgasmically in the hints of degradation and decay I heaped upon myself. Little touches of neglect, the rustle of anchor chains as I furtively cast myself free. I no longer brushed my teeth, and displayed a rapidly yellowing grin. My fingers were becoming heavily stained with nicotine and I was developing a slight paunch due to a combination of a hopelessly unbalanced diet and a lack of planned exercise. I seemed to have become the victim of a spontaneous eruption of dandruff, the flakes glistening like snow in my unkempt hair.

On Saturday afternoons, Betty and I would embark on shopping expeditions along Argyle Street, pressing through sweating throngs, barging into waddling women, stepping on small children. At the end of the day we would slump exhaustedly on the soft seats of our favourite lounge bar, resting throbbing feet, sipping badly needed drinks. We would be surrounded by a barricade of plastic and paper carrier bags which contained our purchases: cheap shirts, gaudy dresses, cotton T-shirts emblazoned with Union Jacks and inane slogans, cardboard denims, sun hats, paper-thin beach towels: all the paraphernalia of the Summer Holiday Season. We would also have some knick-knacks for our flat: clumsy, mass-produced paintings in rococo frames, a tin bread box, glass animals, a tea caddy with a portrait of the queen stamped on the side, a new nameplate, multi-coloured Venetian blinds, a table lamp in the shape of a dolphin, cutlery with plastic handles, a floral dinner service, imitation roses and tulips, rolls of bizarre wallpaper, a doormat, a formica coffee table, a nylon polar bear rug, a chiming doorbell, a sunburst clock, a set of glasses with gold leaf rims and a bamboo motif, two matching shepherdesses for the mantelpiece.

I developed a rash on my toes from wearing nylon socks encased in cheap shoes. My feet also began to smell rather badly. I hid my cigarette lighter and my fountain pen and bought a gold-coloured biro and a novelty box of matches with a picture of a girl on the label which moved obscenely when held at a certain angle to the light. I wore a leatherette coat with a trailing belt, and I drew it luxuriously around my body in the sweating summertime, listening to it rumble and squeak like a disturbed intestine as I squirmed on bus seats. I bought newspapers which displayed photographs of naked women on the inside pages, and read roguishly of sex ordeals, hearing the beery slap of belly on belly, breasts spread, clothes rucked.

Returning from nights of drinking, I would drag Betty into close mouths and slap wet kisses on her protesting lips, pausing to belch, nipping a fleeing buttock. The matchbox rub of our shoes would echo on the stairs leading to the flat, and we would giggle as I fumbled for the lock, toppling helter-skelter into the bacon-rind hall. Grappling and moaning, unbuttoning and unbuckling, falling into the trench of the bed where we creaked and shook our way into sleep.

Unbelievably, a new day would dawn, leading to new adventure. I stared at the world with the wide, lascivious eyes of the newly awakened, savouring the seconds which all too quickly expanded into minutes and hours. My three-day jamboree compressed into a sensuous moment which contained all of the sensations which had previously existed only in the form of vague longings lodged deep within my body, purring, quivering unnoticed. But then I returned to limbo: the four-day stretches which completed the week and rolled interminably onwards towards what seemed like an impossibly distant rebirth. My life would flow on in its normal course, but half-whispered hints would galvanise my senses and I had to quickly discipline myself to show no emotion. I would lapse into silence and slyly dart my eyes here and there in search of signs of recognition, but my safety was preserved. A half smile would present itself on my face, the smile of one who knows, who truly knows, the smile of one whose life is more than the surface trappings displayed to the world, a smile born of the sense of superiority of the traitor.

I could function in their world, function well, but I possessed something more: a secret. You might scurry from mousetrap to mousetrap, longing for the cheese which tempts you with its pungent aroma, but I could lift myself from the common throng, secretly scorning the mad scramble, living for two, my dual nature generating a sense of barely controlled power so great I had to restrain myself from shouting to the heavens in delirious joy. I was perfection: I could mould myself at will, revelling in the basest instincts which sprang with such vitality from the depths. You are Cain or Abel; I am both, swirling the tinctures of life around my palate, scratching repressed itches against the knots of a tall tree. I had struck a blow for freedom and its secrecy added to the intoxicating thrill that I felt as I marched along the connecting corridor between two lives, peering here into a window, peering there, selecting pleasures, scorning consequences. My will reigned supreme and I rejected all bonds and ties, savouring a sense of liberated individuality which knew no bounds.

As I slunk from darkened corner to gloomy sidestreet I bathed in an inner light which, unseen to all but myself, burned with the godlike intensity of a flame which required no fuel but that which was generated by pure will exerted on the movement of life. Alone, I conquered the world. Unseen, I manipulated my environment. Soundlessly, I screamed my triumph as my calm exterior presented an unchanging image to those who surrounded me. I did not desire the acclaim of others. I knew. That was the only matter of consequence. I was alive, life amongst death, vitality amongst corpses. I knew.

Why

The traffic lights turned to green just as Pat found himself stranded in midstream, and cars roared past him to his left and right. He could see faces peering at him from back windows as they reached into the hazy distance. leaving him swaying in their wake. Balancing like a tightrope walker on the white dotted line which divided the road, he drew in his chest and belly as a bus lumbered past, spewing noise and noxious fumes into the night air. As its square body shuddered round the corner, Pat dashed haphazardly across that half of the road remaining between himself and the pavement, only to be pulled up abruptly as a sleek Triumph sports car screeched to a halt to avoid a collision. Its front bumper nudged Pat just below the knee as he toppled headlong over the bonnet. From staring at the metallic blue sheen of the bodywork, he raised his head with a conscious effort and stared through the windshield at the occupants of the car, a couple in their mid-twenties, the girl hanging onto the driver's arm in shock at the near accident.

"Fucking bastards!" Pat slurred, making vague threatening gestures. "You think you own the fucking road." He stood for a moment before the car, blocking the traffic, angry horns sounding behind the Triumph. "Come on out, you bastard!" he shouted towards the white-faced driver, rearing backwards and forwards, steadying himself with a hand on top of the radiator.

The car inched forward, causing Pat to stumble backwards, almost overbalancing. He pulled himself up to his full height and swayed backwards a few degrees, jerking his head forward to spit towards the windscreen, but the saliva dribbled from his mouth to drip impotently from his chin. The car accelerated, brushing him aside, and he aimed a kick at the passenger door as it passed but missed and careered backwards to land with a crash on the edge of the pavement. The traffic flowed once more, the passengers in the cars staring at the helpless figure on the ground gasping for breath. As the lights changed again, pedestrians crossed the road, parting before Pat like a river drifting past an islet in midstream.

A middle-aged man in a worn duffel coat stepped off the pavement, hesitated, then turned back towards Pat, bending down to grip his upper arm with a firm hand: "Come on, pal, up you get."

"Leave us alone," slurred Pat, attempting to shrug himself free, his leg still splayed in the gutter.

"Come on, son, you'll get lifted."

"So fucking what?"

"Come on. You put yourself in a taxi and get off home." Despite himself, Pat was raised to his feet, the man supporting him with two strong arms. "Your wife'll have the polis out looking for you. Screw the bobbin."

"Fuck the wife; fuck the polis. and fuck you too! Who do you think you are, Jesus Christ or something?" Pat broke from the man's grip, waving his arms to fend him off: "Leave me alone, will you?" he demanded aggressively, sucking the saliva from his chin with his upper lip. "Who asked for your help anyway?"

The man seemed about to say something but instead shrugged his shoulders and turned away, leaving Pat standing flat-footed on the street corner. The back of his coat was now covered in brown slush from the fall and he exhibited all the symptoms of the hopeless drunk. His limbs contorted like a spastic toy soldier as he tumbled down Union Street past couples bonded together against the cold. He stopped before the window of a clothes shop and stared at his reflection among the dummies: hair matted, eyes swollen and pig-like, a dark streak of grime down one cheek. He mumbled something to the figure he saw before him, patiently explaining a universal truth with extravagant gestures, strangling words with a rubber mouth.

He was passed by a pair of policemen in rustling waterproofs who paused then moved on, having conducted a noiseless conversation with one another by means of two or three movements of their eyebrows. What's the use? Shrug.

At the corner of Union Street and Argyle Street a figure lay slumped in the doorway of Boot's the Chemist, his arms wrapped round his body for warmth, clumsy feet protruding from the ends of ragged checked trousers. A jumble of hair stood up from the top of his army greatcoat and choked snores were being emitted from behind an unkempt beard. Beneath his body there trickled a small stream which mixed with the half-melted ice on the pavement, discolouring it further. Pat glanced at the tramp from the corner of his eye and staggered past quickly, suddenly chilled.

As he passed over the bridge towards the South Side of the city, putting more and more distance between himself and his home, he spotted vague shadows flitting round the benches on Custom House Quay. One held what looked like a bottle high above his head, keeping it out of the reach of the second smaller figure who danced round him making vain leaps into the air, clawing at his arm. He heard a shrill voice:

"You fucking bastard . . . I paid for that . . . You fucking bastard . . . Give us that . . . You fucking . . ." Pat passed on.

The lights on the south bank of the river danced on the water but Pat was oblivious to them. He hacked up a blockage in his throat and paused on the crown of the bridge, leaning over to deposit the slime into the blackness. The Clyde was dark and moved silently onwards, emptying the city of its refuse. It looked strangely sinister, like a half-remembered image from an old film, and in its stillness it flowed powerfully, a black thought in Pat's mind. Below, unseen, pieces of refuse spun in eddies, pausing for a second, caught in time, before continuing their inexorable passage towards the deep, cold sea beyond the estuary.

In Bridge Street a couple emerged from the slash of a close mouth and were briefly caught before Pat in the glare of a street lamp. The woman looked sullen and businesslike, her shrewish features impassive; the man, his round, flaccid face flushed, glanced furtively along the deserted street. Wordlessly, the two parted company, the many hurring past Pat towards the city centre, the woman slowly edging round a corner into a side street.

Pat crossed the road and passed under the railway bridge which carried traffic to Central Station, his footsteps echoing up to the metal girders where pigeons strutted and pecked at imaginary crumbs. A taxi, its light above the windscreen lit for hire, ticked past like a clockwork hearse.

At the corner of Commerce Street and Nelson Street stood a squat pub, its doors barred, but with lights still showing from behind grilled windows. From inside could be heard laughter and shouting and the clink of bottles. Across from the pub new trucks and lorries hibernated under the snow in silent rows behind a wire mesh fence, corralled for safety. Also in the compound was a watchman's hut, and through its window Pat could see the blue flicker of a mute television set.

Just before the high level Kingston Bridge which lifted the inner city motorway over the Clyde was a concentration of Co-op buildings, Victorian edificies sitting incongruously beside modern pillboxes. Almost unseen to the pedestrians below, vehicles slid over the river, travelling fifty feet in the air, within a few inches of the Co-op Superstore. On an island in the middle of Morrison Street and Paisley Road lurked the Funeral Department, occupying prime advertising space.

Pat walked along Paisley Road towards the Toll, grateful for the noise of the traffic on the flyover which broke the eerie silence of Morrison Street, 200 yards as dead as only a late-night commercial area can be. The buildings lay inert, awaiting the human touch which would reanimate them. A few yards past the bridge was a temporary police station housed in a Portacabin. To avoid it, Pat crossed to the Clyde side of the road, walking past the closed doors of what was once the Kingston Public Library but was now a hostel for down and outs. Outside on the steps some customers who had arrived too late or too drunk to gain admittance huddled together against the cold. At the side of the building a narrow cobbled lane led towards the derelict iron ore terminal on the river bank, and from the gloom Pat could hear scuffling and muffled shouts, followed by the sound of breaking glass. He passed on.

At the Toll, he paused, suddenly realising he was following the route he travelled each morning towards Linwood. Another eight miles and he would be there. No more. Somewhere on the north side of the city lay his wife and children, snoring in bed. Somewhere, he no longer knew where exactly, Moran was sitting discussing politics and union schemes. Somewhere, Stewart was sipping a nightcap before retiring to bed for a well-earned rest. Somewhere, Sam Dunbar was trying to forget whom he had arranged to meet in the Horseshoe Bar. Somewhere, old Archie Campbell was trying to erase bad dreams from his mind. In millions of homes throughout the country people were talking, talking, talking, but not of him. They did not know him, never would. What would they care if I threw myself under a bus? Fuck all, that's what they'd care.

As Pat thought that last thought, a small boy — selling the following morning's papers beside the bus inspectors' hut at the junction of Paisley Road West and Govan Road — jumped. Pat had kicked a lamp post with steel-capped boots and the ring broke the boy's dream. Snow mixed with rain was beginning to fall, plastering Pat's hair over his forehead, sobering him. Underneath layers of clothing he was sweating. He turned back towards the city.

As he repassed the hostel, the men outside were still curled in identical positions. The noises from the alley had stopped. Just beyond the old library were two shops, the solitary remnants of an old tenement which had been demolished. On waste ground behind them Pat saw a light warmly beckon him. Before the light, figures were silhouetted, and through the drizzle Pat could see them raise cups to their mouths. A mobile chip van! Here? What the fuck's it doing in a place like this? Suddenly he felt hungry. He had eaten practically nothing all day. As he moved closer, the smell of what seemed to be Bovril or oxtail soup drifted towards him.

Approaching the van he saw an old man serving behind the counter, ladling steaming liquid into paper cups and handing out chunks of bread. Christ, it was a fucking soup kitchen! The thought of going to such a place was an affront to his dignity, and he was about to turn away when the smell of the soup caused his mouth to water. He moved closer. Pressing through the small crowd of men who, like second-hand moths, flapped in rags before the light, he fumbled in his pocket and, withdrawing a 50p piece, rapped on the counter, calling for service.

"Hey!" he shouted towards the old man who stood with his back towards him, busy at the stove: "How's about some soup?" The old man turned silently and stared at Pat with steady, almost colourless eyes. Pat averted his gaze and instead gave another rap on the counter: "Chop, chop!" he shouted, giggling nervously as the down-and-outs looked on, munching soup-soaked crusts with soft gums. The old man lifted the ladle and poured some soup into a cup, placing it before Pat and laying a thick slice of buttered bread beside it.

"How much, pop?" asked Pat in a cocky voice. The old man shook his head and made a crosswise movement with his hands. "Look, I want to know how much." The old man silently repeated the gestures. "Look, I've got money, see!" Pat held up the 50p piece as if to an idiot: "Money," he spelled out: "I pay. Comprendo?" The old man again shook his head. "Listen, you old cunt, I don't want your fucking charity. What do you think I am, some sort of dosser or something? I'm no wino." The old man remained impassive, his eyes suffering. "Do you think I can't afford to pay for my own grub? Fuck that! Here's the money. Go on, take it. No? Well here's what I think of your soup." Pat slowly tipped the steaming liquid on to the snow-patched ground then picked up the bread, sending it spinning towards the dossers who stood back as spectators, fascinated by this novel turn of events. "Feeding time!" Laughing at his joke, Pat turned back towards the main road, but before he reached it he heard footsteps hurrying behind him. Spinning round with his fists clenched he saw the old man running towards him.

"Just keep your distance, you old bastard, or I'll put your head in." Despite this threat, the old man continued to approach him holding his arms outstretched, palms upwards, a crazy beatific light in his eyes. Suddenly, Pat feared more than violence: "I'm warning you, keep back or I'll fucking do you." The old man reached Pat and placed his hands on his shoulders. Violently shrugging them off, Pat backed away, stumbling on some rubble, falling backwards into the snow, desperately trying to scramble away from this terror. As the old man bent down to pick him up, Pat lashed out with his boot, catching him on the chest. The old man groaned and staggered, placing one hand on the ground to steady himself, the other holding the area where the steel toecap had made contact. Pat jumped to his feet, stood back, and kicked the old man full in the face, causing him to crumple to the ground, blood showing bright on the snow.

"I warned you! Don't tell me I didn't warn you!" Pat looked round desperately and ran for the road, disappearing into the blackness.

After a few seconds the dossers, who had scattered for cover at the first signs of violence, crept closer to the figure which lay moaning on the ground. The old man seemed to be mumbling something, but blood and loose teeth made the words incoherent. Silently, two or three of them drifted closer, eyes darting in all directions, as if anticipating Pat's return. The old man was trying to speak, was making weak gestures with his hands. One of the dossers, younger than the rest, knelt beside him, pressing his ear close to the old man's bloodied lips, but heard only laboured breathing. He reached for the old man's left hand and placed his fingers on his wrist as if feeling for a pulse. Quickly he unbuckled the old man's watch and thrust it into his pocket. Seeing this, the second and third dossers crouched down and rifled through his pockets, lifting out his wallet, discarding a set of keys, spilling loose change on to the blood-soaked snow.

Swiftly completing the search, they noiselessly flitted away into the nooks and crannies of deserted buildings. Above, larger flakes of snow were falling from clouds which scudded unseen across the black, starless sky. The brief thaw was over. It would freeze again that night.